Transmonstrified

R.L. Naquin

Bottle Cap Publishing

This book is a work of fiction. All names, places, and characters are products of the author's imagination or are used fictitiously. Any resemblance to real people, living or dead, is coincidental. No part of this book may be reproduced, scanned, or distributed in any way whatsoever without the written permission of the author, except as brief quotations.

Edited by Sara E. Lundberg

Cover design by Karri Klawiter

Published by Bottle Cap Publishing

Copyright © 2015 R.L. Naquin

All rights reserved.

Additional copyright information is available at the end of this collection.

For Dad.
Thank you for always catching me when I fell.
Saying "I love you" will never be enough.

Table of Contents

Introduction	1
"Shampoo Girl" — A Monster Haven Short Story	3
"Baked Goods"	18
"The Button War"	19
"Fool's Gold"	22
"Unmatched Cupid" — A Mount Olympus Employment Agency Short Story	31
"Hidden Holidays" — A Monster Haven Short Story	37
"How Greg's Chupacabra Became a Small Town Legend and Ended Up Between the Wooden Eye and the Wig Collection at the Caney Valley Historical Society"	51
"Snow Kissed"	56
"Cast Off"	63
"Distressed Denim"	65
"Reaper's Tale" — A Monster Haven Short Story	68
"The Dream Eaters"	79
"Bargain Basement"	82
"Escalating Heaven"	91
"Cursed by Beauty"	94
"What Zoey Doesn't Know" — A Monster Haven Short Story	96
"Cosmic Lasagna"	111
"Undercover Gorgon" — A Mount Olympus Employment Agency Short Story	115
"Voices on the Wind"	130
"Just Right"	133
"Ill-Conceived Magic" — A Monster Haven Short Story	139
"Prune Juice Sestina"	165
About R.L. Naquin	167
Other Works by R.L. Naquin	168
Additional Copyrights	169

Introduction

Over the last several years, a lot has happened for me. One minute I was sending out short story submissions to magazines and anthologies, the next, I sold my first novel. Six books and four years later, I have a completed book series, a pile of short stories both old and new, and a million ideas filling my head for new stories I want to tell.

This collection offers a wide selection of strangeness. Some of the stories are ones you may have read before, but a lot of them will be new even to people who already love my work. (Hi Mom!) It's a snapshot of where I've been, and a peek at where I'm going next.

Come with me and meet the people in my head. If they start talking to you, too, maybe I can finally get some sleep.

—Rachel

"Shampoo Girl"
A Monster Haven Short Story

Kam is one of my favorite characters from the Monster Haven series. This story takes place between book five, Demons in My Driveway, *and book six,* Phoenix in My Fortune. *I thought it would be nice to see what Kam gets up to when she's off by herself.*

Ghosts. Spirits. Lost souls. Whatever. I called them *runners*.

I learned on my first soul chase that barging into a place of business and telling the owners I was there to collect a runaway soul freaked them out. It wasn't like I'd burst through the door with a proton pack strapped behind me like a Ghostbuster, waving the nozzle thingy around and cracking jokes. I could be subtle.

Okay, maybe not. I wasn't so hot at subtle. Subtle was boring. But, seriously. If a spirit were chasing my customers away, I'd want somebody to come get it.

Modern humans confused me.

I stood outside the Bella Notte Salon and Spa in the fancy part of Chicago and inspected my ponytail. Should I risk it? I couldn't remember the last time I'd had my hair done—1986? No. Before that. Sometime in the '60s?

I checked the bracelet covering the magic gems embedded in my wrist, then slid it down my arm and squeezed the soft metal, tightening it to keep the jewels concealed. Only two of the gems were charged. The third was completely black. I'd been using a lot of magic for stupid stuff lately—like doing my hair.

My friends were always giving me shit about conserving my magic so I could reach a full charge. It would take all three of my gems to open a portal to the djinn world and return home. But sometimes I wanted to feel *pretty*. Was that so wrong?

I shrugged and tossed my long, dark hair over my shoulder. Fine. I'd go undercover as a client and let a human cut my hair while I tried to track the missing soul in their shop.

If they totally screwed up my look, I'd still have two full gems of magic to fix it.

I may have flung the door open a little hard when I walked in. Sue me. I was excited. I didn't get to hunt on my own very often, and I never got to do fun undercover stuff. Well, there was that one time when I got to pretend to be a construction worker and wear a hardhat. That was cool. Construction workers were usually pretty hot. Not the foremen, though. Those were all old guys. Not nearly as nice to look at.

The receptionist looked at me over her rhinestone-covered glasses and scowled. "May I help you?" Her hair was short on one side and longish on the other.

The place smelled like chemicals trying to disguise themselves as potpourri. I swallowed hard to keep from wrinkling my nose. "I'm here to let you cut my hair." I gave her an enthusiastic smile.

Her upper lip quivered as if the smell of the place had finally hit her, too. "Do you have an appointment?"

I blinked. "Do I need one?"

No, it wasn't the smell. That was definitely a sneer she was giving me. "We're fully booked." She didn't even look at her computer.

I crossed my arms over my chest and stood my ground. "When's the earliest you can fit me in?"

She sighed as if I were bothering her. Maybe this had been a bad idea. Maybe I should've waited until after hours. Undercover was fun, but breaking in and slinking around in the dark, pretending to be a burglar—that was a kind of undercover, too.

That way I could take the screws out of the bitch's chair so she'd land on her snooty ass when she came in the next morning. The thought cheered me up.

She pressed her bright red lips together and eyed me up and down. "I'm afraid we're booked solid until next—"

A shriek from around the corner interrupted her. A second later, a woman in a gorgeous green cashmere sweater and designer jeans raced into the reception area with a black cape flapping in her wake. Her sweater and hair dripped, and her makeup ran down her face. A redhead with a distraught look on her face hurried behind.

"You really shouldn't get fabric like that wet," I said, trying to be helpful. "Your sweater will lose its shape."

No one paid any attention to me.

The customer tore the cape from her neck and threw it on the floor. "I have never been treated so poorly in a salon before." She turned on the receptionist, speaking through her teeth. "Have the owner call me when he wants to apologize."

The receptionist and stylist stood mute. I didn't think to ask where the customer got her sweater until much later.

The way the lady threw the door open and stalked out was a thing of beauty. The urge to applaud was nearly overwhelming.

She was magnificent.

But I stayed cool. I gave the bitch behind the counter a sweet smile. "Looks like you have an opening after all."

Her face was pale. It made her lipstick stand out like a bloody incision. She sighed. "Fine. What's your name?" She moved to the computer and tapped a few keys.

"Kam." I smiled. "With a 'K'."

She sniffed. "Well, Kam-with-a-k, this is your lucky day." She typed something else, then regarded the redhead holding a dripping, crumpled cape. "Tina, I'll call Antonio and let him know it happened again. Will you take care of Ms. Kam?" She turned away, dismissing us both, and picked up her phone.

The redhead gave me an embarrassed smile. "This way, please. May I get you something to drink?"

I didn't answer. I was too in awe of everything I saw as we walked to her station. It was all so shiny and wonderful. How had I not come to one of these places before?

We passed a section of comfy-looking chairs where some women sat with their feet in tiny, foot-sized hot tubs. Others read glossy magazines while someone buffed their toenails and painted them in gorgeous colors.

In another area, women lay with their eyes closed while someone applied mud to their faces with fat brushes. A third area, furnished in small tables with bright lamps, was populated with chattering ladies getting their hands dipped in warm wax and their fingernails extended into shiny, improbable lengths.

My friends Zoey and Sara had a lot of explaining to do. They'd never told me how far beauty salons had come in the decades I'd been locked up in a box by my old master.

I wanted to try it all.

Tina stopped and gestured for me to have a seat. I plopped into the make-me-pretty-chair, excited beyond anything I'd ever experienced. Hair products of all kinds lined the shelves on the side of her station, and a hair straightener, curling iron, and the shiniest blow dryer I'd ever seen sat at the ready.

Tina pulled the scrunchy from my ponytail and fluffed my hair with her fingers. "So, what are we getting done today?"

I lifted my hands, fingers splayed, and locked eyes with her in the mirror. "I have no idea. What can we *do*?"

We settled on a cut and style, and she shuffled me out of the magnificent chair over to the line of sinks to wash my hair. She hesitated, flicking her gaze left, right, and overhead.

I peered at the ceiling with her, but I didn't see anything. "Are we waiting for something?"

She shook out one of those black capes I'd seen on the soaked lady. "No. Not at all. We're fine." Her movements were jerky and nervous as she Velcroed the cape around me.

Unlike with the angry lady, Tina put the cape on me with the opening in the back. It looked stupid that way, but I could see how it would be more useful in keeping my clothes dry. Maybe the other lady had started off this way and the opening had shifted around. That was disappointing. I'd really wanted to wear a cape.

With my hands tucked under the waterproof fabric and my head tilted back in the sink, no one could see me reach under my T-shirt and stroke the soul stone hanging from a chain around my neck. While Tina lathered shampoo in my hair, I examined what I could see of the room. If I could spot the runaway soul while touching the stone, I'd be able to see it from then on, hands free, as long as it was in the room.

Soul chaser powers weren't nearly as good as reaper powers, but we used the same stones. There were perks.

"Is the water temperature okay?" Tina asked.

"Sure. It feels nice." I wasn't paying much attention. A jerky movement in the far corner caught my eye then disappeared.

"I'm a little out of practice." She shut the water off and pumped some other product into her hands, then massaged it into my scalp. "We had a trainee in here who did most of the shampooing, but..." She paused, both in speaking and rinsing, then resumed. "But we lost her."

Ah. That was what I wanted to hear. "Lost her? Did she get fired?"

I knew she hadn't been fired. Behind Tina, the nozzle to the sprayer on another sink lifted over her shoulder, aiming directly at me. I rubbed the soul stone under my shirt, and the outline of a woman appeared. As I watched, the rest of her filled in, revealing a slight frame, a blonde pixie cut, and a serious face.

Her gaze moved from my hair to my face, and her eyes grew wide. Apparently, she hadn't expected anyone to be looking at her. She dropped the nozzle, lifted herself from the floor, and disappeared into the ceiling.

Tina finished up and wrapped my wet hair in a towel. She glanced over her shoulder as she ushered me back to her station. The muscles in her face and shoulders relaxed once I was safely returned to the make-me-pretty chair.

I'd never understood how humans could get their hair cut so often, knowing they didn't have magic to fix it if it all went wrong. It all seemed so daring and reckless. I was a mess watching Tina cut long strands of my dark, straight locks in order to give me layers. She promised it would give it *movement* and *lift*. As she cut, she chattered, and I guided the conversation to get her to talk about the girl I'd seen.

"So, the shampoo girl. How'd she lose her job?"

Tina ran her comb through a section of hair and snipped off about six inches. "She didn't." She lowered her voice and waved her comb toward the sinks. "She died. Right over there."

I raised my eyebrows in mock surprise. "How do you die in a salon?"

Tina stopped cutting and gave me a serious look in the mirror. "Choked on her gum. Right in the middle of a shampoo."

"Didn't anybody help her? Somebody could've done that Heimlich thing or something. Seriously." It all seemed highly unlikely to me. And yet, I'd seen the girl myself. Come to think of it, her face did have kind of a blue tinge to it.

Tina scowled. "I wasn't here at the time, but I heard everybody ran to help the client, instead. Mrs. Titweiler is high maintenance and rich—most of them are—so when she started screaming about soap in her eyes, she got all the attention. Poor Kelsey was dead before anybody noticed."

Great balls of fire. People needed to get their heads out of their asses.

"So, what was with the lady who ran out of here and gave me her spot?" I knew what her problem had been. Dead Kelsey would have sprayed me, too, if she hadn't caught me looking at her and freaked out. But I needed to hear it from Tina.

Tina ran her fingers through my wet hair—what was left of it—then leaned close to me, almost whispering. "Something weird keeps happening. We're not really supposed to talk about it, but the sprayers in the sink keep dousing people." She stopped while a stylist walked by with a client, then continued once they were out of earshot. "We've had three plumbers in here, and nobody can find anything wrong."

She straightened and resumed cutting, adding Cleopatra bangs across my forehead. I would definitely have to use magic to fix this when it was over.

I kept my voice low. "So what do *you* think is causing it?"

She didn't answer right away, and it took her a full minute before she would look me in the eye. "I think Kelsey is haunting us."

As if on cue, someone screamed from the direction of the sinks.

"There goes another one," I said. "I guess I got lucky."

Tina's hands shook, and a chunk of hair fell to the floor that I didn't think she'd planned to cut. "It doesn't happen every time. Twice in one day is a lot."

"How long has it been going on?" My hair was now shorter on one side than the other. When I'd told her to do something artistic, I hadn't expected this sort of asymmetrical shenanigans. Humans were insane.

She shrugged. "Maybe a week or so. Kelsey died last month."

Yeah. That tracked. Runners usually took a little while to adjust to their new circumstances before they started worrying about *why* they'd run. They all thought they had unfinished business, and this one was no different. Apparently, leaving some snooty bitch unrinsed was enough for her to refuse to cross over.

Dumbest unfinished business I'd ever heard of.

I didn't say much while Tina dried my hair, then touched it up with a straightener. My hair was already arrow straight, but she knew her business better than I did. In fact, I kind of liked the cut, once she was done. It was weird, but when had I ever shied away from weird?

My jeans and T-shirt were all wrong for it, though. I'd need silver go-go boots and a shiny dress. Maybe gold lipstick. No, definitely gold lipstick. My hair was totally rad.

The lights flickered, making me blink. Overhead, Kelsey flittered past in the direction of the shampoo stations, a look of concentration on her pasty, transparent face.

"Hold on to your butt," I said.

"What?" Tina ripped open the Velcro on my cape and shook it loose of hair.

"Nothing." I smiled and touched my bizarre, angularly cut hair. "I love it! It's so different."

Tina opened her mouth to answer, then snapped her jaw shut when someone shrieked from the direction of the sinks. I hopped out of the make-me-pretty chair and ran around the corner in time to see Kelsey drop the spray thingy and disappear through a closed door behind her.

The soaked woman in the chair sat up and accepted a towel so she could blot her face dry. The stylist next to her shifted from foot to foot, eyes darting around the room while she apologized repeatedly.

To her credit, the lady in the chair didn't seem too upset about it.

Tina stood next to me, watching. "That's three times today. It's getting worse."

I pointed at the door I'd seen Kelsey float through. "What's in there?" I crossed my fingers, hoping she'd tell me it was the bathroom so I could get in there without much explanation.

"Storage closet. Why?"

My heart sank. Nope. There weren't any reasons I could come up with for her to let me in the storage closet. But, odds were, Kelsey had chosen that closet as her home base. Stray souls could go anywhere they liked when they made a run for it from their bodies, but once they quit running, they usually chose a grounding spot where they could recharge their energy.

I'd seen Kelsey disappear into the ceiling and into the closet. So, if she wasn't based in the closet, she'd probably chosen the crawl space on the other side of the ceiling tiles.

Please, oh please, don't make me climb around above ceiling tiles.

I hated those places. I could put up with the mice, dirt, and tight space. But I'd already fallen through those stupid, flimsy cardboard tile things on two separate hunts.

Either way, this chase wasn't going to end right now. If I couldn't think of a reason to get into their storage room, I sure as hell couldn't make an excuse to climb up into their rafters.

The lights flickered again.

Tina put her hand on my arm. "Come on. Let's get you rung up and out of here before something else happens."

As we wound our way through the different stations, I glanced over my shoulder at the door to the storage room. Kelsey's face pushed through the wood, and she watched me with an intensity that would make anybody nervous. Unless they were a soul catcher, of course.

I grinned and winked at her. Her eyes grew wide, and she ducked out of sight.

At the counter, snooty lady rang me up and presented me with a bill that explained the level of snot she'd been giving me. I had the money in my account, but she'd pissed me off. Judgy McJudgerson.

Pretending to scratch an itch, I poked a finger beneath my wrist cuff and touched one of the fully charged gems in my arm. A tiny electric spark licked my skin, and a slight sense loss tugged at me. If I'd pulled aside the bracelet, I'd have seen one of my gems was now a little duller than the other.

I reached into my purse and pulled out my new, magically minted platinum card and handed it over, trying my best to look nonchalant and a little bored.

One of the receptionist's eyebrows gave a small twitch, but otherwise, she didn't react. I imagined she'd probably expected me to pay in dollar bills and change. I could have, actually. I'd been working undercover as a waitress three days before while I figured out where the soul of a pissed-off fry cook had holed up.

Silly cow didn't seem to realize she was a receptionist, not the ambassador to the Queen of the Fairies. Nothing wrong with being a receptionist, but receptionists shouldn't be looking down their noses at waitresses.

I'd been right to slip her the platinum card. Despite her feigned lack of surprise to find me carrying the coveted bottomless credit card, her entire attitude shifted. "Is there a time you'd like to schedule for you next appointment?" Her red lips split apart in a ghastly grin. "Perhaps I could schedule you for a facial or manicure?"

My heartrate sped up at the thought of trying mud on my face or letting someone else paint my nails. I sighed. No. I doubted I'd have time to stick around for pampering. "Not today, thanks." I watched her run my card through, then I signed the name embossed on its shiny surface: Kamerona Hogglesworth.

I kept my lips pursed to avoid smirking while I signed. Sometimes my magic put a spin on things I didn't expect. Fake names and IDs were where it came up most. I couldn't use my real name, of course. If anyone knew my real name, they'd have the power to lock me up in a vessel and force me to use my magic on their behalf. Having already spent a century in that condition, I did everything I could to keep my name private. My magic, however, liked to come up with the stupidest names possible.

I added a hefty tip for Tina—it was magic money anyway—and strode toward the door. At the last second, I turned back and scanned the waiting area. Sure enough, Kelsey hung in the air, directly above the counter, watching me go. Her gaze moved from my face down to my chest, her eyes growing wide. I glanced down and realized my soul stone necklace now rested outside my shirt.

Kelsey bit her lip and poofed out of sight.

"Something else we can help with?" the now-accommodating lady behind the counter asked.

"Yeah. One question. What time do you close?"

~*~

The funny thing about runners was, they really weren't that hard to catch, in theory. My partner, Darius, often told me I made it way more difficult than it needed to be.

While the soul is recharging at its anchor location, a soul catcher only needs to get close enough to let the soul stone make the capture. Simple.

Where I tended to complicate matters was when the soul's unfinished business tugged at my heart. I often let go of perfect opportunities to nab a runner because I felt bad and wanted to help them finish up with their earthly business before going wherever souls go. I collected the soul eventually, but not without a lot of complicated errands, chats with the deceased's loved ones, and a hell of a lot of annoyed eye rolling from Darius.

But this catch didn't have to be complicated. Her unfinished business was simple—Kelsey was caught in a weird obsession with rinsing shampoo from wet hair. Fine. I'd let her wash my damn hair if that's what it took to make her happy.

TRANSMONSTRIFIED

Everybody should be happy before they cross over, right?

Breaking into the shop was fairly simple. Back in the '80s, during one of my short escapes from my master, I spent some of my time running around with a guy named Stan, who owned a pawnshop outside of New Orleans. He taught me to ride a motorcycle, make gumbo, fish for crawdads, crochet potholders, and pick locks. That last came in handy a lot more often than I'd expected at the time. The potholders would've been my first guess.

But there are other barriers besides locks. A high-end beauty salon would have a high-end alarm system. However, not every business in the building did. Earlier in the day, I'd done some scouting and found the pet groomer six doors down didn't have an alarm set up. It cost me a little jewel juice to do a thorough check of the building, but not nearly as much as if I'd used my magic to get inside. I didn't mind using a little on a job, but a full jewel is hardly worth the pay the Board gives me for each soul I catch for them. So I'm willing to spend magic on snooping, but not on anything bigger.

So, the back door to the pet grooming shop was easy to unlock and didn't set off any alarms. From there, I climbed a sink, shoved aside a ceiling tile, and pulled myself into the crawlspace. Earlier, I'd dreaded the idea of maneuvering over those ceiling tiles, but this time I didn't mind the long scuttle across the beams and through the spaces from one store to the next. I'd dressed the part, all black and slinky with a mask over my eyes like Batman wore. Not so I wouldn't get caught, really. I just thought I looked cool. Like Catwoman. Costumes made everything better.

Still, six stores was a long way to crawl. By the time I reached the salon, my palms and knees hurt, tufts of pink insulation clung to my clothes, and my lungs were full of dust.

After I moved a ceiling square aside, I reached into the messenger bag strapped to my side and pulled out a can of hairspray. I leaned down and pressed the nozzle, waving my arm in an arc to cover as much area as possible, then popped the can back in my bag.

It wasn't like I actually *expected* a bunch of crisscrossed laser beams to show up in the sticky cloud below, but I hoped. And I'd always wanted to do that, so it seemed like a good chance. I had to admit, I was a little disappointed not to see a red laser grid I'd have to do crazy acrobatics to get past.

Maybe my next runner would hide out in a jewelry store or a bank vault.

I dropped out of the ceiling into a low crouch, impressed with my landing and how much I was sure I looked like Catwoman, minus the ears. Arching my back, I struck a pose with my hand mimicking a cat's paw, claws out.

"Meow," I purred in my best Julie Newmar. That was as far as I got before all that hairspray hit my lungs, and I folded up in fit of coughing that lasted a full five minutes.

Totally messed up my entrance.

Once I got myself together, I pulled my mask off and dabbed my eyes with it before stashing the thing in my back pocket. The moment was ruined. Time to get to work.

I wandered through the dark shop, running my hands over the smooth counters and vinyl chair backs, smelling products, and poking at styling tools. There was enough ambient light from the street to see well enough, but it was dark enough that no one should be able to see me. I took my time making a few circuits of the shop, hoping Kelsey would show herself, but she stayed out of sight.

The door to the storage closet was locked, but I had it open in seconds. Nothing was in there but towels and bottles of hair products.

"Fine." I headed toward the row of sinks and plopped into a chair. "Sure could use a shampoo while I'm here." I leaned back and waited.

The cold porcelain of the sink dug into my neck, and the chemical smells of old-lady perms lingered from the previous workday, stinging my nose. And still, Kelsey didn't come. I shook my decidedly shorter, asymmetrical hair, hoping to get her attention. Nothing.

"Oh, for Gozer's sake." I couldn't wait around all night. Obviously, Kelsey's unfinished business wasn't to shampoo someone, it was to rinse them. I flipped over to my knees and reached for a bottle of what I hoped was shampoo, then leaned forward, spraying my hair with the nozzle until I was soaked.

I had, of course, forgotten to put on one of those cool capes.

The bottle I'd chosen turned out to be shampoo after all, and I dribbled it into my wet hair. I worked it into a good lather, hanging my head forward over the sink. Then I squirmed around until I returned to the normal position with my neck cradled in that sink dent that's nowhere near as comfortable as the designers meant it to be.

I didn't have to wait long, reclining in the stiff chair with my soapy head in a sink and my eyes closed tight to keep them safe. Unlike the victims in the salon during the day, I didn't have a live stylist standing at my sink in Kelsey's way, so she didn't park herself a sink away. Cool water splashed into the sink from the nozzle until it was warm, then steady hands guided the water through my hair, thoroughly rinsing it until it almost squeaked. The spray turned off for a moment, and I heard her take another product from the shelf. Next, she spread whatever it was—conditioner, probably—through my locks, followed by a relaxing scalp massage, then another rinse. She wrapped a towel around my head, then helped me sit up.

I opened my eyes and found her standing next to me, a pensive look on her face.

"Thank you, Kelsey." I reached under my shirt for my soul stone. "I feel great. I bet you feel better, too."

She blinked. "Why would I feel better?"

I slumped back into the uncomfortable chair, disappointed. "Your unfinished business. You needed to finish shampooing someone." I pointed at my turbaned head. "Uh?"

She shook her head. "You had soap in your hair. I wasn't going to just leave you like that. "

I rolled my eyes. "So what's the problem, Sunshine? Why are you sticking around? Don't you have better things to do than hang around work for eternity?"

She folded her arms over her chest and bit her lip. "You'll laugh."

"I laugh at everything. It's more a judgment on my sense of humor than on anything you do or say. I'm just like that. Try me." I gave her what I hoped was a dazzling grin with a hint of whacko thrown in.

The poor girl shuffled her feet, twisting a chunk of short blonde hair between her fingers while looking like she was about to ask for the moon. After a moment, she gathered her courage. "I never got past the shampoo stations. It's not fair."

I frowned. "I don't get it. I've seen you all over the shop. You got past the sinks earlier today and flew right over my head while my hair was being cut."

She stomped her foot in frustration. "I could have cut your hair. I have the training, just like Tina. In fact, we graduated together. But she got a job as a stylist, and I'm stuck rinsing and trying to work my way up." She scowled.

I sighed. What did I have to lose? "Do you think you could work with mine? I know Tina did it earlier today, but I bet you could make it even better."

Kelsey's face brightened. "You'd let me do that?"

I shrugged. "Sure."

"Could I..." she hesitated. "Would you like some highlights?"

Trying to be nonchalant about it, I loosened my bracelet and peeked at the magic levels in my jewels. No telling how much juice it would take to regrow my hair and repair the damage of bleaching and coloring it. I was no expert, but my hair was nearly black. She'd have to strip it first to do anything to the color.

One jewel shimmered steadily in the subdued light, but the other pulsed with about half a load. It would be enough, I supposed. Resigned, I slid the bracelet back in place and nodded. "I'm game. Let's do this."

She clapped her hands and bounced on the balls of her feet in excitement. "Yay! Come with me."

A minute later I was seated comfortably in a make-me-pretty chair while a ghost wrapped a cape around me and let my hair out of turban captivity. We were in the farthest corner away from the windows so she could turn a light on to see what she was doing.

I made a face at the mirror when I saw the hack job Tina had done. My original assessment that my hair was totally rad was actually totally bogus. It hadn't looked that bad dry, but now that it was wet, what was supposed to be artistically asymmetrical simply looked crooked. I really had nothing to lose here with Kelsey. It couldn't get any worse, right?

We were there for hours. Since my hair was wet, she had to dry it first, in order to color it. Next, the dye had to process, then it had to be rinsed and my hair conditioned before the cut and style. Thanks to the crazy shenanigans from the first cut earlier in the day, Kelsey had to trim a lot more in order to even it out. Absolutely nothing could be done about the bangs slashed straight across my forehead. By the time she was done, I had a curly bob that hung below my ears and had streaks of orangey yellow darting through it all.

It wasn't great, but at least it was interesting. Thank the gods of Hollywood I hadn't blown my magic on breaking into this place. It would take years to grow out my hair to what it had been eighteen hours ago.

Nevertheless, she was fluffing my new curls and grinning. No need for me to be rude about it. She'd done her best.

"Fantastic!" I beamed at her. "I love it."

She narrowed her eyes. "You sure?"

"Positive!" I reached under my shirt for the soul stone. Now we could wrap things up.

Kelsey took the cape off of me and shook it out. "All right. Well, if you'll follow me, please."

I frowned and dropped the stone. What could she possibly have left to do? Stretching my cramped muscles, I rose from the make-me-pretty chair and followed her through the darkened shop to the front counter.

My ghost stylist reached under the register and pulled out a receipt pad and a pen, then jotted a few figures on it. "Here's your total." She smiled and pushed the paper toward me.

After all this, I had to pay for it, too? I squinted at the figures in the dim lighting. She'd written several squiggles, a hashtag, and a happy face. I glanced at her face and saw she was waiting for something, even though she hadn't actually written a number.

Sometimes the dead were a little confused about the world. And sometimes they had unfinished business, but weren't entirely sure what it was. It was looking more and more like that was Kelsey's case.

I handed her my credit card, hoping that was the right response.

She grinned and swiped my card through the machine, even though the machine was turned off for the night, waited a few beats, then handed the card back to me.

I tucked it away and gave her a hopeful look. "So…I guess that's it, then."

She nodded and sighed. "I guess so."

One of the saddest sights in the world is a restless, escaped soul with no idea what her unfinished business actually is. I should have pressed harder when I'd first met her and not assumed the obvious. My hair would be a lot less fluffy. And orange.

I leaned my elbows on the counter and gave her my most serious face. "Listen. We haven't come right out and talked about it, but you know why I'm here, right?"

Kelsey sighed again, long and deep. "Yes. I know."

"I don't want to take you until you're ready, but if you can't figure out what it is you need to do, I need to take you anyway. It's almost daylight. People will be coming in soon."

That was a slight exaggeration. It was a little after four in the morning. Still. I was bone tired and itched like crazy because of all the tiny hairs from two separate haircuts. If Darius had been here, he probably would have barged in during office hours, forced her into the stone, then left. Instead, she got me. I'd been a good sport through all this, but enough was enough.

Kelsey's form had been pretty solid ever since she'd rinsed my hair, but she shimmered now, as if she were a hologram about to blink out. "There's nothing left for me to do here." She wavered a second time, then solidified again. "I guess I just hoped if I proved myself, Connie would regret never letting me do more than shampoo."

I tilted my head. "Connie?"

"She's the manager. She usually works behind the counter."

"You mean the snooty lady with the tacky glasses and tiny lips?" The bitch hadn't even wanted to let me in. I was not a fan. "I thought she was a receptionist. She's the manager?"

Kelsey folded her arms across her chest. "She's a terrible woman. Pretends she's above everyone else, as if being in the same room with us is slumming it."

I nodded. "That's the impression I got of her, too."

Kelsey leaned closer, dropping her voice to a whisper, as if someone might overhear us. "She's not, though."

"Not what?"

"Not better than the rest of us. In fact, I happen to know she steals products and goes through everybody's stuff when they're busy. You should see all the loot she's got stashed in her locker."

I narrowed my eyes. "Show me."

Kelsey led me to the break room and flipped on the light. On one side stood a fridge next to a counter with a small sink, drawers, and a microwave attached to the underside of a few cupboards. A table sat in the corner with several chairs clustered around it. A line of lockers hung on the far wall.

Kelsey stood in front of one of the lockers, pointing. "That one. I peeked inside and saw a bunch of stuff, including my missing MP3 player. But it's locked, and she never opens it when anyone's around, so no one knows she's the one stealing."

I fingered the padlock on the little door and smirked. "No problem." My tools made quick work of it, and the lock popped open without a fight. I swung the door open and gasped.

Keychains. Stuffed animals. Jewelry. I counted three watches and two MP3 players. And at the back, six bottles of hairspray and more colors of nail polish than I cared to count.

Kelsey whistled. "I didn't realize there was so much in there. I only saw a little of it."

I closed the door and snapped the lock in place. "Come with me." I led her back to the front counter and flipped on the flashlight app on my phone to search. "Got it."

Taped to the front of the register was a piece of paper with *Antonio* on it, followed by a phone number.

Kelsey hovered over my shoulder. "What are you looking for?"

"You're going to make a phone call to the owner," I said. "An anonymous call in the middle of the night, traced back to his own shop where the alarm hasn't even gone off? That'll get his attention. You've already made a name for yourself as a ghost, spraying all those people. Let's really leave a mark for you."

She gave me a nervous laugh. "Oh, I couldn't possibly talk to the owner. Nobody but Connie is allowed to talk to him."

"Honey, that's part of how she controls everyone. Call him." I picked up the shop phone and dialed Antonio's number, listened for it to ring, then handed it to Kelsey. "Tell him."

She took the phone, sweat beading on her ghostly skin. "Hello? Antonio?" Her voice shook, and she paused to listen to someone speaking on the other end of the line. When she spoke again, her voice held more confidence. "No, you listen to *me*. It doesn't matter who this is. If you want to keep your salon from financial ruin, it would be in your best interest to check your manager's locker. I think you'll find it very interesting." She hung up and gave me a tentative smile.

"Good job." I squeezed her shaking hand. "I think that should do it."

Her hand felt less solid than it had, and her face relaxed into peace and contentment. "I'm done."

I gave her a dubious look. "That's it? You don't want to stay and watch?"

She shook her head. "He'll come in the morning. I know he will. I don't need to see it happen."

"Really? You're sure?"

She nodded. "This wasn't about revenge, just about what was right."

I slipped the soul stone from beneath my shirt. "Well, then. Thank you for doing my hair."

She tilted her head to the side. "Sorry I took up so much of your night."

"It was fun hanging out with you."

I rubbed my thumb over the stone in my necklace, and Kelsey shimmered into a sparkling silver cloud, then flowed into the stone until she was gone. In a few days, I'd be near a dump site, and I'd empty the stone's contents into the receptacle so Kelsey and the three other souls sharing space in there would be sent on to wherever it was souls went.

For a moment, I considered leaving the shop by the front door. That would set off the alarms, and Antonio was sure to show up. Instead, I left the way I came, despite being tired as hell and not really thrilled about the six-store crawl through the ceiling. I wanted Kelsey's mystery call to live on as part of the ghost stories that would forever be told about this place.

Even though I'd been up all night, I waited around outside for a few hours until daylight. There was a quiet coffee shop across the street, so I had a front row seat when Antonio arrived.

At least, I assumed it was Antonio. He had keys to the place, long, luxurious boy-hair, and a pompous walk. I was on my third cup of coffee when Connie showed up, and my fourth when the cops escorted her off the premises. She didn't look so snooty anymore.

I touched the stone through the fabric of my shirt and smiled. "Good job, Kelsey." I tossed my paper cup in the trash, feeling a little jittery from all the caffeine.

On my way out the door, a woman looked up at me from her phone. "Hey, I like your hair," she said.

"Thanks." I smiled and patted my orange-streaked curls. "I just had it done."

"Baked Goods"

The doctor said I'm anemic,
that the diabetes has affected my eyesight.
"More red meat, no sweets."
Ironic advice for a vegetarian confectioner.

An arthritic old woman
can't sit for hours in the damp woods,
waiting for deer and rabbit to happen by.
A tragic waste to kill
such lovely creatures,
with so much life to give.

I eat the world's leftovers.
For this, they call me Witch.
They forget the children were sent to die.
With me, at least they are warm,
their swollen tummies filled with treats
before they leave this earth.

I have set the bait with what I know:
sparkling windows of sugared glass,
enticing shutters of cream filled cookies.
Cheerful peppermints line the path,
as if to say
"Welcome.
Here you are wanted."

"The Button War"

This is a flash piece that first appeared at the Confabulator Cafe website with the original title "Buttoned Down."

On Monday, Edwina Snagroot found the gate unlatched. Her prized hellboar, Terrance, had wandered into the garden and helped himself to every last fruit in her buzzberry patch.

As everyone knows, buzzberries are toxic to hellboars. Terrence fell ill and died by afternoon tea.

Edwina was devastated. She was also suspicious. Every night before bed, Edwina locked the gate as part of her routine. The gate should not have been unlatched.

Upon inspection, Edwina found a shiny silver button engraved with the letters "W.H." in the grass next to the fencepost.

Edwina was furious. Her bright pink hair blew in the wind as she shook her gnarled fist at the house across the street.

"Winifred Houndswaggle, you will pay for this!"

~*~

On Tuesday, Winifred Houndswaggle opened her front door to find that every last black rose in her garden had been beheaded. Winifred cried out in dismay and threw her pointed hat to the ground.

It took years for each rose to bloom, and she'd waited patiently so she could use them to rid herself of a nasty case of hexzema. She scratched her scaly arms and examined the dying plant. Several strands of bright pink hair wafted in the needle-sharp prickles.

Her eyes narrowed. "Edwina, you wretched cow," she whispered. "You won't get away with this."

~*~

On Wednesday, Edwina returned home from the market to find the thatching on her roof infested with golden star-aphids. They'd already eaten through a good portion of roof above her kitchen by the time she discovered them.

It took all afternoon and all of her carefully hoarded supply of unicorn sweat to banish them.

Exhausted and needing the services of a good thatcher before the next rainstorm, Edwina pondered her neighbor—now her greatest enemy.

This insult would not go unanswered.

~*~

On Thursday, Winifred, having forgotten all about her feud with Edwina, marched across her lawn to fetch the morning paper.

The smell hit her square in the face. She glanced down at her pointed shoes and scowled at what she'd stepped in. Dozens of dung beetles rolled their prizes across nearly every inch of the yard. It seemed they'd brought the contents of at least three cow pastures to her doorstep.

It took hours to shovel it all out and the lawn was ruined.

~*~

On Friday, Edwina found her fishpond filled with blood. Every last swamp lily lay across the surface, wilted and brown. Every frog, salamander, and fish floated belly up. It was a huge blow. Edwina had built the pond herself, digging and filling it, then stocking it with plants and animals she needed for her work.

Gone. All gone. How could someone do something like that? Why would someone do such a thing?

She buried the dead animals and drained the blood, considering her next move.

~*~

On Saturday, Winifred's speckled goat, Miranda, gave sour, green milk flecked with purple spots. The goat made one sickly bleat and keeled over dead.

Winnifred wept. She'd raised Miranda from a kid and had spent a great deal of attention and supplies on her to cultivate a perfect product. Winifred bathed her feet in the milk every half moon, and it eased her ingrown toenails. Now that was lost.

Her feet already ached in anticipation.

~*~

On Sunday, before the sun rose, Edwina marched out to confront Winifred before she had a chance to retaliate.

Winifred stomped out before dawn, carrying two buckets of brimstone and heading that way.

They met in the middle of the street and glared at each other.

"Winifred," Edwina said through pinched lips.

Winifred put down the buckets and tipped her head toward her enemy. "Edwina."

They stood that way for some time, shooting silent hatred at each other from their eyes.

Winifred wiped her hands on her apron and broke the silence. "You killed my goat."

Edwina scowled. "You bloodied my pond."

Winifred narrowed her eyes. "Well, you covered my yard in cow poop."

"After you infested my roof!" Edwina took a step forward, her hand clenched in a fist, ready to pop Winifred in her pointy nose.

"What was I supposed to do? You cut all my roses! I needed those!" Winifred, too, took a step forward, her hand raised to strike a blow.

"Only because you opened my gate and let Terrence out! You might as well have killed him with your own hands, letting him into the buzzberry patch like that!" Edwina pulled her arm back to strike.

"Well, you had it coming after you..." Winifred dropped her arm, confused. "Wait, what? I didn't open your gate."

"Don't try to lie about it! I found your button. You wanted me to know it was you!"

"Button?" Winifred frowned. "Show me."

Edwina pulled the silver button from her pocket and handed it over. "See? It has your initials on it, plain as day. W.H."

Winifred examined the object, turning it in the growing first light of the morning. She scowled, then her face transformed into a grin. She cackled and handed the button back. "You idiot. You read it upside down. It's H.M."

The two women stood on the street, and together they turned toward the house on the corner.

"She thought she got away with it. I bet she's been watching us the whole time," Winifred said.

Edwina nodded. "Oh, she's going to pay for this."

~*~

On Monday, Henrietta Manticore found the gate unlatched.

"Fool's Gold"

A lot of Todd the leprechaun was an early blueprint for Walter the brownie, Molly's husband in the Monster Haven series. Also, Dirk the Daring was a real gerbil, and his backstory is absolutely true. He didn't exactly drown in the toilet, but he did die shortly after he and his cage were knocked in by a cat. Marian's words are the same words I spoke at his memorial. No one came to that service, either. This story first appeared in the March 2011 issue of Daikaijuzine.

Very little ever surprised Marian, so when she found the pot of gold buried in her yard, it wasn't so much its presence that startled her, but how small it was. When her spade hit it, she took it for a small rock until she turned the earth over and sunlight caught the object, making it catch the sun's rays in a thousand minuscule rainbows.

Mildly curious, she plucked it from the small hole she'd been digging, freed it of a few clumps of clinging soil, and dusted it with her fingertips. It was roughly the size of a shot glass. Elaborate curlicues decorated the golden curves, and chips of diamonds and emeralds dotted the surface. A thin gold wire served as a handle. Peering inside, Marian saw the miniature pot was filled with tiny rocks that looked like gold nuggets.

Interesting, Marian thought. Heaving herself up from her squatting position, she reached into her pocket and produced a length of garden twine. She threaded it through the pot handle, tied a knot in the end, and put it around her neck for safe keeping. She shrugged dismissively and hunkered back down to finish her work.

The hole she was digging didn't need to be very large, so she finished the work in only a few minutes. A small cardboard box sat beside her. It had once held a coffee mug, a gift from some forgotten Employee of Christmas Past. The mug was long gone, probably one that declared something trite like "#1 Boss" or "Hang in there, baby!" The box, however, had been kept safe in a closet filled with other such cartons. One could never have too many boxes. Mugs she could do without.

She patted the container affectionately and placed it in the fresh hole. Gathering the loose dirt, she scooped it over the box, creating a small mound, then patted it down. She took a piece of the garden twine and joined two sticks together to make a little cross. She poked it into the dirt before standing up to brush her palms across her knees. A slight breeze kicked up, cooling her sweating brow and rustling the leaves of the tree above her. She closed her eyes and breathed deeply, mentally preparing herself for the next step.

"Dearly beloved, we are gathered here today," she said, her voice taking on a booming Southern Baptist preacher tone.

"Who's gathered here today?" asked a voice. "Looks to me like you're all alone."

Marian, never quick to startle, calmly looked around and saw no one. She scanned the area before her, walked all the way around the trunk of the elm tree, and finding herself alone, she took her place again at the foot of the tiny grave. "We are gathered here today to pay our respects to…"

"Down here, woman. Are you blind?" the voice said.

Marian let out an exasperated sigh and looked down. At the base of the tree, a man, roughly eighteen inches high, stood with his arms folded and one foot propped on a gnarled root. He wore jeans and a red-and-white striped polo shirt, and his dark brown hair was in need of a barber. Marian frowned at the shirt and had the passing thought that she had at last found Waldo.

"You're interrupting," she said. "If you don't mind?"

"No, by all means," he said, tipping his head toward her. "Proceed."

She cleared her throat. "Here lies Dirk the Daring. He was brave and adventurous, but he could not swim. An escapee from Petland, Dirk was found in the storage room of a shoe store. He had traveled through many obstacles, crossing half the mall before he was captured, but he never lost his adventuring gerbil spirit, even after coming to live with us here. His inability to tread water until he could be found and plucked from the dangers of the toilet was his downfall. He shall be greatly missed."

Marian bent over and dropped a handful of dirt over the grave. "Ashes to ashes,"

"Hey!" the man said. "You're spilling my gold, you stupid woman! Have a little respect!"

"Oh," she said, clutching the pot of gold to her chest. "I'm terribly sorry." Keeping one hand on the container, she squatted down and picked up two tiny nuggets. "Is that all of them?" she asked, eyeing him over her shoulder.

"No. You missed one over by the 'headstone.'" He snickered as he raised his hands and made air quotes around the word. "And you know, you're supposed to drop the dirt on the box, not on the covered grave. Also, that bit about 'dearly beloved' is for weddings. Oh, and one more thing…it's a gerbil, you idiot!"

"You're really not a very nice man, are you?" Marian put the last gold nugget back in its container and turned to walk back to the house. She despised air quotes.

"Hey, don't walk away from me!" The man had to run to keep up with her. "We have business to conduct, you and I. You have my gold! There are wishes! We have to deal and stuff!"

Marian ignored him and went into the house. Before she closed the door, she looked down at the man. He was out of breath and his hair poked out in sweaty spikes. "You shouldn't leave your things lying around like that. I've had a hard day and I'm going to take a nap now. I'm in mourning. No business will be conducted during the mourning period. Have a good day." She shut the door in his face. Smiling to herself, she stood a moment at the door.

"But there are rules," she heard him say in a miserable tone. "Nobody respects the rules anymore."

~*~

The next morning began early, as it always did in Marian's house. She would welcome the luxury of sleeping in from time to time, but past experience taught her the noise would gradually increase to unmanageable levels and it would take hours to make amends enough to quiet everyone down. She rose at five, showered and pinned her slightly frizzy, graying hair to the top of her head where it would, for a few hours at least, stay out of her way. She spent little time in front of the mirror these days and only stayed long enough to cover the basics of good hygiene. When she was younger, Marian had been pretty enough—nothing men swooned over, but she could hold her own. Now, at forty-seven, time was creeping in and erasing what little she'd had going for her. The thirty or so extra pounds she carried weren't enough to plump up the sagging bits, and the wrinkles kept appearing out of nowhere. She looked in disgust at a zit that was forming on her chin. Pimples and wrinkles at the same time seemed more than a little unfair. Ah, well. Nobody she knew cared what she looked like anyway, least of all herself.

The first order of the day was always breakfast. It would be nearly an hour before she herself could eat, but again, experience taught her there was an order to things, and doing them out of order had dire—and loud—consequences. The living room was large and cluttered but had very little furniture other than a rocking chair and countless tables of various sizes. Every surface held a cage or two, a tank, a Habitrail. Birdcages hung from the ceiling, and floor space was reserved for larger habitats. Gerbils, hamsters, and domestic rats gathered in neat rows along one wall, with a chinchilla, guinea pig, and two rabbits claiming the space beneath them. Doves, canaries, zebra finches, and parakeets swung overhead. Two enormous fish tanks stood side by side along another wall, their occupants a bright kaleidoscope of slow-moving confusion. Further along the wall sat a third, smaller tank that housed frogs and turtles in a mixed terrain of both water and dirt.

Marian pulled the blinds open around the room and dragged covers off the birdcages. As if by magic, the room came alive with joyful twitters, squeaks, grunts, and chatters.

For the next hour or so, she busied herself dispensing various types of seeds, vegetables, fruits, worms, pellets, and flakes. She had a kind word for the occupants of each domicile, forgetting no one, but she was not prone to cuddles or baby-talk and did her work with single-minded efficiency. As always, she ended with the fish tanks, being a firm believer in the old adage "the squeaky wheel gets the grease." Fish hardly ever make a fuss at the chow line.

When her work was complete, she moved to the kitchen and put a teakettle on to boil and bread in the toaster. As she waited for her breakfast, Marian noticed a faint tapping coming from the window over the sink, as if a bird were trying to peck its way in. Curious, she moved the yellow curtain aside. There stood the little man from yesterday, a defiant look on his face as he peered back at her. His lips were moving in agitation, but she couldn't make out what he was saying. Moving the latch to the side, she lifted the window and leaned close to the screen.

"Yes?" she asked.

"It's about time, woman," he said. "I've been banging on this thing all morning. Are you going to let me in or what?" Marian stood a moment, considering it. His manners certainly hadn't improved, but he seemed to be harmless. She took a moment to slip back to her bedroom and retrieve the pot of gold. The night before, she had replaced the twine with a black silk cord to make it more comfortable to wear. Placing it over her head, she returned to the kitchen and opened the back door.

"Would you like some breakfast?" she asked as he trudged in and shinnied up a chair leg.

"It's the least you can do," he said. His breathing became labored as he pulled himself up the linen tablecloth. She watched in fascination, wondering whether she should offer to help or if he would be insulted. It's probably a no-win situation, she thought. He'd be insulted either way. She shrugged and turned her back, deciding she'd better make some eggs to go with the toast or he'd raise a stink that she was trying to starve him.

"My name is Marian," she said. "Not 'woman,' if you don't mind. How do you want your eggs?"

For a moment, the man seemed to be at a loss for words. "Uh...scrambled...please?" he said. There was a long silence. "Todd. My name is Todd."

Marian paused with her spatula raised. She turned and looked at him. "Todd?" she asked. "Todd?"

"Yes, why?"

"Well, it just seems so…I don't know."

"You look disappointed."

"No, it's not that, it's just…you're Irish, right?"

"So Leprechauns are all supposed to be named Patrick or Seamus?"

"No, I…yes. I'm sorry. I've insulted you. I sincerely apologize for my oversight, Todd. It's a very nice name."

She turned back to the stove. In a few minutes, she had slices of toast cut in quarters and a generous helping of scrambled eggs heaped onto a cake plate. Filling a shot glass with tea, she added this to the plate and carried it over to the table. She pulled a few of her collected boxes from the closet and selected two of varying sizes. Together, they made a pretty good fit as a table and chair for a man about a foot and a half high. A linen napkin draped over the little makeshift table added a bit of elegance and she moved the plate of food to it. She filled her own dish and sat at the other end of the table. As Marian scooped eggs on her fork and brought it to her lips to blow on it, she glanced at Todd. He was just sitting there, staring at his breakfast with a sheepish look.

"Is it ok?" she asked. Her face colored as she realized his problem. "Oh, I'm so sorry. I didn't even think…" She cast her eyes around her kitchen, grasping for a solution. "Of course you can't eat with your hands. How could I be so inconsiderate?" Marian was mortified. Her first Leprechaun and she was a horrible hostess. Leaping to her feet, she was a flurry of activity, opening and closing cupboards, rummaging through drawers, slamming them shut and muttering to herself when their contents proved useless.

"No, no…it's fine," Todd said, making an effort to be heard over the chaos. "Sit down. I've got it."

Marian turned and looked at him, doubt and embarrassment mingling on her face.

"Just sit down," he said again.

Using a segment of toast, he shoveled eggs over a second slice, added the first piece to the pile and made a sandwich. He looked up at her and smiled. "See? It's fine. Now sit down and eat your damn breakfast, woman."

She lifted an eyebrow.

"Marian. Sit down and eat your damn breakfast, Marian. Happy?"

She was, in fact, very happy. Marian had lived alone since the death of her husband eight years before, and kept pretty much to herself. They'd owned several car rental agencies together, and after Hank's fatal accident while parking one of the rentals, she'd wanted nothing more to do with the business. Between the considerable insurance and the money from selling off the stores, she had plenty to keep her and her collection of animals going indefinitely. With the exception of trips to the grocery and pet stores, Marian didn't see many people anymore, and until Todd came for breakfast, she hadn't realized how much she'd missed having company around.

"So, tell me about Leprechauns," she said, sipping her tea. "It's obvious that I'm woefully ignorant, and I don't want to insult you again."

Todd belched. "What do you want to know? That's a broad subject and I'm not Wikipedia, you know."

"Wait, you have computers?"

"Oh, we have a lot of things. Why do you think they call it Microsoft? We had it first. There was a lot of debate over whether to call it 'Macrosoft' when they brought it to you people."

"I see," Marian said, disbelief clearly painted across her face.

"Look," he said, scraping together a second scrambled egg sandwich. "I can see this is hard for you to believe, but my family's been in this country for six generations. You're not living in a log cabin and making your own cheese, so why should my family be living in hollow trees and dancing jigs all day? I'm just saying we've advanced right along with you."

Marian considered this for a moment while she chewed. "Would you like more toast?" she asked.

"I'm fine," he said, licking his fingers.

"So…Leprechauns are modernized. Then what's with this thing?" she asked, patting the pot of gold around her neck.

Todd's eyes narrowed. "That," he said, "is my heritage and my magic. When we come of age, we have to design a pot to hold our inheritance of gold. When the design is approved, a master jeweler creates it. At the ceremony, the pot, the gold, and the Leprechaun are joined, and it becomes the source of magic for that Leprechaun. He…or she…must then find a hiding place for it, because anyone who captures the pot of gold captures the Leprechaun. In order to get it back, the Leprechaun must grant one wish in exchange."

Marian leaned forward and eyed Todd with suspicion. "One wish?" she asked. "I always heard it was three."

Todd sighed and rolled his eyes. "Yes, in the old days, it was three. You want three wishes, you have to go to Ireland. After six generations of dividing it up between offspring, there's not nearly as much to go around."

"Ah," she said, leaning back and nodding her head. "That explains it."

"Explains what?" he asked, his face turning pink.

"Nothing. Forget it."

"No, say it. You were wondering why it was so small, weren't you!"

"No, of course not!" Marian had always been a terrible liar. She fiddled with a stray tendril of hair and made a show of trying to pin it back on her head. She glanced at him and saw he wasn't going to let it go, so dropped her arms to her lap in defeat. "Yes, fine. You caught me again. I'm the unwitting victim of propaganda and stereotypes. I'm sure the size of your pot of gold is in no way a reflection on you personally."

Todd puffed out his chest. "Damn right it's not." He held out his shot glass. "Could I get a refill?"

Marian busied herself with the tea to cover the awkward silence. She set it carefully back on his table and took a deep breath. "So. One wish, huh?"

"Yes," he said. "One wish. I guess if they were small, I'd have enough juice to grant three, but they'd have to be really small. You know, like ordering a pizza or refilling the toothpaste. It's up to you." He shrugged. "In the meantime, I've gotta go to work."

"You work?"

"Yes, I work. Haven't you listened to a word I've said this morning? Thanks for breakfast. I'll be back for dinner around six. I'll bring my own utensils."

Marian sat stunned as he slid down the tablecloth, hopped off the kitchen chair, and left through the open back door. Huh, she thought. Dinner. I should go to the grocery store.

~*~

Todd arrived just after six as he'd promised. Marian had spent the day cleaning cages and worrying over what to cook for an uninvited Leprechaun, and finally decided to keep it simple. In all honesty, she was glad he was coming but didn't want the grumpy little bugger to know it. Still, he seemed to appreciate the meatloaf and mashed potatoes in a way that made Marian wonder when his last home-cooked meal had been.

"So," she said, trying to sound casual and not at all like she was prying. "Won't your family wonder why you're not eating at home?"

"Dead," he said, shoveling potatoes into his mouth. "All dead, except for my brother, Ted, and my sister, Peggy. They moved to Chicago."

"Why didn't you go with them?" Marian's brows knit in concern. No wonder he was so grumpy. She took a closer look at his frayed jeans and disheveled hair. She shook her head and mentally chided herself. He was a grown man—uh, Leprechaun—and she was not going to turn this into some warped version of "The Shoemaker and the Elves." The mental picture of her trying to sew clothes for him made her smile until she realized he was scowling at her.

"Why bother asking me a question if you're not going to listen?" he said, growing red in the face. "And what are you smiling about?"

"I'm sorry, Todd. I got distracted for a moment. What did you say?"

"Nothing important." He was sulking now, pushing his fork across the empty plate. "I was just saying that Chicago is too cold. I like the weather in California."

Marian smiled. "Me too," she said, clearing the plates. "There's cake, if you want some."

~*~

After dinner, she set the dishes in the sink to soak, then wondered what would come next. She and Todd spent an awkward moment looking at each other and then at the kitchen clock, making noises like it was getting late.

"I guess I'll get going then," Todd said.

"I suppose," Marian said. "Or…I was just about to watch the news…if you'd like to stay for a bit?"

Todd brightened, then composed himself into a carefully crafted expression of boredom. "I suppose I could stay for a little while."

She led him through the living room to get to the family room and he stopped in mid-step. His jaw dropped and for a moment he stood speechless as he looked around at the menagerie.

"What the hell is all this?" he said with dismay.

Marian was uncomfortable and defensive, but entirely aware of how odd the room looked. "It's my collection," she said. "This is where all the homeless animals come."

Hands in his pockets, Todd took a stroll around the room. He peered into the cages on the floor, then shinnied up a table to wander across it, letting out a low whistle. "So this is what you do all day?"

"Yes," she said. "Mostly. I don't know where half of them come from. They just show up in a box on my doorstep. Apparently, people have decided it's my job."

Todd stiffened and eyed the shadows with suspicion. "So, you're a widow and you have all these animals." A rabbit below him twitched, rattling its cage, and Todd jumped back from the edge of the table, visibly shaken. "Just how many cats do you have then, and why haven't you warned me?"

"Cats?" she said pulling herself up straight, more offended than she'd been in her life. "Now who's full of stereotypes? A woman living alone must have dozens of cats, is that right? Perhaps you'd like to see the pink tutu I made for the guinea pig? Come around next week, I'm nearly done teaching Hamlet to the mice. We'll be ready for their first performance on Tuesday. And have I, in any way, given you a reason to doubt my sincerity as a hostess? Did anything I've done so far make you think I wouldn't take your safety into account, even if I did have cats?" Marian fumed at Todd, her arms folded across her chest. "I am not a crazy cat lady."

Todd stood considering her for a moment, head cocked to the side. "Hamlet?" he said. He snorted, then started to giggle.

Marian's lips twitched. Todd covered his mouth but couldn't keep his laughter from erupting through the cracks between his fingers. Marian, attempting to retain what little dignity she had left, tried to contain her amusement. Her shoulders shook like a diesel engine, until the pressure bubbled up and escaped in a breathless cackle. This caused Todd to double over, holding his sides. They continued for some time, hooting and chortling, not even sure what had been so funny in the first place, each feeding off the other. When their laughter finally ran out of steam, Todd wiped his eyes and cleared his throat.

"So...no cats then?" he said.

"No," she said. "I'm allergic."

This caused an aftershock of hilarity, not as severe as the first, but no less cleansing. When they'd pulled themselves together, they moved to the family room and caught the end of the news, followed by reruns of sitcoms, then Letterman. They talked all evening, arguing over politics, talking about their families, Todd's dissatisfaction with his job as a telemarketer, the embarrassing antics of young starlets. Marian didn't want the evening to end, but they both needed to be up early the next morning. She saw him to the door and thanked him for coming.

Todd smiled up at her, then frowned, eyeing the pot dangling around her neck.

"Decided on a wish yet?" he asked.

Marian shifted from one foot to the other. "No," she said. "See you at breakfast?"

His eyes lit up. "How about blueberry muffins?"

"Muffins it is."

He nodded. "See you at breakfast."

"Unmatched Cupid"
A Mount Olympus Employment Agency Short Story

This story is a quick peek into the world of the Mount Olympus Employment Agency series. I originally wrote it for the 2013 Valentine's Day project for the Here Be Monsters website. The only requirement for the project was to match the theme "Heart-shaped Box." I ran with it, and the box itself barely played into the story. I'm a rebel like that.

Ellen flounced into the office, rosy cheeked and self-satisfied. She hung her wings on the hook beneath her name, and rang the bell next to the wipe-off board. The entire freaking office went wild with applause.

Except for me. Oh, I gave a polite clap, sure. But I didn't bother to offer even a fake smile, and had she deigned to look my way, she'd have seen the poison darts I was pretending to shoot at her out of my eyeballs.

Because Ellen was obnoxiously petite, the bosslady had set up a stepstool for her. I watched barely five feet of bubbling cuteness climb the step to draw another tick mark beneath her name on the board. She flashed a grin over her shoulder at the rest of the room, then added two more ticks.

The room erupted again. She smoothed her little pink-and-white cardigan, then hopped down.

I stared at my computer screen in despair. I wasn't cut out for this. Every match I tried to make blew up in my face. I was the worst matchmaker in the Cupid department. And if I didn't make a match soon, I'd be demoted and transferred to somewhere far worse.

Honestly, I wouldn't have taken the job if I'd had any other choice. There were only two ways into the Mount Olympus Employment Agency: you could be sponsored and brought in by a blood-related god—like Ellen did—or you could have unknown god blood somewhere in your heritage and hit rock bottom in your life.

That was how I got there. Apparently, I was related to some minor god, and when I found myself homeless, unemployed, and alone—boom. Some bum I'd never met before grabbed me and dragged me into an abandoned building. Except the building was different inside—huge, clean, and filled with people. I couldn't say which was more terrifying, abduction by a bum or the magic office, complete with gorgon receptionist.

I suppose I could have run, but I didn't have much choice. I had nowhere else to go. I didn't get to choose my new profession, either. They made me a cupid. And I sucked mightily at it.

I pushed my sweaty bangs away from my eyes and focused on the screen. It was no use. I'd been trying to fill the grid for so long, I'd lost track of where I'd started. Better to start from scratch. Tapping the reset button, I watched the sixteen portraits of lonely men and women shuffle like cards and spread themselves to the edges of my screen. The grid in the middle emptied its rows and columns for me to refill.

The Fates department had determined through whatever weird methods they used down there that several of these people were meant for each other. They did not, however, say which ones. Those of us working in the Cupid department were left with these gaping Sudoku grids that we had to sort through and attempt to place the right couples together in the right squares.

I squinted at the profiles beneath the photos. Derrick of the smoldering eyes was a dentist. I dragged his picture to the upper-left square. Felicia, a redhead with a lovely smile, was a veterinarian. I dropped her next to him. Hey, she obviously had good dental hygiene, a fact I was certain would appeal to Derrick. To her right, based entirely on her job as a veterinarian, I placed Stan, a blonde surfer with a golden retriever. But the grid line between the two blinked red.

No good. I took a closer look. Okay. So, Stan was gay. I tried placing him underneath Derrick's picture. The screen remained steady.

"Interesting." I tapped the screen with a chewed fingernail. "Dr. Derrick goes either way, don't you, buddy?"

Except that I could see absolutely nothing compatible between Stan and Derrick other than the fact that they both enjoyed the company of men. I sighed and dragged Stan to the bottom left corner of the grid for holding.

The Fates department probably thought this entire process was hilarious.

Stephanie, a stockbroker, was originally from a small town in Alabama—a much more likely match for Derrick, who came from a different small town in Alabama. I placed her picture where Stan's had been, directly beneath Derrick.

The key now was finding another match that might fit beneath the veterinarian and to the right of the stockbroker.

This was always the part that hung me up. Whenever I made it this far, I panicked. How could two different men be possible matches for the same two women?

I scanned the other twelve faces staring at me from the screen. Ah. Dave. Long hair tied in a ponytail. Charming grin. No job. Dave was an artist who made beaded jewelry and sold it to tourists on the boardwalk for cash, then couch surfed for a place to sleep.

Dave was a *project*. Two successful women. One handsome freeloader. I dropped Dave's photo next to Stephanie and beneath Felicia.

I groaned. Putting Dave in a middle spot instead of on an edge meant I would have to find four women who were potential love matches for him. I really didn't want to give this lowlife that many shots at love. Where was the justice in that? Smoldering-eyed Derrick with an education, a career, and an open mind only got two possible mates.

Maybe it was the right answer, but I wasn't going to be responsible for it. I hit reset. Maybe if I started over with someone else in the corner—Deadbeat Dave, for instance—I'd get a better idea of where everyone was supposed to go.

Gods, I sucked at this.

Two hours later I had a reasonable grid setup that I thought was, if not right, at least partially right. The next step would be fieldwork. As much as I hated setting the grid, donning the Cupid wings and running around town invisible to meddle in people's lives was worse.

I was worse.

On one assignment, I'd helpfully tipped over a man's coffee on a woman because I had the vague idea that this was what they called a "meet-cute" in the movies. Her hand was badly scalded, which meant she was unable to make the flute audition for the Miami Symphony Orchestra. She lost her dream job, then sued the pants off the guy who'd spilled his coffee on her. He lost his construction business and moved back to his parents' house in Missouri.

Not a meet-cute.

In the seven months I'd been in the Cupid department, I'd made three successful matches. Two of them were during training, so I'd had help. I was on very thin ice.

I glanced up at my assigned wings hanging on a hook next to Ellen's. Her cutesy giggles drifted across the office and over the wall of my cubicle. Ellen was cut out for this. Ellen had an instinct. Ellen was freaking adorable.

As I rose to make my reluctant way to grab my wings off their hook, I backed my chair into something solid. When I turned, I found the mail guy pushing his cart right behind me.

"Oh, sorry, Rudy. I didn't realize you were there."

He grinned. "My fault, Dory." He reached into his bag. "Got a package for you."

Rudy handed me a red velvet box, no bigger than a grapefruit and shaped like a heart.

I frowned. "Who's it from?"

Rudy shrugged. "No idea. I just make the deliveries." He skipped away, every few steps lifting off the floor with the aid of his winged sandals.

I dropped back into my chair and stared at the box. It was beautiful in its simplicity—the dark red almost a burgundy. The point on the bottom was rounded, giving the heart a more friendly feeling, like a bubble or a twelve-year-old girl's dots above her letters.

The velvet was smooth and luxurious against my fingertips as I lifted the lid. I had no idea what to expect.

Candy. Jewelry. Someone else's present delivered to me by mistake. Even a dead mouse. Any of those things could have been in the box and barely fazed me. What was really in there shocked the hell out of me.

At first, I thought the box was empty. A light flashed from its inky depths, and I dropped the damn thing on my desk. Lavender smoke puffed out, laced with sparkles and the smell of roses.

The smoke cleared and a moving image of the bosslady smiled up at me. "Please see me in my office, Miss Anderson. And bring your wings with you." The face dissolved.

Bosslady hadn't been in the office in months. I shivered. This was probably a very bad thing. I'd once heard of a woman in the Muse department who couldn't complete her artist quota. They'd demoted her to Hades and made her a poop scooper for the three-headed dog, Cerberus.

As much as I hated cupid duty, I did not want to scoop monster-sized dog poop.

I moved to the wall and unhooked my wings. They seemed so light in my hands for being so large. If I slipped them on, I'd be invisible once I left the building. I shook my head. There was nowhere to hide. They'd find me eventually.

And maybe scooping dog poop the size of a bowling ball would turn out to be my calling. Cupid sure wasn't it.

I knocked on the office door and waited for the sensual voice of my boss to invite me in. The door opened on its own.

When you're in the presence of a goddess, it's difficult to figure out where to look. This particular goddess was an even bigger problem.

Aphrodite, the goddess of love and beauty, adorned the pink, frilly office like a centerpiece at a wedding reception. She was breathtaking, smelled like a botanical garden after a spring rain, and sounded like a purring kitten. She was also practically naked by current cultural standards. The frothy bit of fabric she had draped over her hid nothing.

"How wonderful to see you, Miss Anderson. Please. Set your wings on the table next to you and have a seat."

I did what I was told, swallowing a lump in my throat and keeping my gaze on her pink marble desk. Disappointing a goddess—especially *this* goddess—was the most embarrassing and shameful thing I'd ever done. It was worse than the time I'd tucked the back of my skirt into my pantyhose on a dinner date with a chiropractor named Chip. The maître d' stopped me, but not before I'd marched clear across Andre's waving my baggy white granny panties at everyone in the dining room.

Yet, this was worse.

Aphrodite stared at me until I met the gaze of her lavender eyes. She cleared her throat, and it sounded like a choir of harmonizing lilies. "As you know, Dory, your success rate has been...unfortunate."

I nodded. "Yes, ma'am." In comparison, my voice was a hoarse, unlovely whisper.

"Oh, now. It's not a tragedy. No one's going to chain you to a rock and let a vulture eat your liver over and over." She laughed and it sounded like adorable white mice ringing miniature golden bells in their tiny paws.

She clapped her hands and the door opened again. I twisted in my chair for a better view. In strode a tallish man with brown hair and large brown eyes behind a pair of gold-rimmed glasses. He pushed the glasses up the bridge of his nose and cleared his throat.

"Dory, I'd like you to meet Ben."

He nodded at me and smiled. "Hi, Dory."

I didn't say anything. My jaw felt frozen shut.

Aphrodite rose and handed Ben a file with my name on it. "Ben will be taking you to your new assignment." She continued to speak behind me, but I hardly heard her. Something about Hercules being my new supervisor, and cleaning Augean stables or something.

She seemed to be waiting for me to respond, so I lifted my hand to acknowledge her. "Okay," I said. "Thank you."

Ben's eyes sparkled like a disco ball at a skating rink. He smiled and touched my hand. "Shall we go?"

I nodded. My heart thudded in my chest, and my stomach danced the Macarena.

We walked through the office, and behind me I heard Aphrodite's voice again. "Well done, Ellen. Ben was a perfect choice."

I glanced over my shoulder at Ellen. She gave me an adorable grin and wiggled her fingers at me in a cutesy wave. I didn't care in the least. She'd done me an enormous favor.

"What do you say we try to get you a better assignment?" Ben took my hand. "Do you believe in Fate?"

I smiled up at him, and the warmth of his gaze spread over me like a soft fur. "They're two floors down, right?"

Behind us, someone rang the matchmaker bell long and loud, and the office went wild.

"Hidden Holidays"
A Monster Haven Short Story

This holiday-themed Monster Haven short takes place between book two, Pooka in My Pantry, *and book three,* Fairies in My Fireplace. *It was previously published in 2014 as a single.*

While I'd been busy at work helping a bride who'd gone over budget, the ghosts of Christmas Past, Present, and Future had vomited themselves across my living room. The mess left me nowhere to step without crunching a glass ball underfoot. My head spun from a sensory overload of color, sound, and texture.

I stood on the threshold, wondering if I should go around back and enter through the kitchen door instead. Or maybe get a hotel until Christmas was over and Maurice, my closet-monster roommate, put everything away.

Maurice leaped out of a mound of lights, and the grin on his face was so large it took up half his head, dwarfing his big yellow eyes. "You're home early! I wanted to surprise you!"

"Surprise." I gave him a half-hearted smile. "I could leave and come back later."

Brenda Lee belted from Maurice's iPod, insisting that everyone should be rocking around the Christmas tree.

He shook his head, and several loops of colored lights slipped to his shoulders. "The tree will be here in a few minutes. You can help me decorate it." Shuffling his legs through the piles of decorations so he didn't step on anything, Maurice reached the chair closest to me and cleared it of boxes. "Sit, sit, sit. I'll get you something to drink."

I waved my hand at the mess around us. "I'm fine. The living room isn't. I'm not going to dehydrate and blow away."

As it stood, I couldn't imagine where the hell a tree was supposed to go.

The floor had no path to the kitchen or to the hallway. My options were few. Or rather, two—leave through the front door or have a seat. I stepped around a three-foot tall nutcracker in a Santa hat and sank into the chair, clutching my purse to me as if it were a shield.

A strand of tinsel puffed into the air and floated past my head.

"Maurice, where did you get all of this?" My eyes and face felt as if they'd stretched into an expression of shell-shocked horror. I did my best to force the muscles to relax.

But there was so much of it. Piles of gold and silver and red garland. Boxes of ornaments in individual compartments. Three electric angels sat side by side on the mantle, their wings squeaking open and closed in tandem. Nutcrackers in all sorts of designs and sizes. I counted six nativity scenes around the room in various materials—cornhusk dolls, ceramics, carved wood, and even LEGO bricks. A stack of wreaths covered the coffee table, and the sofa was a mass of tree skirts, stockings, Christmas-themed throws and pillows, and no less than five stuffed Rudolphs.

Maurice, looking satisfied with his haul, put his hands on his hips and winked at me. "I got it all out of the closet." He flipped a wall switch and the lights trailing around the room all went on at once, nearly blinding me.

Multicolored lights, white lights, strands of all blue, all green, and all yellow. Tube lights. Neon lights. Dripping icicle lights. Old-fashioned outdoor lights with enormous bulbs. Glowing, flashing, twinkling, chasing in every pattern possible. A family of lawn-ornament deer in the far corner came to life, their heads nodding, white lights glowing from their wire frames.

I groaned and closed my eyes. My eyelids were far too thin to block out the bombardment.

My resident closet monster had gone on a closet raid.

"You stole all this stuff?"

Maurice puffed out his chest in indignation. "*Borrowed*. Only from people who won't need it this year. I'll put it back."

I opened my eyes in alarm and regretted it. "Oh my God, Maurice. Turn those off. Please?"

He flipped the switch, leaving us in blessed early-evening light. "You okay? You don't look so good."

"It's just a lot." I smoothed my fingertips over the crease that appeared between my eyebrows. "I think I need some air."

Maurice's grin downgraded to a bewildered smile. "Yeah. Okay. Go take a walk." His smile grew an inch. "Iris will be here with the tree soon, and Molly and the kids are coming over to help decorate. We'll have it all fixed up by the time you get back."

I pulled myself to my feet. A motion-activated snowman ensemble rang tiny bells and sang Frosty the Snowman. "I'm sorry, Maurice. I don't mean to bring down the merriment. Christmas hasn't really been my thing for a long time. I'm a little overwhelmed."

He reached across the coffee table, knocking a few wreaths aside, and grabbed my hand. "I understand. We'll save you a few ornaments to hang when you get back."

Even with my empathic walls up, Maurice's disappointment leaked through my filters, squeezing my heart and giving me a good dose of guilt.

On my way to the door I managed not to break anything, and the only thing I knocked over was a mesh-covered kangaroo draped in colored lights and red ribbons.

Once my feet hit the gravel on my driveway, I took a deep breath to clear my head.

A lot had happened in the last six months or so. A lot had changed. I'd lived alone in my quiet house by the bay, mostly only social when my business partner and best friend, Sara, forced me into it. I hadn't known I was an empath, that the world was full of magical creatures, and that I was an Aegis whose job it was to take care of them.

I didn't mind. I embraced the change. I was happy. I even had a boyfriend who, though a soul-collecting reaper, was still the most stable and normal guy I'd ever gone out with. I had a closet-monster roommate, a skunk-ape bodyguard, and a family of brownies living in a mushroom in my backyard. My life was pretty awesome these days.

None of that meant I was prepared for a ginormous family Christmas with all the trimmings and over-the-top celebrating.

I turned toward my backyard and let the breeze coming from the nearby water blow through my hair and coax away some of the tightness in my chest. My scarf and gloves, while excessive farther inland in Northern California, were necessary for a December walk along the water. I looped the pink and green knitted fabric around my neck, pulled on the black and yellow-striped fingerless gloves, and buttoned up my wool coat.

As I made my way through the grass toward the tree line, I mumbled to myself like a crazy woman, paying little attention to my surroundings. Still, I'd lived in the same house nearly my whole life, so I knew the way to the beach and made it there mostly on autopilot.

My green skirt fluttered around my ankles and caught on the rubber soles of my Doc Marten boots. I tripped and took a nosedive into the trees.

I rolled over. From the pine-needled floor, I gazed through the canopy at the grey, darkening sky.

That's what you get for being a sour Scrooge when people are trying to be nice.

I snorted and sat up. In the distance, twigs snapped and bushes rustled in rapid succession. Iris, my skunk-ape bodyguard, burst into the clearing a few feet away. He towered over me in all his shaggy glory.

Iris squatted beside me, his brown eyes filled with concerned. Although I couldn't understand the exact words for the clicks and grunts he made, I understood his meaning.

"I'm fine." I unhooked my long skirt from where it was caught on my low heel. "Just clumsy."

Iris held out two huge hands covered in dark hair. Despite his size, he was gentle and tugged me to my feet without any jarring movements. He growled low in his throat and released one of my hands, then pulled me through the woods past towering eucalyptuses, stubby bushes, and thick oaks. A few yards in, he came to an abrupt halt. I bumped my nose into his upper arm.

Even up close, he smelled like a florist shop.

His thick lips pulled into a grin, not unlike the one Maurice had been sporting earlier. He chuffed and waved at a pine tree a few feet away. A small axe leaned against it, as if someone—Iris—had been preparing to cut the tree down before being interrupted.

And that's where I came in with my ninja ballerina moves. If my lack of enthusiasm doesn't kill Christmas for everyone, my lack of grace will keep them distracted.

"Is this the tree you picked out for us?"

He nodded, his eyes serious. When I didn't say anything right away, he shifted his enormous feet and his smile wavered.

He wanted me to love it. I pushed aside my concerns that a tree that size wouldn't make it through my door or stand upright in my living room. I ignored my worry about bugs, snakes, mice, and other woodland creatures the tree might be harboring.

I squeezed Iris's hand—which was to say, I flexed my hand that was buried inside of his huge one. "It's really lovely, Iris. Thank you." I swallowed thoughts of how much real estate the branches would take up in my living room and smiled. "You did a wonderful job picking it out."

He grunted, and pride puffed from him in a cloud, settling over us both in a soft mantel. Iris let go of my hand and grabbed his axe to get me the biggest, nicest Christmas tree I would probably ever have.

I watched a moment as he swung for the first cut. The axe looked so small in his grip. I shook my head and resumed my walk.

At the edge of my property, before reaching the path down to the beach, I passed the hip-high mushroom that housed my friend Molly and her kids. The brownie family fit comfortably inside, with several rooms carved from the mushroom and tiny wooden furniture to make them comfortable. Lights burned in the window cutouts, and little Abby sang louder than her older brothers, with no concern for the actual words.

"Bells on Bob's tail ring! Making cherries bright! What fun it is to ride and sing a spraying song tonight! Oh!"

I stifled a giggle and walked past. I didn't want to interrupt.

My boots crunched on the gravelly sand of the winding path to the beach, and my skirt snagged twice on the overgrown branches of the bushes guiding the way.

I wasn't a Grinch about the whole Christmas thing. My heart didn't need to grow three sizes before I could join the Who feast and be the one to carve the roast beast. I wasn't a Scrooge who needed a lesson in my past in order to preserve my future.

I was well acquainted with my past. At eight, my mom disappeared. I now knew the Board of Hidden Affairs had tampered with our memories so we wouldn't know where she went, but it didn't keep us from feeling the hole she left, especially around the holidays.

Dad had tried his best, but he was too confused, too hurt. He never fully recovered from Mom's loss, and Christmas after that was a low-key event. We put up a few decorations from my childhood—paper snowflakes Dad had cut from construction paper leftover from a school project I'd done on Nefertiti. A pair of cups and saucers Mom and I had painted in red, gold, and green at a ceramics shop. A blobby nativity scene I'd made out of homemade clay when I was four. The tree got smaller each year until I hit high school. By then, it was a sad, tabletop affair as pitiful and limp as Charlie Brown's tree before Linus and the gang showed it some love.

The idea of Iris's ginormous tree in my living room made me a little claustrophobic.

After Dad died and I moved back home, I didn't do much more than put out the sad little artificial tree with a few ribbons and gold balls on it. I liked Christmas. I even liked big gaudy trees. But I liked them at the mall or in the ski lodge where Sara and I usually spent the entire week of Christmas and New Year's. It was tidier that way.

I plopped onto my favorite rock and let out a tired sigh. This year I had a lot more than myself and Sara to worry about. I wouldn't be running off to hide at a ski resort.

Not that I skied much. Mostly I sat inside by the fire drinking hot chocolate laced with Irish cream. Heavily laced.

This year, Sara would be going without me. She might as well. Skiing was more her thing anyway. I'd miss her, though. It would be our first Christmas apart in ten years.

I stretched my legs and dug my heels in the sand, wishing it were warm enough to take my boots off and bury my toes. Tilting my head back, I let the wind blow away my grumpy mood and inhaled the intoxicating scents of the salt water, pine, and eucalyptus.

Gulls squawked. Waves crashed. A foghorn groaned. Someone sniffled and sobbed.

I snapped my head around to look. Not far away, a scrawny teenaged boy huddled against a large rock, gazing across the water and crying. Also, as was often the case with people I came across lately, he was naked.

My life is so weird.

The kid was curled in a ball, arms wrapped around his legs. He rocked in time with the movement of the waves. He didn't react as I approached, but he paused his rocking to rub his forearm across his face in an attempt to clear it of snot and tears.

Thick, dark hair curled around his ears and trailed a few inches over his shoulders. The wind tossed it away from his face, giving me a clear view of his profile. From a few feet away, I could see the moisture clinging to his impossibly long eyelashes. The kid probably would break a lot of teenaged hearts once he filled out.

"Hey." I kept my voice soft, trying not to startle him.

He jerked his head toward me, and his dark brown eyes grew wide.

"I'm sorry!" His voice was rough, and the words were more like a bark than any human sound. He moved to stand, bracing his palm on the rock behind him.

"No, sit. You're fine." I held out my hands and smiled to reassure him. "I won't hurt you."

The tops of his feet were covered in a down of dark fuzz, and his toes were webbed. Hobbit? No. For one thing, hobbits didn't like water. And for another—as far as I knew—hobbits were fiction.

Like skunk-apes and closet monsters and brownies.

To show the kid I wasn't a threat, I folded my legs and sank into a sitting position. Cold, damp sand soaked through the back of my skirt within seconds. I tried not to wiggle and make it worse.

The kid resumed his seat but kept his muscles bunched as if ready to flee at a second's notice. "I have to watch, in case they come back." He glanced at me from the corner of his eye, then went back to gazing out at the water.

I watched with him for a few minutes, though I had no idea who we were waiting for. The sun completed its descent, and the last sliver blinked out.

"Did you hear it?" I asked.

He tilted his head toward me. "Hear what?"

"The sun. It sizzles when the last bit drops into the water."

Human or not, teenagers have a universal language of facial expressions reserved for adults they think are complete idiots. I'd never been the recipient of such a look before now, but I didn't hate it. It meant I had his attention at least.

He snorted at me and returned to whale watching—or whatever it was he was doing. He shivered and clutched his arms tighter around his legs.

"It's kind of cold to be sitting out here naked. Do you want to borrow my coat?"

He swiveled his head toward me, and his big eyes filled with liquid. "I have my own coat." A sob caught in his throat, and he swiped at his face to dry a stray tear. He swallowed hard. "I used to, anyway."

I took off my coat and tossed it toward him. "Take mine until yours turns up. At least I have clothes on."

Not a lot of clothes, but more than Naked Boy.

I didn't think he'd take my offering at first, but he shivered again and snatched up the wool coat, draping it around his shoulders. "Thanks."

I scooted closer, as casual as I could be with a wet-sand wedgie creeping up my backside. "I'm Zoey."

He nodded. "I know." His fingers clutched the fabric tighter around his thin frame. "I'm Owen." He paused, and the muscle along his jaw tightened. "We were coming to look at you."

I frowned. "Look at me? Who's 'we'? And why were you coming to see me?"

I hoped by "look at you" he meant they were coming for a cup of hot cocoa and some of Maurice's delicious Christmas cookies.

I glanced at the kid's weird feet. So, not human. And he and someone else had been on their way to see me when some unnamed tragedy struck and left him naked and alone half a mile from my house, afraid to move a muscle.

Out in the bay, a splash caught Owen's attention. He sat up straighter and froze.

"Owen." I touched his shoulder. "Who are we waiting for?"

"Brynn and Rhys, my sister and brother. They got scared and swam away."

I squinted at the darkening waves. "What do they look like?"

"Seals, of course. They wouldn't be swimming in their human forms, not with that undercurrent."

"Oh." I'd only been part of the Hidden world for less than six months. In that time, I'd come across quite a few types of mythological creatures and urban legends. I didn't always know what the hell they were, but I'd read about selkies—seal people who shed their pelts and became human for short periods. Granted, I'd always been under the impression that selkies were all female, but at least I was able to follow his conversation. Not all the Hidden were that familiar to me.

My skin, already cold from volunteering my coat, felt like ice. "You lost your coat."

He nodded, miserable. "We came ashore and shed our pelts." He bit his lip. "Today is the Feast of Llyr, so we danced on the beach in celebration. When we were tired, we were going to climb the path to your house to look at the new Aegis. We went to get our pelts to wrap around ourselves and…" He stopped and bowed his head.

Waves of sadness rolled off his skin and choked me with its intensity. "Oh, Owen." I squeezed his hand. "Your pelt was missing?"

He nodded, head still hanging over his knees. "The other two were still there. We must've interrupted the thief. My siblings would've stayed, but I told them to go. I was afraid whoever took my pelt would be back. And maybe they could go for help." His voice broke, and his shoulders shook, this time with emotion rather than cold.

"Oh, honey, I'm sorry." I put an arm around him, and he tilted into me, crying. My other arm wrapped around him, and I held him until he was cried out, like my mom did for me when I was little.

There wasn't much else I could do, though. I was furious that someone would do something so awful. Stealing a selkie's pelt was on the list of lowest things a person could possibly do. In fairy tales, fisherman did it to force selkies to be their wives, which was definitely not cool.

Owen sniffled and sat up, wiping away his tears. "They're not coming back, are they?"

I had a mother who disappeared and never came back. I was not the one to ask about family loyalty.

"How about we get you safe and warm, get some food in your stomach? Then maybe we can try to figure out who took your pelt and where your family is."

He nodded, and we helped each other to our feet.

"I guess if they come back, they can find your house, right?" His eyes were so hopeful, begging for reassurance.

I gave him steady, firm look. "Owen, everybody finds me, eventually. Don't you worry."

As we turned away from the water to make our way back home, two things happened at once.

Ahead of us, twigs snapped and trees shook, as if something very large and very angry were tearing through the woods toward us. Behind us, frantic voices shouted Owen's name.

We both halted in mid-step. Owen spun around, my coat flapping like a cape. He glanced over his shoulder at whatever terror lurked just out of sight in the forest, then tore back to the water. A naked girl and a naked boy, both a little younger than Owen, stood grinning in the waves, water splashing around their knees.

The terrible thing in the woods crashed from the tree line, growling and snorting. I took two steps back before I realized it was Iris.

Iris dangling a short, stocky man in the air by one foot.

I turned toward the kids and gave them a signal I hoped they'd understand to mean they were safe to come up from the water. Without waiting to see if they'd follow, I picked my way up the path to inspect what Iris had caught for me.

The man twisted in Iris's grip, but he didn't struggle much. The dark suit was good quality, and the one shoe the guy still wore looked expensive. Blood had rushed to his chubby face, flooding it with pink—a terrible look for someone with such orange hair.

A gold shamrock pinned to his lapel twinkled in the twilight.

I groaned. "I thought I got rid of all you guys a few months ago."

A mob of leprechauns had rolled into town and tried to set up a protection racket in Sausalito. Several people were hurt or killed when they refused to pay. After collecting all their lucky shamrocks, I'd booted them out of town and told them not to come back. This guy showing up in my backyard was not a good sign. Maybe I wasn't as scary as I'd hoped.

The man blinked at me from his inverted position, and a slow smile spread across his face. "Fin. Fin Jones, at your service, madam." He pulled a business card from his inside coat pocket and held it out to me.

Iris chuffed and gave me an incredulous look. I shrugged and took the card.

Finnegan Jones
Acquisitions and Treasure Hunting
If you want it, I'll find it.

I made a sour face and tucked the card in my blouse. "Mr. Jones, give me a reason not to let my friend snap you like a twig. The Leprechaun Mafia is not welcome on my property. Your people have been warned."

His salesman smile didn't waver. "Madam, there's no such thing as this 'Leprechaun Mafia' you speak of. And if you're referring to that small incident with the Sacramento Brotherhood, those events occurred in Sausalito. I'm an independent contractor, unassociated with the Brotherhood." He had the audacity to wink at me. "And this isn't Sausalito, either."

I bent low to look him in the eye, and I spoke through gritted teeth. "You're in my woods, and a selkie pelt has gone missing. Theft is not a business model. Hand it over or I let Iris beat it out of you."

Iris shook the leprechaun for emphasis. I nearly ruined the effect by smiling at Iris. Having backup was awesome.

Fin held his hands out. "Please, no. The suit is expensive and I've already lost a loafer. If you'll have the gentleman put me down, I'll hand over the pelt. I don't want trouble."

I nodded and Iris dropped Fin. On his head.

The small man took a moment to shake sand from his hair and brush the wrinkles from his clothes. He reached into his pocket for a flat box, about the size of a woman's wallet, then pinched it open. A pile of fur sprang out, as if it had been under pressure. The pelt was far larger than the box, but since I owned a magical purse with similar properties, I didn't question how it fit.

"My pelt!" Owen ran past me in a naked streak, scooping the pelt into his arms and rubbing it against his face.

Brynn and Rhys appeared on either side of me, their pelts draped around them like blankets.

Brynn grinned at me, and her dark eyes lit her face. "We went for help."

I frowned. "How did you talk to Iris from the water?"

Rhys puffed out his chest. "We found a sea serpent. She said she knows you and would take care of it."

"Frannie." I smiled. "I haven't seen her since she and her baby rescued me from sharks after I fell overboard from a dinner cruise."

That sounded ridiculous, even to myself. And I'd lived it. The kids didn't even blink.

How a sea serpent had gotten word to a skunk-ape I had no idea, but I knew the two were friends. It made a weird sort of sense, given the context of my currently wacky life.

"Can I go now?" Fin stood to the side watching us, his arms folded across his chest.

I squinted at the sky. Full dark was nearly here, and I had to get back home before I couldn't see my way through the trees. Maurice would be worried soon.

"Here's the deal, Fin." I gave him the full-on force of my most serious stink-eye. "You get the hell out of this town. You do not operate your business anywhere in the Bay Area. If I hear anything about you, even a whisper, I will find you. Iris is not the only scary friend I have, and I will not hesitate to send some of these terrifying people after you." I intensified my stink-eye. "You understand?"

The leprechaun nodded. "I understand."

"Leave."

He backed away from us and disappeared into the woods. Iris grunted a question at me.

"I agree. Follow him out to make sure." I patted Iris on the arm. "Thank you."

Iris took off into the trees, silent despite his size. When he wanted me to hear him, the trees rocked and crashed. If he didn't want to be heard, like now, he could walk right next to me and I wouldn't hear a whisper.

When I turned to the kids, they were already wiggling into their sealskins. Owen paused and gave me a soft smile. "We need to swim now. Thank you for keeping me company."

I shrugged. "I couldn't let you sit there all by yourself." I glanced up the hill in the direction of my house. "If you ever need anything…"

"We know where to find you!" Brynn's chubby cheeks sprouted whiskers, and her tanned face grew darker with fur. Before my eyes, all three melted into their seal forms, then flopped across the beach into the water.

I heard splashes, but the light was too dim for me to see. The selkies were gone, and I was alone in the dark with a hike through the woods to get home. I picked up my discarded coat, brushed the sand from it, and slipped it on.

Maurice was probably having a heart attack with worry.

I picked my way up the path, then stepped into the dark woods. To my surprise, the trees came alive with dancing lights along the path home. As I walked, fairies from behind flittered past me, lighting the way ahead.

Somebody was always looking out for me.

A few minutes later, I was back in my own yard. The house itself lit my way from there, though I noticed Molly's mushroom sat in darkness. Cheery music floated toward me and drew me toward the warmth of my house. From that far away, I still couldn't make out the words or the tune being played.

It didn't matter how much of a mess the living room was. If Maurice wanted to have a big, gaudy Christmas, then I would share it with him. I'd been selfish earlier. Maurice was family now. Maybe it was time for some new traditions.

And we'd figure out how to make Iris's ginormous tree work, as soon as he finished chasing off the leprechaun.

From the porch, the music was much louder, but still nothing I recognized. I took a deep breath with my hand on the knob, then opened the door to step inside.

In the few hours I'd been gone, the room had transformed into something entirely new and utterly lovely.

Somehow, Iris had managed to get the tree there before the leprechaun/selkie fiasco. Apparently, getting it through the door hadn't been the problem I'd imagined and, while it did take up a lot of real estate, the tree didn't overwhelm the room.

The tree stood in elegance, adorned with colored lights, red-velvet ribbons, gold and silver ornaments, and a shimmering star on top that was lit from within by a warm, golden light. The star didn't even touch the ceiling. The fit was perfect.

Twinkling white lights lined the mantel, windows, and doorways. Everywhere I looked, my gaze landed on something beautiful. The piles of stuff were gone, and only a small percentage remained. Maurice could have gone overboard, but he hadn't.

"Oh, Maurice." I stepped inside and unbuttoned my coat, trying to see everything at once. "It's so pretty."

He moved behind me to pull off my coat and take my scarf and gloves. "Do you like it? I was worried."

"I love it."

"We helped!" A small voice drifted from the other side of the couch, and Molly's littlest, Abby, hopped from the floor to the armrest. A few seconds later, Molly popped into sight, then was joined by Aaron and Fred, her two older boys.

"Happy Wintergreen, Zoey!" Aaron said.

Fred nodded and smiled, a bit more subdued than his younger siblings. "We brought the bunny fluff," he said. "Would you like to help us?"

"Bunny fluff?"

Molly waved me over. "It is our tradition. This time of year, there is often less of the things we need. We celebrate Wintergreen to remember to be grateful for the things we *do* have rather than worry for the things we do not." She directed me toward a basket filled with fluffy white down. "Rabbits share their undercoat with us so we will not be cold when winter takes hold. For the festivities, we decorate with it."

Molly and the kids each took handfuls from the basket and tucked it between branches and pine needles. I took a little and placed it here and there, but mostly I watched the kids. Their laughter blew the last of my grumpiness away, and I laughed with them when they jumped from branch to branch like little birds, stuffing bunny fluff into the greenery.

When they were done, it looked as if we'd had a light snow in the living room.

"My turn!" Maurice appeared beside me with a grocery bag. "Reach in and grab one."

I craned my neck to see inside. "One what?"

He snapped the bag shut. "No peeking. Just pick."

I crooked an eyebrow. If something alive squirmed inside, harmless or not, I'd have to pop him. But if I couldn't trust Maurice, I couldn't trust anyone. I held my breath so I wouldn't scream if something startled me, then plunged my arm into the bag.

My fingertips brushed pieces of fabric. I fished around until I found an especially soft piece and drew it out.

The ugliest hand-painted tie I'd ever seen dangled from my hand. A trout with wonky, mismatched eyes leapt from a stream as a bear chased him. I rubbed the fabric. "Silk?"

"Now, tie it in a bow and make a wish," Maurice said. "If you wish hard enough, Saint Cedarchip might grant it."

"What?" I stared at him.

"Oh, my gods, Zoey! Hurry before the magic runs out! Tie it, quick!" His face wasn't nearly as distressed as his voice pretended to be.

I tied the men's neckwear into the best bow I could muster, considering it wasn't meant to go in that shape, then closed my eyes for nearly a minute.

I opened one eye. "Okay, now what?"

He took the tie from me and arranged it on the tree in a cloud of bunny fluff. "Now we have hot cocoa. Duh. Sit, sit, sit!" He gave me a small push into my favorite chair. "Wait here."

While I waited, there was a tap on the window, so I wandered over to see who it was. I pushed the curtain aside, and Iris's big grinning face stared back at me. I opened the window.

"Hey, Iris. The tree is gorgeous. Is Fin gone?"

Iris snorted and made chuffing noises I didn't understand.

Molly hopped to the sill and sat with her legs crossed. "He says the man is gone and will not return. Iris has a souvenir for you."

Iris held out his enormous, hairy-backed hand. A gold shamrock lapel pin glittered in the soft light. Iris chuffed again, this time with laughter.

I winked and took the pin from him. "How about we make it a new tradition, Iris?" I scanned the room for the right place to show off the leprechaun's lost luck. One of the red velvet bows had fallen from the back of the tree, so I pinned the shamrock to the center of it, then stuck it on the frame over the front door.

"Christmas luck for all who enter or leave," I said.

"Sit, sit, sit!" Maurice brought a tray of mugs filled with steaming hot chocolate and placed it on the coffee table. Someone knocked on the back door, and he tilted his head. "Sara and Riley aren't due for another few hours. Are you expecting anyone?"

I shook my head. Frothy whipped cream clung to my upper lip, and I licked it away.

Maurice returned to the kitchen and came back with three teenagers in tow.

"Blessed Feast of Llyr!" Owen said.

Rhys waved a square basket in the air, and the smell of fish wafted across the room. "We brought the blessing creel. Do you have a big pot for the crabs?"

"I'll clean the fish!" Brynn snatched the basket from her brother and skipped into the kitchen.

I settled in my chair and sipped my cocoa. The brownie kids hopped from branch to branch, rearranging bits of fluff on the tree. Maurice directed the selkies in the kitchen while they cooked up the fish and shellfish they'd brought.

Behind me, Molly and Iris chatted in grunts and chuffs while she wove the hair around his face into braids, then attached tiny silver bells below his chin.

So many different traditions. So many different holidays.

"Hey." Maurice knelt next to me with a small cardboard box in his hands. "I thought you might like to add this stuff."

I reached for the flaps on the box, then frowned, hesitating. "Where did you get this?"

"From the garage. I was looking for an extension cord."

My heart squeezed in my chest. I knew the box. A lot of Christmases had come and gone since I'd last seen it.

I pulled the flaps open and peered inside. My blobby, clay nativity scene was long gone, but the baby Jesus remained. It didn't look like a baby Jesus, but I knew what it was supposed to be. Small as it was, it still felt heavy in my hand. One of Dad's fancy paper snowflakes, heavily creased, unfolded to reveal the elaborate shapes he'd cut from the pages of my Nefertiti report. I shoved aside a few ribbons and half-used candles to get to the wad of paper at the bottom. I peeled the paper away and found mom's hand-painted china cup in gold and red and green.

I took those three things, forgotten over the years but no less precious, and put them all on the mantle. I tucked some bunny fluff around them to keep them safe.

Wiping away a stray tear, I turned to face my family.

"Happy Wintergreen Saint Cedarchip Feast of Llyr." I squeezed Maurice's hand.

"Merry Christmas, Zoey." He kissed my cheek. "What did you wish for when you tied your Saint Cedarchip bow?"

I sighed, content. "Nothing. I didn't wish for a thing."

"How Greg's Chupacabra Became a Small Town Legend and Ended Up Between the Wooden Eye and the Wig Collection at the Caney Valley Historical Society"

My ex-husband is a great guy. You'll never hear me say a bad thing about him. But the truth is, we're from two different worlds. He called me up one day and asked if I'd heard what happened. I had not. "Somethin' ate my damn goats," he said. I don't know what it was about how he said it, but I couldn't stop laughing, and "Greg's Chupacabra" was born from those four words. This story originally appeared in the September 2010 issue of Seahorse Rodeo Folk Review. *Sorry about your goats, Mike.*

Greg pulled himself into the bed of his rusty Ford and peeled the tarp from the coagulating mass of flesh. He covered his nose and mouth with the back of his hand in an attempt to stifle the stench. Four other men gathered around, jostling each other.

"Sure is an ugly son-of-a-bitch," Roger said, crinkling his weathered face in disgust.

"Stinks, too," Steve said. He pulled a bandana from his back pocket and tied it around his face, then climbed into the back of the truck. He hunched down for a closer look. "What the hell is it?"

Greg nudged the carcass with the toe of his work boot. It made a wet, squelching sound. "Dunno. Bastard's been killing my goats, so I shot him. I was hoping one of you might know what the hell it is."

Trevor tipped his ballcap backward and scratched his head. "Ate your goats, did it? Might be one of them chupacabra things they got down in Mexico."

Steve scooted back from the body in alarm and nearly toppled over. "In Kansas? You've got to be kidding me. What the hell would it be doing this far north?"

"Couldn't say," Trevor said. "But there was a lady down in Texas found a dead one last year. It was all over the news. Killer bees, pythons—everything's moving north. Global warming, they say. Can't see why the goat suckers wouldn't move north, too."

Jimmy shook his head in disgust. "That's the stupidest thing I ever heard. There ain't no chupacabras. And that lady in Texas had the DNA tested. They said it was a mangy dog or fox or something. Probably same as what Greg's got here."

"Think what you want," Trevor said, nodding his head wisely. "If the university couldn't say what the DNA was, they wouldn't likely admit it. Probably just called it a dog to avoid a panic."

"The way I see it," Roger said, turning his head to spit, "doesn't really matter what it is as long as it's dead. Any idea if it was on its own? I heard it was a pack of them down in Texas."

Greg had been feeling self-satisfied and victorious up to that moment. His face fell. "I guess there could be more. Makes sense. Maybe I better get back home and keep an eye out." He pulled the blue tarp back over the carcass and secured it in place with a few bricks.

"What're you going to do with it?" Steve asked. He jumped down from the truck and pulled the bandana from his face.

"Bury it. Burn it. Dunno," Greg said. "Thought maybe I'd take some pictures first. See if the newspapers might be interested."

Jimmy snorted. "I hear they pay good money for pictures of bald, dead coyotes."

"Don't you let them do DNA tests," Trevor said. "Won't do you any good. They won't tell you the truth anyway."

Greg jumped in the cab and started the engine. "I'll let you know," he said. "I better get back. I can't afford to lose any more stock." He pulled out of the parking lot at the Short Creek Bar, dust clotting the air in his wake.

The four men watched him go, his taillights glowing through the veil of settling dirt.

"Think there's more of them?" Steve asked.

"There's always more," Roger said. "Even Bigfoot has a wife."

~*~

In small town Kansas, a man can't throw a rock without hitting somebody he knows. With a population just under two thousand, Caney was no exception. Three days later, Roger and Steve were right out front of Caney Agri shooting the breeze when Greg pulled into the parking lot to pick up a supply of feed.

"Well, hey," Roger said. "How's that chupacabra, Greg?"

Greg swung out of the cab and shut the door. He leaned his shoulder against the truck and folded his arms. "Doing just fine. Dropped it off in Edna this morning, in fact. I'm having it stuffed."

Steve choked. "You what?"

Greg gave a self-congratulatory smile. "Took it to a taxidermist."

"Thought you were going to get rid of it," Roger said. "Whatever they do to that ugly thing, I guess it'll still stink."

"Probably so," Greg said. "The wife's not too happy about it."

"I bet not."

Steve strolled over and gave a cursory glance at the truck bed. "Find any more?" he asked.

"Now that's a funny story," Greg said. "After I saw you the other day, I ran right home, parked my truck by the barn, and sat on the porch half the night. Kept my rifle right by me, just in case."

"Did you see anything?" Steve asked, hands stuffed in his pockets and eyes wide.

"No," Greg said. "But I heard something. A weird, scratchy whine coming from several directions. I don't mind telling you, the hair on the back of my neck was standing straight up and saluting."

Roger was notably quiet but moved closer.

"I grabbed my gun and started to move off the porch when it sounded like something had jumped into the back of my truck. There was a snuffling sound, the crinkle of the tarp, and then a loud yip. When I got there, they were gone, but the tarp was pulled off the carcass. I haven't seen or heard anything since."

Steve sounded out of breath. "What do you suppose happened?"

"I'll tell you what happened," Roger said. "It scared them off. Scared them good. And now they're at my place. I've lost two ducks, and my cow is so spooked she won't hardly let me close enough to milk her."

Greg considered this. He tucked his hands into his armpits and crossed his ankles. "Sorry about your ducks, Rog. You want to borrow it after I pick it up? Maybe they'll leave your place alone if you have it over there a few days."

Roger looked relieved. "I heard that scratchy whining myself last night. I'd appreciate the loan."

"I'll bring it over soon as it's done. No problem, buddy."

~*~

Within a month, the stuffed carcass was a sought-after commodity. Roger kept it in his yard for four nights before Steve came over with Greg for his own turn with it.

"Take it," Roger said. "Did the trick the first night out. Within two days, Gertie's milking was back to normal, and I haven't missed a single bird."

When Roger showed it to him, Steve swallowed hard and backed up three steps. "What the hell is that?" he said, trying not to sound like a little girl.

"Scary, huh?" Greg said. "The taxidermist tried to make it look natural. Said he had to get creative, not knowing what the hell it was in life."

It bore little resemblance to the squashed mound of flesh Steve had seen before in the truck. The bluish-black skin had a sparse covering of thin, white hairs. These had been fluffed out to look almost like quills. The claws were polished to an ebon sheen, and the ears pinned to look fierce. Lips were peeled back to better display vicious fangs, and the cloudy, cataract-laden eyes had been replaced with glowering red glass.

"It was gross before, but now it's down-right terrifying. My wife's going to pitch a fit when she sees this out back." He paused. "Can't afford to lose another pig though. It's worth it, I guess." Steve looked queasy. Whether it was the sight of the animal or the thought of his wife's ire, they weren't sure.

The carcass spent just three nights at Steve's before it was passed to Trevor.

"Two of my best hunting dogs were in a terrible scrap with something out there, and one of my wife's cats has gone missing," Trevor said.

"Help yourself," Steve said. "It scares the hell out of my wife, and the pigs have quieted down. Sounds like the pack has moved on to your house."

Greg's chupacabra became a town legend. It was no secret that something was out there stirring up livestock, and whoever had the ugly thing on their property didn't seem to have any trouble afterward. Despite Greg's decision not to call the papers, they eventually found out and pestered him for interviews. When he wasn't forthcoming, they moved on to other Caney residents and printed whatever rumor and hearsay they could dig up.

Jimmy was noticeably loud in his opinions. "I saw it before it was stuffed," he often said to anyone who would listen. "It ain't no chupacabra. Just a mangy dog that's been fancied up by the taxidermist. Ain't no such thing, and you can quote me." Jimmy's negative press was probably the biggest favor he could have done for Greg. The story died down after a few months.

And the chupacabra continued its grand tour of Southwest Montgomery County.

After six months, most landowners in the area had, in turn, displayed the macabre trophy somewhere on their property. It was a point of pride to be able to call a farm "Chupacabra Free," and local real estate agents had even begun using it as a selling point.

Mostly, the animal wasn't needed anymore, and Greg kept it under a blanket in his garage. Weeks had passed since the last person had come by to borrow it.

TRANSMONSTRIFIED

The knock on the front door was almost timid. Greg, not even certain he'd heard it, opened the door and peeked out. Jimmy stood with his Royals cap in his hands, worrying it around in a circle.

"Hey, Jimmy," Greg said. "What's up?"

"My chickens are dead," he said, staring at the ground.

"Sorry to hear that, buddy." Greg smothered a smile and tried to look serious. "What do you suppose happened to them?"

Jimmy scuffed his feet and mumbled into his hat.

Greg leaned forward and cocked his head toward him. "Sorry, didn't hear that. What'd you say?"

"I said, 'Can I borrow it, please?'" Jimmy's voice was louder and a little defiant.

"Borrow what?"

"Fine," Jimmy said. "You want me to say it? I'll say it. Can I borrow your damn chupacabra?" He jammed his hat over his head and stood fuming.

"Of course you can, buddy. All you had to do was ask."

~*~

With nothing worse than the occasional fox or coyote roaming their lands, the farmers around Caney had no more use for the stuffed chupacabra. Greg himself didn't want to look at it anymore, and not even taxidermy and the passage of time could completely eradicate the stench. The Caney Valley Historical Society was both pleased and baffled by his donation. With so many pieces of historic value, Greg's gift was badly suited for the rest of their collection. In the end, they tucked it in a cramped corner with Amanda Brighthouse's wooden eye and Daphne Taylor's wig collection. It sits there still, collecting dust and staring out through its crimson, glass eyes. And it's ready, should anyone find the need.

"Snow Kissed"

Fairy tales are the truest stories I know. When I was a kid, someone gave me an enormous book of fairy tales. I read most of the stories over and over under the covers with a flashlight when I was supposed to be asleep. "Snow Kissed" is very loosely based on the Hans Christian Anderson story "The Little Match Girl." Something about the original always struck me as so beautiful and tragic, and it stayed with me my entire life. Not only do I still have that book today, it has an entire shelf of friends to go with it.

Wren flew through the trees with no other destination but *away*.

She ran blind, and her lungs labored against the assault of frigid air she gasped with each step. Her feet, clad in boots far too large and stuffed with burlap to fill the holes, chuffed through the deep snow, leaving behind a trail even the town drunk could follow.

The cold, the damp, and the signs she left in her wake were nothing to Wren. Her only thought was *away*.

In another time, another place, Wren might have had fancy dresses to wear. Her hair of sun-lit gold might have spilled down her back in perfect curls held in place by colorful, satin ribbons. She might have had handsome suitors plying her with trinkets and sweets to win her favor.

This was not another time, another place. This was now. This was here.

Wren scavenged or stole whatever scraps of cloth she could find to protect herself from the cruel northern winters. When her body began to change, her hips and breasts beginning to round and soften, the miners took notice. They reached to touch the soft, yellow ringlets, snatching bits of sunshine to keep them warm through the brutal winter. Wren retaliated with a sharp knife, hacking and sawing until nothing remained but a head of hay stubble, far too short for even the cheeriest of bows to brighten.

Despite her self-mutilation, she could still have her choice of suitors—if she didn't mind the coal-smudged fingers of men more than twice her age. There were no trinkets or sweets to be had, but they were quite willing to ply her with lumps of fool's gold and beads strung together on deer sinew.

TRANSMONSTRIFIED

Wren broke through the trees at the edge of the lake and could go no farther. She leaned against a tree to catch her breath, and the cold bit her ears and cheeks. The scrawny woolen coat she wore gave little warmth, but she drew it closer around her thin shoulders.

Her lungs ached with the effort of trying to warm the air wheezing in and out of her chest. She slid to the base of the tree and huddled there, gazing across the frozen lake.

She'd have to go back soon. There was no food or shelter within twenty miles of the small mining town she'd fled. Eventually, she'd have to trudge back to the tiny room behind the bar where she slept. Back to the grasping hands, the careless kicks, the hopeless future. Back to the unfinished beating Stavros was waiting to give her.

It would be dark in a few hours, and they'd come search for her if she didn't wander in on her own. All it would take for Stavros to remember she was gone was a single spilled mug with no one there to answer his command to mop it up. The men living in Buehler's Pass were clumsy. It wouldn't take long.

Wren's bleak passivity settled heavy on her shoulders. She squinted at the lake, her vision smudged with unshed tears. In the chill, her eyes were reluctant to give up the liquid warmth that would surely freeze the minute it was released.

Through her blurry eyes, the lake seemed to swirl and undulate, though Wren knew that wasn't possible. It was frozen solid this time of year. There were no waves or currents.

She blinked away her tears, enduring icicles on her face in exchange for a clearer look. The lake still rippled as if teased by unseen creatures beneath its solid depths. She crept forward on hands and knees.

The wind picked up, and mist, a mixture of condensation and dusted snow, drifted across the ice. Wren drew closer to the edge as the drifts twirled and danced in puffy clouds and shapeless faces. The formless figures gathered and became denser, then turned to ice crystals, spinning about each other in the air. When the mist and snow were gone, all that remained were shimmering, icy fish.

They swam above the lake, drifting with the air currents, nudging and jostling, darting from one side to the other. The setting sun shot through their crystal bodies, sprinkling prisms across the clearing.

Wren gasped and clapped her hands with joy. She had never imagined anything so lovely.

One tiny creature, no bigger than Wren's index finger, broke away from the rest and swam toward her. It hesitated at the edge of the lake, then fluttered its fins and crossed into the clearing, where it hovered inches from Wren's nose.

Wren held her breath. From this close, she could see every crystal scale in detail, each gill-fold a dark slash through the clear body.

The fish regarded her with golden eyes, then pushed forward to nudge first one cheek and then the other. Warmth spread from her melting tears across her face and thawed her frostbitten ears. Heat swelled and moved through her, down her arms and legs to her stiff fingers and toes.

For a moment, there was darkness. Then the light returned.

Wren found herself in a small cabin with a crackling fire. No longer was she huddled in a drift of snow. She sat cross-legged on a rug of woven cloth scraps, her gingham dress billowing around her like a fabric cloud. A harmonica played, and she looked up to find her Papa dancing around the small room. He wasn't sad like he had been before he died.

She craned her neck to watch him and realized the rocking chair next to her was occupied. Wren sat at Mama's feet, while Mama darned socks and bounced her head to the music Papa made. Mama's cheeks were rosy and plump, the way they had been before sickness had eaten her away and put her in the ground.

Every detail was as it once had been. Coffee bubbled in its dented tin pot over the fire. Old Tom slept curled beneath the table, his orange fur sleek and shining in the flickering light. The cuckoo clock above the mantle tocked out the minutes until the next time the tiny figures inside would emerge for a momentary, merry dance.

Mama set aside her darning and took up a wood-handled brush. She sat forward in her chair, smiling, and ran her fingers through Wren's hair before pulling the brush through in long, comforting strokes. Her hands smelled of soap and freshly baked bread.

"Almost bedtime, little bird," she said.

"One last song first," Papa said. He bent and kissed the top of Wren's head, ruffling her hair and eliciting a small noise of protest from Mama.

Papa stepped away and played another song, this time a quieter tune, somehow sad in its slow notes. Mama resumed brushing Wren's hair, laying it neat again.

Wren closed her eyes and listened to the fading strains of the melancholy song. Mama's brushstrokes became lighter until they stopped, and the smells of bread and soap and coffee drifted away.

When she opened her eyes again, Wren was alone and cold in the clearing. The lake was motionless and solid, and the air above it was still and empty. Light was fading.

Wren made her way back to the town and slipped into the bar without anyone noticing she'd been gone. Later that night, she dropped a plate, and Stavros remembered her again, along with the beating he'd left unfinished.

TRANSMONSTRIFIED

She took the beating and those that came after without complaint. In her head and her heart, she was in a little cabin filled with love and warmth. The blows were no more to her than the background noise of a handcrafted cuckoo clock, tocking out the time.

After a week, the memory faded, and she was again firmly rooted in Buehler's Pass, where she was stuck scrubbing stains from wooden tables, and fumes from the lye soap burned her eyes. It was early morning, and the miners had all come and gone—their bellies filled with cold venison stew and hard bread. There would be little business until evening when they returned from their day of digging.

Stavros was out. There was no one to stop her. Wren pulled on her clunky boots and her thin coat and hiked back out to the lake.

It took much longer than it had when she ran there, and she was even colder than before. She squatted beneath the same pine and waited, watching the frozen lake.

Before long, the surface roiled and tossed, mist rolled in, and the dancing ice fish appeared. They looped and spun and darted like a mass of sparkling jewels lit by the blazing sun.

Wren stepped to the edge and waited.

A single fish, no bigger than the length of her hand, broke away from the rest and came toward her. It nudged her frozen cheeks and kissed them with its lipless mouth. Braver now, Wren dared to reach for it and stroked a finger over its glassy skin. The fish seemed to purr like a cat, and it nudged her hand.

Wren looked into the bottomless golden eyes, and the clearing around her went dark. When light returned, she found herself in a garden lit by Chinese lanterns of every color. Tiny lightning bugs flitted in the weeping willows and sparked from the neatly trimmed box hedges. The air was thick with honeysuckle and roses.

Blue satin fell around her in a party dress the likes of which she'd never seen, and her head was heavy with ribbons and curls. She stood to the side and watched the revelers dance to the strains of a lively tune played by a small group of musicians on a bandstand. Wren tapped her foot in time and sipped punch from a crystal cup she found in her hand.

The song ended, and the musicians took up a quieter song. The partygoers pulled closer in a more intimate dance.

"May I have the last dance?" A young man stood before her, his manner shy and hesitant. He bowed and put out his hand. His eyes were the same deep blue as Wren's magnificent dress. She took his hand and allowed him to pull her to the dance floor.

They danced together, their steps in perfect harmony, his hands fitting around her as if made to be there. For the duration of the song, Wren gazed up into those eyes and basked in the adoration she found there.

As the song faded, he loosened his hold and stepped back, his cheeks flushed. He regarded her for a moment, then seemed to make up his mind. Taking her back into his arms, he leaned in and kissed her.

She was surprised but not unhappy at the sudden move. She closed her eyes and drank in the feel of his lips pressed against hers, the taste of fruit punch on his tongue, and the smell of his ironed shirt. It lasted an eternity and only a second. The kiss became less insistent, then faded entirely.

Wren opened her eyes.

She was alone and cold in the clearing at the frozen water's edge. The lovely fish had gone. Stavros was surely looking for her by now.

Halfway through the woods, Wren heard a gruff voice calling for her. Stavros moved through the trees with deliberate steps. When he found her, he cuffed her ear.

He captured her arm and pulled her toward town, but she couldn't keep up with his much larger steps. She stumbled in the snow.

"Lazy, sow," he said. "I'll not have it." He kicked her ribs with his heavy boot.

Wren felt something tear, and pain spread through her body, thick like the smell of honeysuckle and roses. When she pulled herself to her feet, one hand clutching her side, she smiled at the music only she could hear.

This time, the memories sustained her for nearly two weeks. Like the others, they eventually faded and left her alone again, surrounded by cruelty and want.

Late one night, after all but a few of the men had taken their stench and their filthy, grabby hands back to their camps, Wren saw Stavros in earnest conversation with one of his more repugnant regulars, Lester Greeley. She inched closer, wiping the table nearest them so she could listen.

Stavros glanced her direction and looked away, dismissing her. The men haggled for a bit—over what, she wasn't sure. They shook hands, and Stavros remembered she was there.

"Girl," he said. "Finish up and get your things. This is your last night here."

Wren was confused for a moment. For one, she had little in the way of *things*. She finished wiping the tables before fully understanding what had transpired.

When she was done, she went and got her things, as she had been told to do.

And then she ran.

Wren flew through the trees with no other destination but the lake.

In the darkness, the woods were unfamiliar. The branches snagged her coat, and rocks tripped her feet. She ran as far as her lungs could carry her before she collapsed, utterly lost and alone.

The forest was silent. It offered no suggestions.

Her breath heaved out in puffs and sobs. She couldn't go back and live with Mr. Greeley. What little safety she had working for Stavros would be gone. She couldn't go forward, either. The woods were too large and dense to see, even by the light of the waning moon.

She bent her head and tucked her knees to her chin, rocking and thinking.

After a time, she felt rested and calm. Running was no help. She rose and picked her way through the trees, feeling her way as she went, her eyes straining for anything familiar.

Wren walked for hours. The moon moved across the sky above her, making it easier to see. At first, the cold was unbearable, but soon she ceased to feel her fingers and toes.

More than once, voices in the distance called her name. She ignored them. They stopped after the first hour. The men were unwilling to lose themselves in the darkness.

Wren sat in the snow to rest. Bathed in silver moonlight, she closed her eyes and listened to the wind brushing against the needles in the pines above her.

When she opened her eyes, the fish were all around her. In the near darkness, they glowed a tranquil blue and left trails of light in their wakes.

They darted and floated, danced and swirled. One, no bigger than the length of Wren's forearm, broke from the rest and came closer.

It kissed her cheeks and regarded her with its luminous golden eyes.

Wren held out her hand and stroked the fish, feeling its satisfied purr vibrate through its glassy scales. Another fish wandered over and dusted her with fishy kisses. Soon, ice fish both large and small swam to her through the air, surrounding her with a shimmering sapphire aura.

They touched her arms, her fingers, her ears. They kissed her eyelids, forcing them closed.

When she opened her eyes, she stood in a meadow. The sun shone bright and warm. She wore a simple white frock, tied at the waist with a blue ribbon. Her arms and feet were bare and unencumbered. The air was thick with bees and the smell of sweet hay and lavender.

She rose to her feet. In the distance, three figures approached, one of them waving wild arms at her. The figures grew larger, and she recognized Papa as the one hailing her.

Wren flew through the grass and into Papa's waiting arms. They toppled over, laughing. She and Papa pulled each other up, nearly falling over in their shared mirth. She kissed Mama's cheek, which smelled of soap and freshly baked bread.

She'd forgotten three had come. The third person coughed, and she turned away from touching Mama's hair to see who it was.

His eyes were blue, and she basked in the glow of their adoration.

"No last kisses," he said. "Only kisses that last."

He took her in his arms, and his kisses engulfed her, warmed her, and surrounded her in safety and love.

~*~

The search party found Wren the next day, an hour after sunrise. Her small body was stiff, lying curled on its side in the center of the frozen lake. Her lips were pulled up in a contented smile. If she hadn't been so blue from the cold, she would have resembled a marble angel.

Her hand rested partially open, as if cradling something precious.

In her palm lay a single sliver of ice, no bigger than the length of her index finger, in the curious shape of a fish.

"Cast Off"

Pink toes curled within cozy depths
are absent.
Knitted tubes of sweat-soaked cotton
tucked inside for safekeeping
live elsewhere now.
A twin once shared its journey,
but no more do they keep their secrets,
whispering beneath a dusty bureau,
spying from a lightless closet

Past its prime, it lays alone.
Crinkled leaves and powdered glass,
escaped hubcaps and tired gum,
a crumpled candy wrapper crammed inside
give no witness to the tale of its downfall
from blissful days of running and dancing
to this weary existence as roadside refuse.

Perhaps as a joke,
it was plucked from a protesting foot
and hurled from the bed of a moving pickup.
Or creatures from another world,
using futuristic firearms of death,
dissolved the human wearer
leaving one lone item behind.
Likely, it was the work of a witch,
bent and sour,
a sack draped across her hump
as she trudged through town
leaving items of clothing on her path—
a warning for children to eat their broccoli.

Until the street sweeper drones through town
and carries it away in the darkness.

"Distressed Denim"

This story was an entry for the Summer 2010 Writer's Weekly 24-hour Short Story Contest. The writing prompt came in at noon on that Saturday, and we had until noon the following day to send them the completed story. "Distressed Denim" won first place. Here's the prompt I had to use:

"The young girl pulled another pair of pants from the pile of laundry. Between the hot black iron and the fireplace, it was stifling in the small kitchen. The only relief she could hope for was a small breeze coming from the window overlooking the distant waves. Her arm started moving methodically once again and, just as she started to fantasize about a forbidden swim, the iron stopped at a bump in the pocket..."

Throughout the course of this day, I have been drowned, beaten repeatedly against a rock, strangled, and hanged. The only respite I had was spent dangling by my waist, the sea breeze cooling my overwrought skin, caressing and soothing the bruised, abused flesh.

While the wind tossed me about, I sent out a hopeless prayer to the gods that my legs would remain straight and steadfast; to crumple at this stage would invite one last painful indignity. My prayers went unanswered. When I was taken down, I was judged inferior.

I knew what would come next.

She tossed me into a basket with the others. Our limbs tangled together, clinging in desperation. I did my best to burrow to the bottom. There was a chance she would grow weary of her torture and give up before reaching me.

It was dark at first, my security assured at least for a while. But with each snatch of her greedy hands, a little more light reached me in my place of cover.

Once I was able to see her clearly, I noticed her rhythm had slowed. She drew her wrist across her brow, wiping away a line of moisture. Her eyes shifted to the window. I thought for a moment she might quit. The room was stifling for all of us. If she went for a swim, I might make my escape.

It was not to be. She reached into the pile and grabbed blindly. I tried to avoid her touch, but there was nowhere to hide. She pulled me out by the leg and shook me, her cold impartiality at war with the ferocity with which she snapped me straight. She stretched me out across the table, smoothing my skin with hands that were surprisingly gentle.

She paid no attention to my struggles and whimpers of protestation. She took up her instrument and placed it across my bare flesh. I screamed. The heat was worse than I had imagined. It tore through me. I felt it scorch the back of my leg through the front. She cared nothing for my hysterics and carried on with her detached movements, deaf to me. She ran the cruel device back and forth on my body, moving ever higher in her quest to destroy me.

At the front of my hip, she met resistance. The object in my front pocket gave her pause. I whispered another hopeless prayer that she would reach inside and pull it out if she was to continue her torture. Again, the gods refused my petition. She resumed her mission, sliding her equipment over my pocket, pressing down against the object to flatten it.

It began to melt.

I could feel the hot liquid soaking into my skin. I begged her to stop. I pleaded for mercy, but she refused to hear my voice. It was several moments of searing heat and pressure before she took note of the crimson pool seeping out of my flesh and down my leg.

She cried out in dismay.

Already tender from her earlier ministrations, my skin was unprepared for the harsh scrub brush. It tore at me. Bits of skin flaked away leaving bone-white patches. She sobbed in frustration and poured harsh, burning chemicals over me.

I had tried to warn her about the crayon, but she disregarded my advice—just as she had ignored my pleas. Now we both suffered for it.

Exhausted, her face puffy and wretched with tears, she left me. I thought I might escape then, but I found I could not move. I was thoroughly beaten. In the silence of the warm kitchen, my battered mind and body succumbed to the peaceful emptiness of sleep.

I don't know how long I dozed, but when I awoke, the fire in the hearth had settled into glowing coals, and the shadows had grown long. A considerable length of my body, from hip to knee, had gone stiff with cooled wax.

She stood sopping wet in the doorway wearing nothing but her shift. Her eyes glowed in the low light, and her damp hair clung to her face and bare shoulders. Sea water gathered in a puddle at her feet. In her hand she brandished a pair of sewing shears. They flashed with light from the dying fire, their sharp tips glinting with ominous intent.

TRANSMONSTRIFIED

She attacked me before I had time to react. The scissors sliced through me. She was quick about her work, reducing me to a gibbering pile of scraps within moments. I was dismembered as neatly as a rabbit destined for the stew pot.

Those parts of me she deemed ruined were tossed behind the house.

~*~

From the rubbish pile, I can see the sea. It's peaceful. I know eventually I will be set ablaze, but for now, I can await my death in comfort, unthreatened. The rest of me is in another basket.

I am a stack of neat squares piled on top of myself to await her next devious scheme. I cannot fathom what else she might have in store.

She's humming to herself, the earlier demonic frenzy forgotten. She opens the box beside her and removes a spool of thread. The needle in her hand glints in the light of the rebuilt fire.

Her cool hands lift me out of the basket. She spreads me out across the injured knee of another of her victims. As the dull needle pierces my skin, I try not to scream.

I know I will never be free.

"Reaper's Tale"
A Monster Haven Short Story

In Monster in My Closet, *Riley gives Zoey a brief explanation of how he became a reaper. This is how it really happened.*

I saw that girl again this morning. Every time I think I've lost my chance to talk to her, the universe spits her out in my path and gives me another shot.

You can't miss her. Dark red curls dancing around her head to their own beat, brown eyes a guy could stare into forever, and a face like an angel. She stands out in a crowd.

Most women dress like they don't want anyone to remember what they're wearing or like they want you to focus on the skin that's showing instead of the actual clothes. Not this girl. She doesn't give a damn what you look at. And she gives you a lot of choices—like her shoes covered in what appear to be gummy worms, her tights where butterflies fly up the sides of her legs, or her daisy-spattered skirt and neon green shirt.

My favorite is when she wears the blue fedora with the peacock feather. Nothing says "Fuck you" like a woman in mixed prints wearing a hat with a big feather jutting off to the side. I respect the hell out of that.

It all works on her. Her self-confidence shows in her every step. And it shows in how she talks to people.

I stood in line behind her once at the coffee shop. This guy in front of her snapped at the barista, something about soymilk, then kept making impatient, old-guy sounds while he waited for her to ring him up.

The red-headed girl—who was wearing a string of pink beads around her wrist and a yellow beret that day—put her hand on his arm. He turned and scowled at her. I thought I'd have to jump in and save her.

"Sometimes, the most important thing you can do is stop and breathe," she said in a quiet, warm voice. "The rest of the day will go much easier."

I swear, I thought he'd try to punch her. Or at least shake her hand off and tell her to mind her own business. I didn't know. From where I was standing, the guy was an unknown quantity wrapped around a jiggling vial of nitroglycerin.

But she knew something I didn't. The creases in his face relaxed, and I'll be damned if he didn't do exactly what she said. He took a deep breath, held it, then let it out. He smiled, patted her hand, then turned away and got his coffee.

I watched him walk out the door. His shoulders were where shoulders are supposed to be instead of up around his ears. That was one of those moments when I should have manned up and said something to her. Anything. A comment about the weather. Ask her what kind of perfume she was wearing. Offer to buy her coffee.

I took too long thinking about it. My phone buzzed against my hip. I had a text message I couldn't ignore. Someone was probably about to die, which meant I had to get to the address as soon as possible.

The last thing I heard as the door closed behind me was the barista asking for the girl's name. If I'd waited another few seconds, I'd at least have learned that much. But I missed it.

I could only hope the universe would toss her in front of me again and give me another chance.

Turned out I didn't even need to be at that address after all. It was close. Some ditzy blonde in heels that were way too tall fell off the edge of the sidewalk in the path of a taxi. She would have bought it right there, and I'd have had to collect her soul, but a teenaged girl, in shoes that showed far better judgment, yanked the blonde backward where she landed safely on her ass on the sidewalk.

I stood across the street, watching the beauty queen bitch at the girl who'd saved her, to make sure the designated time passed without further incident.

You never know. Sometimes the obvious death isn't the right one, and a secondary surprise creeps in. While my client sweats over the close call he had with a bus, a train could jump its tracks around the corner and a leather trunk full of books might hurdle through the air and land on the client's head. True story. That happened about three years ago. I've seen some weird stuff in my line of work.

This trip, however, was totally wasted. I could have stayed at the coffee shop and talked to my mystery girl after all. Still, the job always comes first. Whenever I get a text, I drop everything and go where I'm told, then text my report back, no matter the outcome. That day's report was of the non-event variety.

No pickup at this time. Client's need was averted.

I checked the time and sighed. She'd be gone already. My window of opportunity to talk to her had closed. I'd see her again, though. I was sure of it.

Being a reaper didn't leave much room for a social life.

It had been eight years since I'd made the agreement that saddled me with a 24/7, on-call gig with no vacations. I'd had no chance to have more than a few drinks with someone before having to bail, and women kind of hate it when a guy takes off mid-date. After the first year or so, I kind of stopped worrying about where a relationship might go. First dates were usually all I got.

I saw so much death. All wanted was a chance at a little life from time to time. That didn't seem like so much to ask.

And there's something special about that girl. Something magical, though she doesn't seem to be involved at all with the Hidden world I know of—reapers and soul catchers, monsters and demons. Her magic comes from inside and radiates out to touch the people near her.

Last week, she wore a yellow sundress with purple polka dots, and she'd piled her hair on top of her head in a haphazard mound. That was when I finally figured out why she fascinated me so much. With her hair up like that, she reminded me of Clara.

I only met Clara once, but she'd changed everything. She had magic, too. The real kind of magic, not just the figurative kind, like the red-headed girl with the fedora and butterflies. Clara saved my sister's life when no doctor possibly could have.

~*~

I was twenty-four back then, and I still hadn't figured out what I wanted to do with my life. I'd changed majors three times and still hadn't found my calling. Business seemed like a smart choice, but halfway through the first semester, I remembered how much I disliked math. Art history bored me. Psychology seemed to be a never-ending path to nowhere unless I made a total commitment to a master's degree or more.

Summers relieved me of the pressure to make a decision. I worked for a roofing company, using my muscles instead of my brain. I could tune everything out and just *be* for a while.

Until that morning when it all turned into a steaming pile of heartbreak and life-changing decisions.

Frank always had a radio blasting a local oldies station while we worked. We couldn't hear it very well with all the banging, but it gave a nice background noise. Sometimes I'd try to work to the beat, if it was a fast one. That day, I was hammering my heart out to "Locomotion" and singing to myself, when the DJ interrupted with an announcement. The guys must have been listening to the song, too, because they all stopped to listen.

"A passenger train on its way to Kansas City has derailed in Woolridge. Iowa authorities are unable to release official numbers at this time, but they look to be upwards of seventeen dead and thirty-five injured."

I swallowed hard and looked at my watch. Mom and Izzy were on their way to Kansas City today. Izzy had won a scholarship to go to a jazz camp for a week at the University of Kansas, and Mom loved the train. They'd driven up to Osceola that morning and splurged.

I didn't bother to listen to the rest of the report. My hands shook as I gathered my tools without a word. The guys all knew Mom and Izzy had taken the train. I'd worked overtime to help them pay for the trip. I climbed down, and Frank met me at the bottom, his hand held out.

"I'll take care of your stuff. Just go on and check on them."

I handed over my tool belt. "Thanks. I'm sure they're fine." My gut wasn't as sure.

"Trains are big, Riley. Lots of people on them. They're probably sitting by the tracks playing cards, waiting for you to come pick them up."

I nodded, grateful for the picture he painted in my head, which was so much better than the wreck of blood and misery I'd been imagining.

My cellphone rang before I made it to the crash site, which was probably for the best. Seeing the crash site in person would have haunted my dreams forever.

A nurse from the hospital had found my name and number in Izzy's wallet. The woman wouldn't tell me anything useful, only that I needed to come to the hospital right away.

I'd never driven so fast in my life.

What followed was a blur. They had no idea about Mom and, at first, they couldn't even find Izzy. The emergency room was packed with crying loved ones, people with minor scrapes, doctors and nurses moving through the crowd, and a flow of EMTs coming through the doors with more of the injured. Gurneys of wounded people lined the hallway, since all the beds were already full.

Eventually, I found her myself, at the end of the hall outside room 106. She looked so tiny and still. A bruise the size of a softball covered her right temple, and her eye on that side was swollen shut. Her blonde curls were dark with drying blood.

From time to time, her shallow, nearly imperceptible breaths gave way to a single, racking intake of air that rattled in her chest, wet and terrifying. One small hand lay above the blanket, curled across her chest. I took it in both of mine as gently as I could. My baby sister wasn't going to last long.

I swung my head around, frantic for someone to help. A nurse strode past, and I grabbed his arm. "Can't you do something for her? Why is she out in the hall like this? Somebody has to do something."

He stopped for me, though he clearly had a million things he needed to do. His blue eyes were sad, but didn't look away from me while he spoke. "We've sedated her to keep her comfortable. I'm really sorry. It's all we can do. There are a lot of injured people here, and not enough of us. We have to concentrate on the people we *can* save." He glanced at my beautiful baby sister, lying so still, and his eyes filled with tears. "I'm really sorry." He patted my shoulder, then disappeared into a room filled with a lot of beeping and yelling.

Logically, I understood what he was saying. Emotionally, I wasn't going to sit there and accept that my baby sister was going to die because her injuries were too extensive, and there weren't any doctors available to spend eight hours operating on her.

I bent and kissed her on the forehead, careful to avoid the awful purple bruises. "I won't go far, sweetheart. I'll find help." In my heart, I knew nobody could help. Staff bustled down the hall and in and out of the rooms in a constant stream. More injured came in every few minutes.

I tried to stop a doctor, two nurses, and even an EMT. With every brushoff, I went back to Izzy's side to be sure she was still with me. Each time she was unchanged—either barely breathing, or sucking in a single, shuddering breath.

At the registration desk, I made a last, desperate attempt. "Please," I said to the tired woman. "Can't you get someone to look at her again? I don't think she's going to last much longer."

The woman took a deep breath, her eyes already scanning a new inrush of people. "We're overwhelmed here. I'm sorry. Normally, you wouldn't even be allowed back there. Go be with her. It's all anyone can do right now." She tried to give me a kind smile, but she wasn't doing much better than I was, I could tell. She was right. The best thing I could do was be with Izzy.

And try not to think about the fact that I hadn't found Mom.

On my way back to my sister, I passed a small group of people who appeared to be checking the injured along the hallway.

"Excuse me," I said, squeezing past a portly, balding man in a bad suit.

He grunted over his shoulder and shifted out of the way. The two men with him ignored me and continued inspecting the orphaned patients.

When I made it back to Izzy, she didn't look any different, but some kind person had left me a chair so I could sit instead of hover.

The three suited men made their way toward us, stopping longer with some patients than others. I held Izzy's hand, listening to her breathe while I watched them. About three patients away, I saw something I didn't understand. The tallest of the three men bent over a small boy and placed his hand on the boy's chest. After a moment, he glanced at the tubby guy and the guy with tortoiseshell glasses, then they looked at the boy's chart together. They pressed their heads close to each other, nodded together, and the tall guy did something really weird.

He placed his palm across the boy's forehead, then pressed the ring on his other hand against the boy's mouth. The motion was quick enough for me to doubt what I thought I saw. He pulled—a quick, short yank—and a silvery substance squeezed through the kid's lips and attached to the gem on the man's ring. For a second, I thought I saw a face in the glittering cloud, then the whole thing disappeared, as if it had been sucked into the ring.

I blinked. They'd already moved on to the next bed, heads bent in discussion. The weird thing happened again, across the hall from Izzy and me. This time, despite the unreality of it, I was sure of what I saw. What's more, an intern stopped next to the boy they'd already visited, took his pulse, then pulled the sheet over the kid's head.

The girl across the way didn't look too alive either, once they yanked whatever it was out of her.

And they were looking right at me.

The guy with the glasses approached me first. "We'll need you to step aside for a moment, please, while we examine…" he paused, frowning at the clipboard in his hand. "…Isabelle. We'll only be a moment." He smiled, but it was a terrifying, ominous smile.

Behind him, the frowning intern pulled the sheet over the girl they'd just examined.

I rose from my chair, but refused to get out of their way. I'd grab Izzy and run with her if I had to. There was no goddamned way these people were getting anywhere near her.

I puffed myself up to full construction-guy size. Probably not as threatening as I hoped, but these weren't muscle men. They were something else altogether. Something not as physically threatening, but far more dangerous. I braced myself and spread my arms out to keep them away from my baby sister.

"You're not getting near her," I said.

The chubby, balding guy rolled his eyes. "Here we go," he said.

The tall man took a step forward. "We're here to help." His voice was gentle, and he stuck his hand toward me. Or toward her. I wasn't sure.

My hands became fists without any thought on my part. The little bald guy pushed forward, coming too close, and my fist connected with his cheekbone before I even thought about it.

"Not another step. I saw what you did." My eyes flicked to the bodies they'd left in their wake. "You don't get to *help* my sister. She's fine."

Baldy stepped back, scowling and rubbing his face. I hadn't hit him hard, but it was enough to get him to take me more seriously.

Glasses squinted at Izzy, then glanced at her chart, shaking his head. "She's not fine. Let us do our job."

I lifted my chin in the direction of the tall guy's hand. "What kind of ring is that? What did you do to them?"

I wasn't budging, and they knew it. They took a step away and pressed their heads together again, this time, no doubt, consulting about me. I suppressed a shudder, hoping they didn't decide the only way to get me the hell out of their way was to use the ring technique on me.

"Look," I said. "Obviously, you guys have some kind of device that does stuff. I'm willing to believe you're even doing a service for people here. But Izzy's not dying today, so unless you can reverse your little handheld device and make her better, you can just back yourselves off and go on to the next patient."

The three of them stared at me as if I were some kind of new species of tree monkey they'd never seen before. They went back to the three-headed formation and consulted again.

The guy with the glasses popped his head up. "What do you do for a living?"

I frowned. "I'm a student, but I've been doing some roofing for the summer. Why?"

He smirked and ducked his head back into the discussion. After a minute, they seemed to come to a conclusion of some sort, nodded their heads in unison, then turned to face me.

"How old are you?" the pudgy one asked.

"Twenty-four. Why?"

They exchanged looks and nodded again. "Do you have family other than this girl?"

My shoulders sagged, and I looked at the floor. The white tiles were scuffed, and someone had dropped a gum wrapper. "I'm not sure. Our mother was on the train, too. Nobody else is close."

Glasses took a step toward me. One of his shoes was untied. "Is she here in the hospital?"

I shook my head. "I haven't found her. And nobody can tell me anything."

"Art," the tall one said to the short, pudgy guy. "Stay here with Isabelle. Mr..." He consulted my sister's chart. "Mr. Banks, if you'll come with us, we'd like to discuss your future, and what we can do for each other."

I took a backward step and bumped against my sister, fists held up. "I'm not leaving her with him. Do you think I'm stupid?"

Art ran his fingers over his face where I'd punched him before. "Pull yourself together, kid."

Tall Guy shook his head. "No, Mr. Banks. We think we can help you in a way that will make everyone happy. You have my word that Art won't touch your sister while you're away."

I gave him a hard look. He seemed sincere, and no one else was willing to help me. The situation was weird, but my only options were to stay with Izzy until she died, or hear these guys out to see if they could do something.

Izzy took another shuddering, wet breath, and my shoulders slumped. I couldn't just let her die and not do everything I could to save her.

I kissed her on the forehead. "I'll be right back, sweetheart. I'm going to fix this."

Tall Guy and Glasses led me away, and Art took my place in the chair watching over Izzy. As I followed the guys in suits, I wondered what it would be like not having a soul. Would I get to keep mine until I died before they collected it, or would they take it today once I signed in blood, or whatever they asked me to do?

It didn't matter. If selling my soul was what it took to save my baby sister, so be it. I lifted my chin and prepared to give these guys the only thing of worth that I owned.

Because the hospital was so busy, the only way we could speak privately was to step outside, into the memorial garden the hospital had built last year. Late afternoon sun didn't do much to warm my chilled skin. Would I be able to appreciate the breeze on my cheek or the smell of freshly bloomed roses once I had no soul?

"Well," I said throwing back my shoulders. "Let's get this over with."

Glasses cleared his throat. "Mr. Banks, my name is Seymour, and this is Carlton. You met our colleague, Art, earlier."

I nodded but said nothing.

Carlton reached into his coat and pulled out a cellphone, glanced at the display, and stuffed it back into his pocket. "What we'd like to do, Mr. Banks, is make you an offer. We have someone in our employ who may be able to keep your sister alive long enough for her to stabilize and receive a doctor's care."

I blinked. "You can't just magic her well?"

"I'm afraid not," Seymour said. "It doesn't work that way. And there's no guarantee we can get our necrofoil here in time to save your sister. Art has already sent for her, though. She'll be here in a few hours. We had to fly her in from New Hampshire."

My shoulders slumped. Izzy might not have hours, but it was my only hope. "If this person gets here in time and saves my sister, you can have whatever you want. Where do I sign?"

The two men exchanged a puzzled look.

Seymour pulled out a folded stack of papers. "Don't you want to know what we want in exchange, Mr. Banks?"

I stared at my feet. "I told you, I'm not stupid. I know what this is. And you might as well call me Riley if you're going to take my soul."

They were silent for a moment, then Seymour snorted.

Carlton chuckled. "Mr. Banks—Riley. We don't want your soul. We want you to come work with us. We aren't in the business of taking people's souls. We merely collect the souls that get stuck after a trauma, then we set them free so they can move on to their next destination."

I frowned. "I don't understand."

Seymour put his hand on my shoulder. "We're reapers, Riley. And if you agree, you will be, too."

An hour and a half later, Clara arrived. She moved like a ghost, gliding across the tile floors toward us, a quiet, comforting air about her. She looked to be in her late thirties or early forties, but she also had a youthful quality to her. It might have been the way she'd pinned her dark red curls on top of her head in such a haphazard pile. The moment she placed her hands across Izzy's chest, the wet, shuddering breaths stopped and Izzy's breathing became less labored.

"She's better," I said, my own breath catching.

Clara gave me a gentle smile. "Death no longer stalks her. I can't heal her, but I can help her body heal itself a little quicker. After a few hours, she should be stable enough for the doctors to reassess her and treat her." Her brow wrinkled in concern. "A lot is broken inside. But I think she can be mended."

I signed the paperwork immediately. Whatever this beautiful woman was doing, the difference in my sister was undeniable.

A smart man would have taken the hour-and-a-half wait to read the contract. A smart man would have read the contract later, before signing. I was too traumatized to be smart. That's my only excuse.

The ink wasn't dry before Art grabbed my elbow. "Well, then. Say your goodbyes so we can be on our way."

I looked at Seymour and Carlton. "What does he mean? I can't leave right now. Izzy still needs me. And I haven't even found out about Mom, yet."

Art dropped his hand, and Seymour put his arm over my shoulders. "Riley, it was in the contract you signed. You have to say goodbye. Not just to Izzy, but to your whole life here. You won't be able to see her again. Not while you're a reaper."

I felt all the blood leave my face. "No," I whispered. "I can't leave her like this."

Seymour turned me to face him, his hands on my shoulders. "Riley, we looked into it. Your mother didn't make it. I'm so sorry. But she felt no pain."

My eyes blurred with tears. But as much as I wanted to mourn the loss of my mother, all I could think about was my baby sister. "Izzy has no one. She's only fourteen. I can't leave her all alone."

I broke. I'd just been told my mother had died, my sister was still in critical condition, and I would be forced to desert her without even telling her why. My shoulders shook, and Seymour hugged me and patted my back while I sobbed into his suit jacket.

When I was done, I pulled away, wiping my eyes, feeling a little embarrassed. "Where will she go?"

"I called your Aunt Alice," Carlton said. "She'll be here by morning."

I nodded. Aunt Alice would take good care of Izzy. She was a teacher and lived on a farm. Izzy would be okay. "All right. I'll say goodbye."

Clara sat with her hands splayed across Izzy's chest, sorrow lining her face. "I'm so sorry for your loss. But I'll make sure Izzy's okay."

My voice caught in my throat. "Thank you." I turned my attention to my baby sister. Her color was better, and her breathing was steady. I leaned down and kissed her cheek. "I love you, Iz. Be well."

She didn't stir, and I didn't look back.

~*~

That was eight years ago. I never broke the rules by contacting Izzy, but someone at Board Headquarters must have had a soft spot for me, because every year or so, I got an anonymous package in the mail with photos and an update. After a rocky start, my sister adjusted to her new life, made new friends, and graduated high school at the top of her class. The last update I got was that she was studying to be a veterinarian.

I suspected the packages came from Art. He ended up being my immediate supervisor. We don't get along very well. He's always pretty high strung, and I'm too laid back for his tastes. Plus, I'd punched him in the face when we first met, so there was that.

Still, I was pretty sure he was behind the anonymous updates.

The sharp pain I used to get when I thought of Izzy has become a dull ache. I can live with it because she'd lived.

Plus, I have a pretty good life now. I make decent money at my regular job as an EMT. I actually enjoy being a reaper, too. It's sort of an extension of my EMT job. If I can't save someone one way, I help them in another.

Still, good or not, it's a lonely life.

But I saw that girl again this afternoon. I was leaning against the wall, drinking a cup of coffee, when she stumbled out of the grocery store across the street. Her hair ringed her head like a fiery halo. Today was a yellow beret day.

I stared at her over my coffee, willing her to finally look my way. While crossing the street to try to catch up with her sounded reasonable in my head, it was bound to make me look like a stalker. Not the first impression I was wishing for.

So I stared, hoping like a fool that she would look.

And then she did, and my whole world change.

Holding my breath, I winked at her, and her smile lit my heart on fire.

I'm finally in.

"The Dream Eaters"

This is a flash story from the Confabulator Cafe. I wouldn't say I'm obsessed with closet monsters, but they—and attic monsters and under-the-bed monsters—are definitely recurring characters in my stories. As much as I love them, I never leave my closet door open at night. I'm not a daredevil. Sheesh.

Devon slept sprawled across the bed with the sheets in disarray and one fisted hand tossed over his head. He whimpered. Beside him Amy lay still, her mouth curled in a slight smile. The blankets fell in neat folds around her body.

A door creaked open, and acid-blue eyes in a froggy face glowed from within the inky vastness of the closet. Beneath the bed, blood-red talons scraped at the hardwood floor dragging a large, furry body out into the room.

The two monsters shared a glance, then took their places beside the sleeping husband and wife. Unwilling to wake the humans, the monsters spoke in whispers.

"Looks like he's having another bad one," said Radley, the under-the-bed monster. "At this rate, I'll have to start jogging."

Felix, the closet monster, nodded. "She seems happy enough, though." He patted his stomach and licked his lips. "I hope she's not having another baby dream. I always feel weird about eating the babies."

Felix hovered over the sleepers, breathing in the exotic scent of dreams.

"Oh, yeah," Radley said. "This is a bad one, all right." He spread his claws and touched Devon's forehead with a light pressure so Devon wouldn't wake. Silver mist escaped from Devon's nostrils and rose above his face in a cloud. Shapes took form, then the dream clarified into moving pictures.

Across the bed, Felix touched a scaly finger to Amy's forehead and watched the swirling mist emerge, forming the images moving behind her eyelids.

Above Devon, a chase scene played out. A humpback whale with gnashing teeth and snaky tongue swam through the air. It snarled at Devon and followed him through a maze of cubicles and tiny offices that were peopled by zombies. The building shook, and paperwork rained down from the tiled ceiling.

Radley pinched the whale between two razor claws, pulled it from the dream, and popped it into his mouth. Whale juice dribbled from the corner of his mouth. He belched softly into his fist and wiped his face with the back of his hairy hand.

Within the dream, the action slowed for a moment. Devon stopped running. Zombie workers looked up from their keyboards and groaned. Devon ran, and the zombies gave chase.

"Dammit," Radley said. "He needs to find a better job. I can't eat this many zombies."

Felix stared at the still-life dream above Amy's head. "I can come help. She's got nothing going on over here. Grass. Trees. A pond."

"Has she been doing yoga again or something?"

"I think so. I got hit in the head with her mat yesterday when she threw it in the closet. I'll come around and help you finish."

Amy sighed and turned over. The picture above her head dissipated in wisps and tendrils of smoky silver.

Radley frowned. "Are you sure? You hate the scary stuff."

Felix shrugged. "Probably need to work on a more balanced diet anyway. My doctor says I'm deficient in vitamin T. Besides—getting a little tired of puppies and babies and rainbows, you know?"

Radley made room, and the two monsters stood side by side, picking off zombies as they appeared. Devon continued to be distressed, and zombies eventually turned to disembodied hands, which, in turn, morphed into a schoolyard of angry, demonic school children.

The frantic pace of new horrors the monsters had to consume nearly overwhelmed Felix. He paused and wiped his brow. "How do you keep up like this every night?"

Radley shook his head. "It's not usually this bad. Something horrible must have happened at work today." He pointed a thumb at Amy. "Something he didn't share with Sleeping Beauty over there."

"He's definitely repressing something big," Felix said, scooping up a handful of vulture-headed business men. He crunched down on them and cringed. "Let me guess. It's an acquired taste?"

Throughout the night they kept their vigil, eating the things that threatened to devour Devon's mind. By morning, the bellies of both monsters were bloated with dead things best forgotten by humans.

When Devon's fears were played out, he fell into an exhausted, dreamless sleep. Amy's soft breathing never altered its slow, even pace. Ignorance truly was bliss.

Radley shook Felix's hand and patted him on the back. "Thanks for your help. I don't think that would have gone too well if I'd been on my own. As it is, it'll be hard squeezing back under the bed."

"Anytime." He turned to close himself into the closet, but hesitated. "You know, if he tells her today, we may have to deal with both of them tonight."

"Maybe she'll drag him off to yoga."

"Maybe. If not, we might need to call the basement for help. Sheldon's probably bored down there anyway."

Radley wrinkled his muzzle. "He smells like mildew. It really puts me off my dinner."

"There's only one other choice." Felix scratched his armpit. "I know you're not crazy about her, but Avery's not doing anything these days but stomping around in the attic and slamming doors."

"She's so uppity." Radley sighed. "Let's just hope for the best. I'm gonna turn in."

Felix rubbed his stomach and grimaced. "I need to hit the medicine cabinet for some antacid first. See you tonight, Radley."

"Sweet dreams, Felix." Radley scooted under the bed and disappeared with the dust bunnies. A few minutes later, Felix stepped into the closet and shut the door behind him.

At six a.m., the alarm clock went off, and the Bangles blared out their odd observance of how very Egyptian everyone seemed to be walking.

Amy stretched and kissed her husband's cheek. "I had the most beautiful dreams."

Devon rubbed his eyes and yawned. "I slept like a rock. I didn't dream at all."

"Bargain Basement"

This is a pretty old story. Several years ago, I had it in my head to turn it into a novel, but I never made it past the third chapter. However, the basic idea driving this story keeps finding its way in one shape or another into a lot of my other books and shorts. By the time I get a chance to revisit this story as a novel, I may have already used it all up elsewhere.

I should have guessed something was screwy the day we moved in. How long it took me to figure it out is an unfair measurement of my intelligence. Things that are so far removed from our comfort zones and experiences are difficult to comprehend and impossible to guess. I thought we scored a great price on the house.

"Where do you want these?" the mover asked me. I'd planted myself near the front door so I could direct traffic. He was a big guy in his mid-forties. A bit sweaty for the mild weather, but then I wasn't hauling boxes and furniture. According to his damp shirt, his name was Roger.

I checked the numbers on the boxes he carried and consulted my list. "In the basement," I said. "That's Christmas stuff. Put it up against the far wall away from any other boxes. The previous owners left some boxes they haven't picked up yet."

Roger nodded. I watched his sweat plop on the carton containing my mother's antique Italian nativity scene. He clumped down the hallway, and I turned my attention to the next load. I checked the items off as they came through and gave instructions: bedroom, office, bedroom, dining room. Roger came back, still sweating on Christmas. He looked baffled.

"Where's the basement?" he asked.

I started to point, but realized the next load would be a few minutes. My sofa was lodged in the doorframe and showed no sign of wanting to budge. "Let me show you."

I led him back down the hall and opened the first door on the left. Reaching in, I flipped the light switch and backed out of his way.

Roger stood looking at me, dumbfounded. He mopped his forehead on the shoulder of his shirt, leaving a smudge. "Ma'am, I swear I looked in there," he said. "I thought it was a coat closet."

I tried to reassure him that he wasn't stupid. "It happens," I said with a shrug. "I always get turned around in a new house. With the light off, it probably looked like a closet. Don't worry about it. We'll leave the door open."

He didn't look entirely convinced as he disappeared down the stairs.

By the time Danny came home, the movers had been gone for hours. I'd managed to put most of the kitchen in order, and the bedroom was fit for sleeping. Otherwise, the house was a hedge-maze of boxes and stacked furniture, and I felt certain I would turn a corner and find a huge wedge of cartoon Swiss cheese in the middle of the floor. I was half buried in a box marked "bathroom" digging for the shower curtain, when he burst through the door carrying a bottle of champagne and a bag of take-out Chinese. I've never loved him more.

Over dinner, I amused him with the story of our couch wedged in the front door. "It took them ten minutes to figure out the right angle," I said. "In the end, they had to unscrew the feet."

"Any casualties?" he asked. "Did we lose a Ming vase or puncture our Picasso?"

I grimaced. "If you've stashed a Ming vase or a Picasso in one of these boxes, maybe you should've clued me in. So far, I've lost three drinking glasses and a casserole lid. Not even worth filling out the claim forms. I'll check on my tiara and scepter tomorrow, my lord." I rose and gave him a curtsey, piling plates and silverware to take into the kitchen. "I'm thinking of keeping all my royal valuables in the basement. If thieves are anything like our movers today, they'll never find their way down there."

"They couldn't find the basement?"

"No. I had to show it to them and leave the door open. Some weird depth perception thing with the light off, I guess. He looked embarrassed. He swore he'd looked and only found a closet."

Danny went quiet, his forehead creased in thought. I touched his sleeve. "Hey," I said. "What's wrong?"

He shook his head. "Nothing. It's just that Dave said the same thing when he came to look at the place last week. He couldn't find the door to the basement. Said it was a closet before I opened it for him."

~*~

I spent the next week moving boxes from room to room, pulling things out, putting things back in. Each day the maze of cartons looked a little more like a home. At last, the only boxes I had left were the ones I had to take downstairs to be stored. I put it off until last more because I hate stairs than any creepy feeling I had for the basement. I didn't believe for a minute there was anything weird going on. I admit, occasionally I passed the door in the hallway and shot my hand out, yanked the door open, and peeked down the stairs. I tried relaxing the muscles in my eyes until the doorway went fuzzy to see if maybe I could make it look like a coat closet. Nope. It never looked like anything but a stairway.

I flipped the lights and grabbed a load of boxes. The wooden stairs were sturdy but narrow, and I had to step carefully to avoid misjudging my footing. I piled my cartons on top of the ones the movers had placed the week before and took a look. The basement was a huge, underground room, stuffy and dank, but well lit by overhead lights. Our belongings were along the far wall, but not alone. Boxes and furniture were stacked in every corner in neat, carefully labeled piles. We'd never met the previous owners, but the realtor had asked if we could store a few things for them until they were settled. It would only be for a few weeks. We didn't mind. I hadn't realized how much they were leaving behind, though.

I went up for a second load and brought it down, craning my neck to see the labels on the other boxes: "Christmas," "Baby Stuff," "Personals," "Old Paperwork." Whoa. Personals. That was hard to resist. Stop it, I chided myself. We were doing a favor for someone and they trusted us not to snoop in their stuff. I went for a third load and brought it down, making sure it was stacked where it couldn't be mixed with someone else's "Personals."

Oh hell. What could it hurt?

I nudged the foreign box with my toe and looked around, as if anyone else would be watching me in my own basement. I peeled back one box flap and peered in. The flaps were tucked over and under to lock them in place, so pulling one up only gave me a peek at what was in there. Huh. Looked like porn. I tugged a little harder, trying to find the best view without actually opening it. All the corners sprang loose at once. I jumped back and looked around, like my mother might be watching, wagging her finger in reprimand. I felt stupid. My house. Nobody home but me.

I crouched down to flip through the magazines and books. Someone had some kinky tastes. At the bottom, I found a large leather collar with a tag that said "Misty" on it. Coupled with the owner's taste in magazines, I assumed "Misty" was not a dog.

The phone rang upstairs and I eyed the box with a guilty conscience. I'd have to leave it until I came back down. I sprinted up the stairs, closed the door and ran around the house searching for my cell—I never leave it in the same place twice.

After an hour-long conversation with my mother (she was not, in fact, wagging her finger at me in the basement. She was still in Tulsa, four hours away), I remembered to eat some lunch. By the time I came back to the basement, over two hours had passed. Clutching the last pile of storage in one arm and the rickety handrail with the other, I clambered down the stairs.

The "Personals" box was closed up tight.

My eyes darted around the room, and I turned full circle. No one was there. My stomach flipped, and the hair on my arms and the back of my neck lifted. Scrambling up the stairs, I didn't pause to put out the light. I slammed the door shut behind me and leaned against it to catch my breath. This is stupid, I thought. Nobody's been in the house. I had the wrong box. There was so much stuff down there, it would be easy to mistake one box for another. I rubbed my forehead with a shaky fingertip.

"Get a grip." I dropped the boxes on the floor.

It took me two days to find the nerve to go back, and I made sure Danny was upstairs within earshot. I didn't tell him what had happened. I felt stupid enough without sharing.

The lights were still on and that was reassuring. I knew I hadn't turned them off on my way out. I stood on the top step, arms full, with my head cocked to the side listening. Nope. Not a sound. I crept down the steps and peered in, noting the empty shadows. Piling my load on the teetering stack, I inspected the room. The box marked "Personals" was still closed. Nothing else seemed disturbed. Maybe we had a ghost who was either sexually insecure or obsessed with the privacy of others. A little creepy, but nothing threatening.

Danny popped his head in the doorway, and I jumped. "You want me to order pizza, babe?" he asked.

I nodded, feeling silly. "Get breadsticks."

I thought my voice sounded a little shaky, but he didn't seem to notice. He pulled his head back out and shut the door. There I was, alone, in a potentially haunted basement, and he shut the door. I took a deep breath and tried not to succumb to irrational panic. Almost immediately, the door opened again.

Obviously, I'd expected my husband. I was mistaken.

I wasn't the only one who had difficulty navigating those narrow stairs. A woman in her mid-sixties came down sideways. She wore white sneakers and baggy jeans with those little socks with the pom-poms peeking out. I didn't think they made those anymore. Her bedazzled floral T-shirt was tucked neatly into her elastic waistband, and she carried a large pile of fluffy sweaters in her arms. Halfway down the stairs she noticed me staring up at her. Her face split in a grin.

"Oh, you're here!" she said. "How wonderful! I was hoping I'd be the first to meet you, and here you are." She picked her way down the rest of the stairs and hurried over to me.

I was puzzled and glanced up at the closed door above us. "Did my husband let you in?" I asked.

She patted me on the arm. "No, dear. I came through my door."

"Your door." I said. "Are we neighbors?"

"In a manner of speaking, yes." She crossed to a section of boxes in a corner and opened a carton marked "Winter." Carefully placing the sweaters inside, she squashed them down with one hand and tried without success to fold the flaps over with the other. Feeling a bit like Alice in Wonderland, I helped her fight the sweaters until they were nestled safely away.

"So," I said, waving my hand around the basement. "All this stuff is yours. When will you be coming to get it?"

"Oh, no. Just what's in this corner. See the little "H" on all the boxes? Those are ours. "H" for Holdstadt. But you can call me Gloria."

She paused and it took me a moment in my lost state to understand she was waiting for a response. "Jennifer," I said, automatically sticking my hand out. She squeezed it with both of hers, then only let go with one, in order to indicate the various groupings around the room.

"That corner is the Campbell area. They keep to themselves, mostly, but if you ever hear kids down here, that's them. Then over here we have William's belongings." Still clutching my hand, she pulled closer and lowered her voice. "You need to stay out of his things, dear. We all poke into a box or two at first, before we know what's going on, but you want to stay out of his filth. He's very touchy if he thinks something's been moved. I might not always be the first down here to close up the boxes, you know."

I blinked at her. Emotions jostled my brain, crowding for attention. I didn't know which to feel first. I was relieved my basement wasn't haunted. Mortified this sweet lady had caught me poking through someone else's stuff—and it was porn. Furious she'd been in my house, uninvited. Confused my basement seemed to be a multi-family storage unit. I took a deep breath but it didn't help.

"I can see you're confused. Did you buy your house from a short man, dark hair, walked with a limp?"

I nodded.

"When we bought ours, fifteen years ago, he called himself Ben Swindleman. What's he calling himself now?"

"His name is Barney Huxter." I frowned, feeling a headache growing in my skull. "What's that got to do with it?"

Gloria looked at her watch. "I really don't have time to explain all this right now, Jennifer. I have a pie in the oven upstairs and I need to pull it out before it burns." She looked at her watch again and shuffled to the steps. "I'll meet you back here at seven o'clock tonight. Bring your husband, dear and I'll bring my George." She hurried up the stairs and paused halfway, turning back. "What time zone are you in?"

"Central," I said, drawing the word out like I was talking to an idiot.

"Eight, then," she said. "Eight o'clock your time." She reached the door and turned to face me again. "One more thing. Keep this door closed. When you leave it open, we're locked out. The day you moved, in I couldn't get the door open all day long." Then she went through the door and closed it behind her. I ran up the stairs two at a time, risking my safety all the way, threw open the door, and nearly hit Danny in the face.

"Pizza's here," he said. "But I guess you heard it. Are you all right, Jen?"

"Did you see her?" I asked.

"Yeah. I gave her a good tip, too. She'll need to deliver a lot of pizzas to pay off those breast implants."

I gave him a blank stare. "What are you talking about?"

"What are *you* talking about?"

"I need a beer with my pizza," I said.

~*~

We kept an eye on the basement door and, when 8:00 pm came around, we were hesitant to go downstairs right away. If people were tracking through our house, we wanted to catch them at it. We also wondered if we should bring some sort of protection, like a baseball bat. At least Danny took me seriously. He may not have understood what was going on, but he never doubted my sanity. I did enough of that on my own.

We went down ten minutes late and unarmed. Gloria seemed harmless, so how threatening could her husband be? Danny went first, taking the stairs with confidence while I closed the door and trailed behind. In theory, the basement should be empty, since no one but us came through the hallway upstairs. In reality, there were five faces turned up, watching us descend. Several folding metal chairs had been set in a circle, and everyone seemed to be milling around a table of food. I could smell pie.

The minute our feet hit the floor, Gloria broke from the herd and pounced on us.

"Jennifer!" she said, beaming and looping her arm through mine.

"This is Danny," I said. I placed my free hand in his and examined his face. He didn't look well. He was pasty and looked lost. I knew how he felt.

Our hostess had us well under her control, bustling us to the center of the room for introductions. "This is my George," she said.

George was a pleasant, grandfatherly type, smelling of pipe tobacco and peppermints. We shook his offered hand and made the mild, meaningless greeting noises of human strangers. He stepped aside, and Gloria introduced us to William Decker, a tall man with a receding hairline, short-sleeved dress shirt, and banana-yellow "power tie."

"Great to meet you both, Dan," William said, pumping our hands with a ferocity worthy of a politician up for re-election. "Great to have new blood in the basement, if you take my meaning. How's your portfolio looking these days, Dan?"

"Oh for God's sake, Bill, give it a rest." A man with kind, hazel eyes stepped forward and shook our hands. He had a firm, decisive grip. "I'm Ted Campbell," he said. "And this is my wife, Grace." Ted and his wife were opposites. She was small and delicate with dark eyes and mousy hair, while he was large and sturdy with a shock of hair like shoe polish.

Grace gave a shy, welcoming smile, but said nothing.

"I know this is all a surprise," Ted said, escorting us to a pair of folding chairs. "It wasn't long ago Grace and I were the new ones, so I know how crazy all this seems. Have a seat and we'll try to explain it."

We murmured our thanks and sat, feeling awkward and vulnerable. Plates of cherry pie and cups of coffee appeared in our hands. I wanted to object, demand answers and cry out in anger, but the entire situation seemed so normal. I had no idea how to react. Danny was in the same state. We did the only thing we could do: we ate our pie, and we listened.

It seemed we'd been the most recent mark in a real estate scam. Our agent, Mr. Huxter, (Swindleman, Conner, Scammington) sold us a house with a large basement and gave us a great price, only charging a little extra for the substantial, underground basement. A comparable house with such a large basement would normally go for a great deal more.

"If you go to City Hall," Ted said, "you'll find the original plans for your house didn't include a basement. It's just not there."

"That's crazy," Danny said. "We're sitting in it right now. There *is* a basement in this house."

Ted nodded. "There's a basement, but it's not in your house. Where do you live, Danny?"

Danny blinked, not understanding the question. "We live upstairs."

"No," William said, pulling out his wallet. "What city? What state?"

"Lawrence, Kansas," Danny said. "What are you trying to say here?"

William crossed the circle of chairs and stood in front of us, brandishing his business card. "My house is right upstairs, too," he said.

The card gave us the number and address of William Decker, Investment Broker, Macon, Georgia.

"Oh my God," I said slowly. "Gloria, where do you live?" I was beginning to piece it together, and I didn't like it.

Gloria smiled. "We live in Cloudcroft, New Mexico, dear. It really is beautiful. You should come up for a visit sometime."

Danny and I exchanged glances. "Ted?" he asked.

"Portland, Oregon," he said. "I know it's a lot to take in."

"How?" I asked. My mouth was dry. I took a sip of coffee.

Ted leaned back in his chair and made himself comfortable. "Well," he said. "The nearest we can tell is this guy sold us all a basement-sized pocket universe. It seems to be keyed specifically to whoever signed the paperwork for the house. We don't know how he does it."

"I think it's the pen," George said, lighting his pipe and eyeing us closely. "Do you remember signing with a heavy, silver pen with a slider on the side?"

We nodded.

George gave Ted a satisfied nod. "Told you," he said, drawing on the stem and puffing thick smoke into the air. "I always thought it was the pen. Probably something to do with our electro-magnetic-whatsits."

"I still don't understand how it got in our house," Danny said.

"Oh, that's the easy part," Ted said. "It's the only thing we know for sure. Ever notice how the doorknob to the basement doesn't match the rest of the knobs in the house? I changed mine out once. Without that doorknob, I lose the basement and gain a bathroom."

"So, now what do we do?" I asked.

Gloria rose to collect the empty plates. "Nothing to be done, dear. We can't call anyone to complain. They wouldn't believe us. And there's no one to sue. He changes his name and keeps moving. So, we make do and share the basement."

I considered the faces in the room. Everyone seemed honest and friendly and he did give us a good deal on the house. She was right. What could we possibly do?

"So," Ted said. "A few rules we like to follow to make this easy on all of us. Don't leave your door open. It locks us all out. Keep your belongings in your designated area and don't leave a mess. Hands off other people's stuff. Really, that's common courtesy and shouldn't even be brought up."

"Always turn the light off when you leave, dear." Gloria said. "That way, if you come in and the light is on, you know someone's already down here. I've had a fright more than once, so it just makes good sense."

"One last thing," Ted said, handing us a sheet of paper. "These are our phone numbers and addresses, in case of emergency. You can add yours when you're comfortable with us, but we like to keep in touch outside the basement. I found Bill huddled in here once during a tornado and brought him out through our door. He stayed with us in Portland till the weather cleared in Macon. We've found ways to use all this to our advantage, and you will too. Sleep on it. It's actually a pretty good deal."

~*~

Over the years, I've grown pretty close with Grace, who turned out to be a chatterbox when her husband wasn't around. We've watched their two boys grow and they call us Aunt Jen and Uncle Danny. Gloria passed away last year, and we were all devastated. We've tried our best to keep George from clanking around in that huge house by himself, bringing him casseroles and having him up for dinner or to watch movies. He probably won't stay there much longer, but he promised to take the doorknob with him if he leaves. Bill fixed us up with a strong stock portfolio, and our money is looking pretty good. He's pushy, but he's good at what he does.

Yesterday I tried to go downstairs, but the door was locked all day. This morning, I found a pile of boxes in a previously empty spot along the wall. With Gloria gone, I guess I'll have to be the new greeter. My pie isn't nearly as good as hers, in spite of all the time she spent trying to teach me.

I hope the new tenants live somewhere warm. I wouldn't mind a vacation in Florida.

"Escalating Heaven"

Another flash fiction piece for the Confabulator Cafe, this one had a challenge attached. I had to use "I think I got everyone" as the first line and "This is better than anything" as the last. Everything in between is mine.

"I think I got everyone, George. Shut her down."

"Got it, Frank."

Edna held her breath and clutched her newly issued, regulation white robe, halo, and harp. The flimsy fabric of the robe crinkled under her grip. She pressed herself against the marble pillar and listened to Heaven's escalator rumble to a halt. The footsteps of the two men receded, and the lights dimmed.

She let out a lungful of air and peered around the column. Empty. Edna dumped her uniform on the floor and stepped on it for good measure.

"Eighty three years," she said, poking the bent halo with her toe. "Eighty three years of hymns, prayer, good deeds, and faithful service to the church."

She ran her hands over her flat belly and smooth hips, reveling in her young body. She'd forgotten what it was like not to wince in pain with each step. She grinned and tapped her strong teeth with a finger of her now age-spotless hand. All there. Just like the good old days.

Edna stepped out into the atrium and adjusted her hospital gown. It didn't fit well. It had been put on her when she was alive, as a frail, bony old woman with sagging breasts. Now it was tight across her perky bosom and full hips. She had a vague memory of what it was like to have a young, healthy body. She hadn't paid much attention to it at the time, nor had she done much with it, except plant flowers outside the church or make cupcakes for the church bake sale. She'd never dated or married. There was too much work to be done. Too many poor to help.

Before her, a pair of silent escalators stretched into the distance. Waist-high gates of gold and pearl blocked off the unmoving steps up. Near the top, golden light broke through fluffy clouds. Edna heard the faint notes of harp music, and she made a face.

The down escalator was blocked by soot-covered gates carved with screaming faces and monstrous creatures. Even several feet from the entrance she felt waves of heat and heard distant screams. Edna backed away.

These were her choices? Fire and torture or an eternity as dull and endless as the life she'd already endured?

When Edna had crossed over, she'd been relieved to throw off the mortal coil and take her eternal reward. She'd worked hard for it. The Judgment Hall was filled with milling, confused people, but Edna had been ready. Her whole life had been devoted to this moment. In fact, her good works and dedication to God had earned her a Judgment Fast Pass, sending her to the front of the long line. St. Peter smiled and welcomed her, stamped her paperwork with a big smiley face, and sent her off to wardrobe and orientation.

That's where it all went wrong.

Her younger body was restored, and they issued her the formless robe and accessories of her new station. She was a disappointed, having expected something a little less cliché, maybe a little more stylish. But a harp? Everyone had one, too. She couldn't imagine a life spent doing nothing but playing a harp with a million other smiling, empty faces.

In orientation they assigned her a cloud number and a chord. A single chord. She wouldn't even be playing songs. Everyone played their small part in the Celestial Harp Orchestra. It was better that way, they explained. Everyone was a piece of the whole, and everyone worked together to glorify God. There was no pride in Heaven.

So, that was it. She'd given her whole life to earn more of the same, only it was even less interesting and even more selfless.

After orientation, a bell had rung and a panel in the wall opened, leading out to the escalators. Heaven's gates were open wide, the steps rolling up to the sky. Hell's gates were still closed. When asked, the orientation instructor had waved a dismissive hand at it and explained that other groups would be going down later in the day.

Edna didn't want to go to Hell, but Heaven now held a nearly equal amount of dread for her. It was then that she slipped from the crowd of Paradise-bound travelers and hid behind the marble pillar at the back of the room. What would it hurt to delay a little?

Edna crossed her arms over her firm bosom and stared at the two sets of closed gates. A particularly noxious wave of sulfur blew up from hell, making her stomach lurch. She sighed. There really was no choice. She was being obstinate and prideful. With reluctance, she moved toward the gates to Heaven, preparing herself for the long walk up.

A bell rang and a section of wall opened, spilling out hundreds of people.

"All right, people, everyone follow me in an orderly manner." A man in a grey suit waved his arms to direct the crowd, his voice booming directions.

Edna stepped behind the pillar.

"You, too, sweetheart." Another man in a grey suit grabbed her arm and pulled her into the crowd. "Don't lag behind."

Dismayed, Edna shuffled along with the crowd and out a door behind the escalators. Her last glimpse of the atrium was a sign above her doorway: *Welcome to Purgatory.*

The door closed and disappeared behind them. The crowd dissipated around her, and Edna stood alone on an unfamiliar city street.

A good-looking man stood on the sidewalk near her. He nodded and smiled. "You look lost, doll."

Edna nodded. "A little, yes."

The man tilted his head toward the bar behind him. "Can I buy you a drink?"

Her eyes grew wide. "Certainly not. What kind of a woman…" Edna stopped. What could it hurt? "Yes, I believe you can. Thank you."

Inside, Edna took a sip of her first alcoholic drink ever, while a strange man eyed her legs with a hungry look.

She licked her lips. "This is better than anything."

"Cursed by Beauty"

Lovely, lithe, exquisite.
No other so fair.
Greedy, they reached,
grasping to possess.
My only escape,
a loveless marriage.

His child danced
before my stricken eyes
trailing curls of night.
Her face, palest ivory,
lips a scarlet rose.
I beheld her winsome form
with astonished grief.
Her curse exceeded even mine.

Hands raw and calloused,
weary with scrubbing and fetching.
Still, her curse grew.
I failed.
Only death could break the spell.
I would keep her heart
cherished and safe
in a walnut box carved of sorrow.

I confused lust for loyalty.
A gentle lie, meant to appease.
Her mewling cries
captured his soul.
Knife twisting in his grasp,
she slipped away in darkness

TRANSMONSTRIFIED

Poisoned comb, corset laces,
shining, juicy apple,
my final effort to keep her safe.
I hold aloft my tools of mercy
cackling to the thunderous sky.
The winds accept the sacrifice.
My own curse is blown away.

"What Zoey Doesn't Know"
A Monster Haven Short Story

This was the first Monster Haven piece I wrote from a point of view other than Zoey's. It seemed fitting that, given his popularity, Maurice should get a shot at talking to us. This peek into a day in the life of a closet monster takes place between book three, Fairies in My Fireplace, *and book four,* Golem in My Glovebox. *It was previously published as a single in 2014.*

The mummy barely waited for Zoey's car to disappear down the driveway before he knocked on the back door. I knew it was him. My monster ears are pretty sharp—probably because of their size. I'm proud of them, even if they do make it hard to wear a hat.

Hats are cool.

The mummy's bandaged feet shuffled up the steps. His gauzed-over knuckles thumped rather than knocked. I opened the door to find Akhenaten waiting, hands tucked into his armpits and head lowered.

"Dude," I said. "I just re-bandaged you yesterday."

Akhenaten moaned. He did that a lot before speaking. Drove me nuts. "I didn't know she was making spaghetti for dinner."

Sure enough. The gauze around his lips had a reddish stain to it, and tiny red flecks covered his chest and chin. It sort of looked like blood, so I was surprised he was worried about it. It added a startling effect.

I ran my hand over my head and took a deep breath to keep from getting angry. "I've got a lot going on today. I'll redo your head, but that's it, okay?"

He nodded. "Thanks." He drew the 's' out extra long, and I considered flicking him in the ear. I didn't. But I thought about it.

"Sit, sit, sit." I pulled out a kitchen chair for him, but didn't offer a drink like I usually did. The game was getting old.

While Akhenaten got himself settled, I ran down the hall and grabbed the bag of gauze from the back of the linen closet. Zoey found it once when she was digging in there for nail polish, but she didn't ask why we had so much of it.

Thank the gods, because she'd kill me if she knew about this.

After I located the end of the gauze from where I'd tucked it in his collar the day before, I unwrapped the bandages from his head to his neck. His blond hair was sweaty from confinement, and his skin was pale from lack of sun.

The guy's real name was Gavin, and why his wife put up with this behavior was beyond me. Humans are weird. I went along with it mostly so he'd leave Zoey alone. She had enough going on without playing counselor to a delusional whackjob who'd accidentally stumbled on the Hidden world and wanted to be part of it.

Zoey wouldn't have humored him. She'd have tried to 'fix' him. My way was easier. He wanted to play dress up and role-play the whole monster thing, more power to him. Not my business. He paid me in peaches or the occasional bag of walnuts from the trees in his backyard. Fair deal, I guess, since Zoey hated when I took stuff from the neighbors' yards without their knowledge.

Once Gavin was rewrapped, I patted him on the shoulder. "Okay, buddy. You're good to go. Try to keep it clean a little longer this time. I'm running low on supplies."

He groaned, long and low. "Thanksss."

"No problem. Make sure nobody sees you. It's broad daylight. Do you want a hat or something?"

He refused the hat and stumbled out the back door, his legs stiff and awkward, groaning and holding his arms out in front of him. I wasn't too worried about people seeing him. The magic bubble surrounding our backyard made everyone and everything inside invisible to people outside the bubble. Gavin only had to go through four yards to get to his own house. As long as he was careful, nobody would see him now that most people were at work.

If he were actually part of the Hidden community, I'd be more concerned. But what was the worst that could happen? Felicia from two doors over might look out her window and see a mummy dragging himself through the trees. If she believed it was a real mummy, she probably wouldn't tell anybody, for fear of being called crazy. If she thought it was a crazy person in a mummy outfit, she might call the cops. Worst-case scenario, Gavin's little fetish would get exposed and he'd be outed as a human.

Not my problem.

Once I was sure he was gone, I grabbed my navy hoodie and zipped myself into the appearance of a passable human. Snagging my eco-friendly, reusable shopping bag, I went out in the opposite direction to make my morning rounds of the neighborhood gardens.

Zoey's told me more than once not to do this. Sure. Her reasons were sound, and I totally respected them. If people saw me picking their produce, they'd show up with pitchforks and torches demanding we hand over their purloined eggplants and radishes. That was why Zoey didn't know about it. Also, it was why I'd never tell her that her favorite pumpkin cheesecake was made from the Deckers' prize-winning pumpkins and eggs from the Hawthornes' chicken coop.

Usually, I made my rounds earlier in the morning, but Zoey had overslept and Gavin had shown up, so I was behind. It meant I had to be faster and stealthier than usual. Speed wasn't a big deal—closet monsters can move faster than the human eye can follow—but choosing which fruits and vegetables are ripe and how many won't be missed required more than faster-than-the-eye thought. Most people don't understand that super-speed doesn't necessarily equate to super-thought.

Zipping to and from each garden was great, but I had to stop to examine things. And that's when things got dangerous.

Most of the neighbors in the area had regular nine-to-five jobs. At my first stop, a quick peek out front to see that Sandra's car wasn't in the driveway told me she was gone. I popped around the side to trim a little rosemary and mint from her herb garden, then strolled to the back to check her tomatoes.

"Psst. Get down!"

A hand grabbed my sleeve and tugged. I dropped to the ground, alert. "What's wrong?"

"She's home, you nitwit. Didn't you check inside? Her car's in the shop."

Startled by the tone, I stopped scanning the area and looked at the guy squatting next to me. I groaned. "Silas, what are you doing here?"

Silas the pooka was bad news. He was the embodiment of bad luck and took great pleasure in causing trouble for the people around him. Sitting next to him meant the very real possibility of an anvil falling on my head while I slipped on a banana peel dropped by a passing black cat.

The dude was seriously dangerous.

Silas rocked back onto his heels and shoved a hairy finger up his nose. "I came to see Zoey. It's been awhile." He inspected the goop on the end of his finger and wiped it on Sandra's grass.

The first time Silas had shown up, I'd been away. Zoey'd had to put up with him, and he'd trashed the house. He was gone by the time I got back, but I'd dealt with the mess. Since then, he'd visited twice—always at mealtimes. The bad-luck thing he had going wasn't nearly as disruptive as the slob factor.

Silas was intentionally disgusting.

"Zoey's at work. And she's really busy, Silas. It's not a good time for company."

He snorted and scratched his belly. "Don't be stupid. Zoey's always busy. And I know she's at work. That's why I thought I'd grab a little breakfast over here. I thought I'd wait until this broad made breakfast, then move in close until my luck got her. Maybe she'd have to run to the hospital." He shrugged. "Or worse. Either way, I'd get breakfast."

I stared at him, appalled. "Dude, seriously? Is that how you usually get your meals?"

He smiled and didn't answer.

I shook my head. "You need to stay away from our house today. I've got a lot to do, and Zoey's under a lot of stress. Go home."

Silas held his stubby arms up with his palms held out. "All right. All right. Don't get all bossy on me. I brought her some information I thought she'd be interested in."

I inhaled and counted to ten. "What information?"

"What are you, her secretary?"

Asshole. "Let's just say I'm her business manager. Everything goes through me."

Silas belched. "Fine. Suit yourself. You ever heard of Mytho-crockus?"

Aside from the fact that Silas was an untrustworthy shit, the word sounded totally made up. I gave him my best eye roll. "You know I haven't."

He examined his filthy fingernails, then used one to pick his teeth. "It's a neuro-virus. Humans can get it when exposed to a large number of Hidden in their vicinity. It's why large populations of us don't generally hang out together around large cities."

I couldn't decide whether to laugh or pop him in the eye. "I'm not an idiot."

He looked at me as if I were, in fact, an idiot. "Ignore me if you want. But that mummy I saw leaving your house isn't the only one infected. Humans all up and down this street were exposed, and I've seen several acting like they think they've got magic powers. Mummy guy is harmless, but Sandra in there thinks she's a harpy. If you don't do something, the lady's likely to jump off her own roof thinking she can fly."

I closed my eyes, imagining how upset Zoey would be that her helping so many Hidden creatures had put her human neighbors in danger. "Well, hell. So how do we cure this?" I looked around. "Silas?"

He'd disappeared without a sound, just as Sandra came around the corner, dragging a ladder with her. She didn't see me crouched in her marigold patch because she was too focused on securing the ladder against the side of the house. She hummed as she worked, an eerie, tuneless song that sounded more like it came from a carnival ride than the radio.

She climbed the rungs, a weird little hop to her step, almost as if she were trying to flap a pair of wings she didn't have. When she made it to the top, she stood tall, flung off her ruffled blouse and industrial-strength bra, and spread her arms wide.

As much as I hated to admit it, Silas appeared to be telling the truth.

Fortunately, I have that monster super-speed thing. Before she jumped, I scurried up the ladder, grabbed her from behind, and dragged her down the ladder and into her house, where I locked her into her own bathroom by hooking a chair under the doorknob. It all took about thirty seconds.

I backed away from the door, breathing hard. She banged a few times, then shrieked, sounding very much like the harpy she thought she was.

She never saw me, so that was something. Still, I couldn't keep her locked in there for long. I rubbed my head. What was I supposed to do now?

"It's an easy cure, you know." Silas sat in the next room at Sandra's kitchen table, stuffing his face with toast that was liberally dusted with sugar and cinnamon. He belched and gulped down a glass of milk. "I can write down the ingredients for you."

"You would do that?" My tone was flat. "What's the catch?"

He made a face as if he were hurt. "No catch. I don't want to see people suffer."

"Dude. You live to see people suffer."

He grinned. "Fair enough. I really do." He wiped his greasy, sticky fingers on Sandra's checked tablecloth. "But I'd rather not see Zoey suffer. You? You I don't care about. But Zoey's cool. I kind of owe her."

Before he could change his mind, I raced through the unfamiliar house and grabbed the first pen and blank piece of paper I could find. "Write it down."

He chewed as he scribbled, crumbs flying everywhere. It didn't take long. He held out the paper, then pulled it away when I reached for it. "Wait."

"I knew there was a catch." I narrowed my eyes at him. "What do you want?"

He shrugged. "Nothing much." He tossed a crust on the floor. "I can't live on toast, you know."

I shook my head. "Dude, I don't have time to make you breakfast. I'm already an hour and a half behind schedule today."

"Dinner, then. Tonight. Steak."

Zoey hadn't exaggerated. This guy was a pain in the ass. "Fine. But not a word of any of this to Zoey."

"Deal." He handed over the list and shook my hand.

I resisted the urge to wipe my hand on my shirt for fear of my hand sticking to the fabric forever. "This is it?"

He shrugged. "You're dealing with a virus. You can't actually cure it. It's got to run its course. That list helps you manage the symptoms in the meantime."

I stared at the short list in my hand. It didn't have a lot to offer, and none of it seemed likely. "Hairspray? Why hairspray?"

He smelled his fingers, as if shaking my hand might have left a residue behind. I tried not to curl my lips in disgust as he licked his palm and fingers with a thoughtful look. "Hairspray is sticky. It helps to 'set' their true identity rather than the delusions their minds are projecting." He stuck his wet fingers into the sugar bowl and swirled them around. "Any brand will do."

I couldn't shake the feeling that he was pulling a prank on me. "What about the calamine lotion? What's that for?"

"Makes them comfortable in their own skin." He stuck a finger caked with sugar into his mouth.

"The mints?" At this point, I was looking for hidden cameras, and I was ready for any answer he gave me.

"You have to give them two. One to freshen them, the other to 're-fresh' them. That should put their old personality back for a few days and give the virus a chance to work itself out."

"No." I'd been ready for any answer but that, apparently.

"Yes." He sucked on his fingers and pulled them out with a loud *pop*. "I know it sounds stupid, but it's really a thing. Ask that hag friend of yours, Aggie. She'll back me up."

A thunk and an ear-bursting screech from the bathroom down the hall told me I didn't have time to consult with Aggie the Hag. I either had to suck it up and trust Silas or call an ambulance for Sandra.

I zipped up the stairs and rummaged in the closets of Sandra's primary bathroom. At the back of the cupboard under the sink, I found an off brand of pump-type hairspray, then tore back downstairs with it.

"So, do I just spray it all over her or…"

Silas was gone. The kitchen was a wreck of sugar, buttery smears, and dirty dishes. I glanced from the mess to the bottle in my hand, then at the hallway where Sandra certainly sounded like a screeching harpy. If the spray worked, she'd be herself again for a while. She'd see the mess in her kitchen—a mess she never made—and possibly call the police. Also, I wouldn't be able to get the lotion on her or get her to suck on a couple of mints, since I couldn't let her see me.

Sandra slammed herself against the bathroom door again, and I worried it wouldn't hold.

Get ahold of yourself, dude. Whatever you're going to do, do it fast.

I trotted toward the front door and threw open the coat closet. I needed mints and calamine lotion before I could do anything else. The more times I had to come back here, the more chances I had of getting caught and exposing the Hidden community to a human—even if that human did currently think she was part of the community.

I stepped into the closet. A bright light shone from above me and my eyes flicked into closet-monster mode. The elaborate network of the Closet Superhighway lay before me in a grid of the world's closets. I narrowed my focus first to the United States, then California, then Bolinas, and finally our little neighborhood.

The Lohman's up the street had two boys, and both had come home from camp last year with poison oak. They'd be the most likely to have what I needed. I touched the square that held their house, chose a door as the location loomed closer, and stuck my head through the closet door of five-year-old Max's room. The coast was clear. I could hear Mrs. Lohman vacuuming downstairs, and the kids would be at school.

Fast as a shooting star, I dashed into the boys' shared bathroom, found what I needed, and made it back to Sandra's before a floorboard had a chance to finish squeaking.

Using that same super-speed, I cleaned up the kitchen, then rummaged in Sandra's purse for a couple of slightly fuzzy mints. I checked the clock above the stove. Less than two minutes had elapsed. I gave myself a mental high five, since my hands were full.

The screeching from the bathroom had turned to squawking. If I didn't do this quickly, Sandra was going to do damage to herself and her bathroom.

I checked the list one last time, but nothing new turned up. No magic words. No special order in which to apply the items. No instructions of any kind.

Thanks for you help, Silas. You're a real prince.

After stuffing the mints and the hairspray in my pockets, I uncapped the lotion and pulled the chair away from the door. Sandra stopped making angry bird noises, but I heard her pacing back and forth.

In one smooth motion, I threw open the door and flicked the open bottle so it splattered lotion on her bare chest. I did this while trying to avert my eyes, because, seriously, I am not equipped to deal with human boobs.

Sandra flailed around for a few seconds, then stopped, rubbing her hands over the lotion in fascination. While she was distracted, I fished the mints from my pocket, defuzzed them as much as I could, popped them both in her mouth, then spun her to face the window so she couldn't see me when the delusion passed.

I gave one last glance around for hidden cameras, then pumped the nozzle of the hairspray, giving her a liberal coating from behind.

"Hey!" She looked down at her naked chest covered in stinky pink lotion and held her arms out in disgust. "What the hell?"

By the time she turned around, I was home, having escaped through her coat closet. I kept the lotion and hairspray, just in case.

I gave the top of my head a vigorous rub and dropped into a chair in my own kitchen. I was two hours behind schedule, the sun was now far too bright to risk making my garden rounds, and I'd left my shopping bags behind at Sandra's house.

The homeless shelter would have to do without the fresh fruits and vegetables I usually smuggled into their pantry in the mornings. They never knew where it came from, but they really needed it. I couldn't risk the trip though. The windows of opportunity both for collecting the produce and delivering it were gone. Margie would have to be disappointed in her anonymous benefactor for today.

I made a mental note to go out early tomorrow and double my usual collection.

Something stank. I sniffed myself and found a streak of calamine lotion across my arm. Wrinkling my nose, I washed it off at the sink, then refocused. My day wasn't shot. Only derailed a bit. I could get back on track.

I preheated the oven. Earlier, I'd thrown together a nice pastry crust, cut it into tiny circles, then lined a muffin tin with them. The tiny crusts, now baked and cooled, waited on the counter. I whisked some eggs, added a little cream, veggies, and cheese, then filled the pastry cups. The oven hadn't finished preheating yet, so I made the beds, vacuumed, cleaned the bathrooms, dusted the furniture, and scrubbed away a new stain in the hallway carpet.

When the oven beeped, I tossed the mini quiches inside and went back into Zoey's room to consider my options.

Zoey was a slob. I knew that when I moved in. I liked things neat. She'd told me several times that she appreciated all I do around here, but that she felt guilty when I cleaned her room.

I could not let this stand, though. Clothes were everywhere. Dirty. Clean. Tried on, worn a few hours, then discarded. Her entire wardrobe was in a jumble on her bedroom floor. If I hung it all up, she'd probably be pissed.

I tried to walk away. I really did. But damn, that girl was like a force of nature in her destruction. I gathered up the clothes, sorted them, and tossed the dark pile in the washing machine. While they ran, I washed her delicates in the bathroom sink and hung them over the shower rail to dry.

When I was done, I checked the time. Ten minutes had passed. I'd been taking my time, since the mini quiches needed fifteen minutes to bake, but I still had a few minutes left.

I made myself a cream cheese and jelly sandwich and sat in the living room to watch a little television and relax.

Relaxing was out of the question. To my horror, a special news report ran on the local station. The cameras went live to the outside of a Sausalito bank robbery in progress. The robber or robbers had hostages, though authorities weren't sure about how many there were of either.

I dropped my sandwich on the plate and wiped my fingers on a napkin. Zoey's office was half a block from there.

I flew through my closet and into a janitor's closet at the bank, opening the door a crack to peek out at the lobby.

Several customers lay flat on the floor, cringing in fear. Two men in dark ski masks paced, their weapons pointed at the ceiling.

Because Zoey is entirely incapable of keeping out of trouble, her yellow beret shown like a beacon from among the hostages. That upped the difficulty level of taking these guys out without anybody noticing. Zoey would definitely notice if I set so much as a sneaker toe out there.

As one of the robbers walked past my closet, I reached through and pulled him in. He was unprepared, blind in the dark, and slow. I was none of those things. I managed to knock the gun from his hand, spin him around, secure his hands with a length of twine I found on the shelf, and stuff a reasonably clean rag in his mouth. Then I turned his ski mask around so his eyes were covered. The golden rule of being part of the Hidden community was to stay hidden. I couldn't have him looking at me when I opened the door and let some light in.

I checked my watch. If I didn't leave now, my mini quiches would burn.

Someone, presumably the other bank robber, shouted in the lobby. The guy at my feet gave a muffled cry.

"Shh." I prodded him with my sneaker. "Don't make another sound. Seriously, dude. You're not in a position to make trouble for me." I peeked out the door again and saw the other guy talking on his cell phone. "Don't move."

I zipped back home, pulled out the tray of quiches, turned off the oven and went back to the bank. In the thirty seconds I'd been gone, the guy in the closet hadn't moved. I wasn't sure what to do. The second guy was out in the lobby, where I couldn't get to him.

I faced the back of the closet and shifted my eyes to see the rest of the bank's closets and cupboards. I found a space on the other side of the lobby that was behind the mail slot on the wall near the bank robber, so I stepped into it. He paced a few more times, then stopped in front of me. A woman on the floor near his feet shifted, and I caught a flash of badge.

Perfect.

I tore back home and grabbed a bottle of vegetable oil, then came right back. The masked man still stood in front of the mail slot, blocking me from everyone else. Quiet as a swamp bogey tracking a flargsnozzle, I tipped the bottle and poured oil on the floor beneath him.

He took one step, slipped, and landed on his ass. As I had hoped, the cop on the floor was quick to take over and, within seconds, had him subdued. I went back to the janitor's closet and shoved the other guy out the door, then ran home, confident it was all over.

As I finished my sandwich, I watched the live coverage on the news of the hostages—Zoey included—coming out of the bank.

I took my plate into the kitchen to wash it. "Not bad for a lunch break."

Zoey's laundry was done, so I tossed it into the dryer, then put her whites in to wash. I hummed while I washed the dishes and popped the cooled quiches into a pretty, napkin-lined basket. As I made my way through the backyard to drop off my gift at the mushroom house where Molly and the rest of the brownie family lived, a rustling in the bushes made me stop.

What the hell? Nate Saunders from across the street stood with his arms in the air, feet planted in the ground. I mean, literally *planted*.

I sighed. Dude thought he was a tree. Or more accurately, he thought he was a dryad.

He wasn't actually doing anything but standing with his arms in the air, so I had a few minutes before I had to deal with him. I continued on my way toward the back corner of the yard, weaving between the empty tents, fire pits, and chairs that had recently housed dozens of refugee monsters and mythical creatures.

A puff of smoke rose in front of my face, and I stopped, glancing down. "Oh, hey, Bruce."

A green dragon, about the size of a collie, lay curled in the opening of a small canvas tent. He snorted a greeting at me, then sent a double spiral of smoke from his nostrils. When he growled, I understood the friendly question, even though I didn't speak pigmy dragon. Molly spoke it, but there was no need to bother her. I knew what Bruce wanted.

"No problem, buddy. The jewelry Zoey and Sara borrowed from you is safe and sound in my closet. I'm kind of busy at the moment." I held up the basket of quiches. "If you're sticking around awhile, can I bring it out to you later?"

Bruce tipped his head, winked, then closed his eyes. Dragons slept a lot. He'd be fine until I had a chance to get his stuff for him, even if it took until tomorrow.

At the giant mushroom, I bent and knocked on the tiny door. Eight-inch tall Molly popped her head out an upstairs window. She craned her neck to look up at me. "Maurice! I forgot you were coming. I will be right down."

She shut the window. While I waited for her to come out, the window opened again, and little Abby waved her chubby hand at me. I squatted so we'd be eye level. "Good afternoon, princess." I bowed at the waist—awkward when one is already squatting.

She giggled and stuck her thumb in her mouth. "Silly." The word was garbled around her hand.

Molly stepped out the front door, brushing wrinkles from her skirt. Hands on her hips, she squinted up at her daughter. "Close the window, please, Abby. It is still nap time!"

Abby ducked inside and disappeared. Molly shook her head, stifling a grin.

I placed the basket of quiches next to her. It was several times her size. "I brought you these for the bake sale. I hope they help."

She peered inside, inhaling the smell of cheese and pastry. "This is very kind of you, Maurice. I am certain they will help a great deal." She shook her head, her face sad. "So many losses in the Hidden community. So many lost and alone."

I rose to my full height and shoved my hands in my pockets. "If I can do anything else, let me know. I'll come by tomorrow to check on you."

Molly smiled. Whenever she did that, all the tense muscles in my body relaxed.

"You do so much, Maurice. Maybe take some time to relax tomorrow." She turned toward the house and stopped. "The world can take care of itself for one day."

The world could do no such thing. I shuffled away, unhurried, until I was sure she couldn't see me anymore. Molly and Zoey were close. If Molly thought I was up to something, she wouldn't hesitate to bring it up to Zoey. Not because she'd rat me out, mind you. Molly simply wasn't the sort of person who kept secrets, even if it was for a good reason.

I raced to our house, gathered a tin of mints, the lotion, and the hairspray. When I got back to the spot where I'd seen Nate earlier, I thought he was gone. That would've been great. It would mean he got over thinking he was a tree and went home.

Or that he was in full dryad mode and was a few yards away, dancing in his altogethers across the lawn.

The weird part was that he'd left his socks on.

Okay, maybe that wasn't the only weird part. I scouted around for his clothes. They were everywhere. Dude must've flung them as he took them off.

One shoe lay in the dirt, the other in the crook of a tree. His shirt hung from a bush, and his jeans were in the neighbor's yard.

For the life of me, I could not find the dude's underwear.

I scratched my head. If I could get him dressed, he'd probably wonder why he was going commando, but probably wouldn't suspect that somebody had taken them. That would be too bizarre. I decided it was safe enough for me to forget it.

For a tree-man, he was pretty strong. It took me fifteen minutes to wrestle him to the ground and get his clothes on him. He moaned like I was killing him when I tied his shoes.

"I can't feel the earth!" He kicked, and his hard rubber sole connected with my jaw. "I'm suffocating!" His wailing hurt my head.

But I managed to get him dressed and half carried, half dragged him around the house to the bushes along our long driveway. Mindful of possibly needing the supplies again, I was more frugal this time.

First, a dab of calamine lotion on the back of his arm. Two strong mints went into his mouth. I gave him a small shove and, while he stumbled forward, I spritzed him with the hairspray.

Nate fell to his knees, landing on all fours. "Ow. What the hell?"

As his head came up to look around, I disappeared into the house.

Zoey's first load of laundry was done, so I scooped it into a basket and transferred the second load into the dryer. I was cutting it close. I may have been able to move fast, but food cooked at the same speed as it always did, no matter how fast I put it together, and laundry always took the same amount of time to dry.

Physics.

While I waited for the dryer to finish, I tossed together some olive oil, soy sauce, balsamic vinegar, minced garlic, and my secret seasonings and stuck the steaks in to marinade for a bit. I'd have preferred to leave them overnight, but Silas had kind of sprung it on me last minute.

I whizzed around the kitchen throwing ingredients together, whipping fresh cream into stiff peaks, rolling potatoes in rock salt, shelling peas, and slicing strawberries. When Zoey was home, she liked to watch me cook, so I had to move slower. Nobody watched tonight, so I went at a quicker pace.

The dryer buzzed as I pulled a lemon Bundt cake from the oven. The whipped cream and strawberries would go on it later, after the cake cooled.

I checked the time. Zoey would be home in a few minutes. More than anything, I wanted to spend the next few minutes folding laundry, but I couldn't let myself have that pleasure. If I folded it, she'd notice. Shoving all those clean clothes into the basket with the rest made me cringe. Sure, they were finally clean, but now they were all wrinkled. I toyed with the idea of ironing them, but time wasn't on my side. Besides, she might notice.

In her room, I replaced everything exactly as I'd found it on the floor. I folded my arms and stood back, concentrating. It didn't look right. I pushed a pair of jeans over a bit with my toe. No. Still not right.

The bathroom! I'd forgotten her delicates. The bathroom was a forest of lace and silk—and a few of those horrible cotton things she wore that I wished I could throw away behind her back. I plucked everything from where it hung and placed it in the basket as if I were some sort of farmer in an unmentionables orchard. Once I dumped everything in her room where I'd found it, I stepped back and nodded.

Perfect. Nothing out of place.

I zipped outside and got the barbecue started, then came inside, turned on the television, and plopped on the couch as Zoey's car pulled in.

"Hey, something smells good." She dropped her purse on the table by the door, and placed her yellow beret on top of it. "What's for dinner?"

I stretched. "I thought we'd grill tonight."

"Awesome!" She smiled.

"Because we have company tonight." I gave her my best sorry face. "Silas is here for a visit."

Her smile faded. "Not so awesome." Her steps were heavy as she clomped across the living room in her hot pink platform shoes. "I need to get changed. I spilled coffee on myself. Again." She plucked at her pink polka dot shirt, then brushed the front of her yellow skirt. "And I think I got gum on me from the floor of the bank."

My jaw twitched. Keeping an innocent expression was an effort. "Did you trip or something?"

She shook her head and her bouncy auburn curls went everywhere. "You won't believe it when I tell you. I got caught in a bank robbery."

"No!"

"Yes! Crazy day. I'll be out in a few minutes." She clomped into her room and shut the door. Not ten seconds later, the door flew open and she called down the hall. "Maurice, did you spray something in here when you made my bed?"

I tried to be honest. "No. I didn't spray anything."

She was quiet for a minute. "Huh. Well, it smells different in here. I don't know. Never mind." She shut the door.

By the time she came out in her comfy—and secretly fresh-washed—jeans and *Star Wars* T-shirt, I was out back turning the potatoes in the coals and getting ready to drop three steaks to sizzle.

Silas sat nearby in a folding canvas chair, swinging his feet and plowing through a bag of tortilla chips. At least outside his mess didn't matter too much. The birds would clean it up in the morning. Still, I eyed the crumbs on the ground and wondered if I should at least sweep them into a pile so the birds could find them easier.

Zoey pulled a chair closer to the barbecue. "So, these two masked guys walked into the bank today and pulled guns on us. I'm surprised you didn't see it on the news."

I poked a stake with my long fork. "I was kind of busy today."

Silas snorted and sprayed tortilla crumbs at me.

Zoey smiled. "The house looks really nice. Clean."

I grinned back. "I got that stain out of the rug in the hallway."

"Awesome." She settled into her chair and eyed Silas with suspicion. "How'd we get so lucky to have you visit, Silas?"

He glanced at me poking at his steak, then to her while he decided whether to tell her after I'd asked him to keep quiet. The steak must've persuaded him.

He shrugged. "Do I need a reason?"

Her forehead wrinkled. "I guess not. Just—you know—try to keep your bad luck whammies to yourself."

As I flipped the first steak, something rustled in the bushes. Dread knotted my stomach. I'd forgotten something, but I couldn't think what.

A long, low moan from the bushes reminded me. Akhenaten—Gavin—burst into the open, dragging one leg and holding his arms in front of him as if he were in a Lon Chaney movie.

"No, no, no, no, no!" I darted off to stop him, but the damage was done before I'd moved. He was already in our yard, moaning and being theatrical.

Zoey caught up with me in seconds. "I didn't know mummies were a real thing." She held out her hand to shake. "I'm Zoey. Welcome!"

It was my turn to moan. "What are you doing here? I just fixed you!"

Gavin let out a high-pitched wail. "Wife won't let me in. She locked all the doorsss."

Great. This was perfect. His patient wife chose now to stop being patient.

Zoey patted him on the arm. "I'm so sorry. We have plenty of room for you here, and we'll do everything we can to help you work things out with Mrs. Mummy."

I sighed. "Zoey, it's not what you think."

Silas snickered. "Understatement." He belched.

"Just...everybody wait right here." I zipped into the house and came back with my supplies. This required a little thought. Gavin's situation was a little different from that of the earlier infected humans. His wife had been putting up with it for weeks.

I shook my head. There was nothing I could do to erase his behavior from his wife's mind. Best I could do was make sure he didn't see me and add a monster sighting to his messed-up-psyche list. He was about to think he needed mental help as it was.

Gavin groaned as I swiveled him by the elbows to face Zoey. "Akhenaten, take Zoey's hands. Don't look away from Zoey. Okay?"

He nodded. "Yesss."

Zoey gave me a questioning look, then took the bandaged hands.

I stepped behind Akhenaten/Gavin and dug around in the gauze until I found the end. As I unwrapped his face, Zoey gasped when she recognized our neighbor.

Silas laughed and tossed the empty chip bag in the fire. "This'll be great."

I dabbed Gavin's cheek with the calamine lotion, popped two mints into his mouth, then spritzed the back of his head with hairspray. He inhaled sharply, then moved his head to look around. Zoey touched his face to stop him as I ducked behind the tent.

"Zoey," he said. "Hi." She dropped her hand and let him look around to get his bearings. "What am I doing over here?"

Zoey's voice was soft and calming. She was good at that—even when she had no idea what was going on. "We're not really sure, Gavin. But I think your wife is waiting for you. You should head home."

"Yeah. Yeah, I should go home." The confusion in his voice made me think of white rooms and padded cells. I felt bad for his wife.

The minute he was gone, Zoey swung around to face me. I didn't give her a chance to say anything. "I'll get the plates!" I ran into the house.

Zoey followed behind. I poured her a glass of wine and met her at the steps.

She frowned. "Maurice, what are you not telling me? What happened around here today?"

"Nothing special. Drink this." I shoved the glass of wine in her hand.

She took a sip. "I don't believe you. Not for a second. Something happened today."

A gust of wind blew over us and from somewhere above—the gutter maybe—Nate Saunders's missing underwear shook loose from where it had been hiding. It flapped through the air and landed on top of Zoey's glass.

I snatched the offending garment away and hid it behind my back, smiling. "Nothing, Zoey. Nothing that doesn't happen any other day of the week."

"Cosmic Lasagna"

I think I love using alternate dimensions as much as I love closet monsters in my stories. This story was originally published in the Fall 2010 Returning Contributors issue of the Seahorse Rodeo Folk Review. *They asked me for a new story, and this is what I wrote for them.*

Last week I walked in on myself in the bathroom. I have to admit, he looked as surprised as I felt. He was reaching to flush the toilet when I barged in. I froze. He froze. Does my mouth really gape that way, like a zombie on valium?

He had blond hair, and his part ran down the middle of his head instead of on the left the way my dark hair does. Blond does not suit me. Like an idiot, I started to tell him so. Not, "who are you?" or, "what are you doing here?" or even, "what the hell is happening?" No, my reaction was to tell my double that blond hair makes him look washed out.

I have to believe it was the shock of it. It doesn't much matter. We only stood like that for a few seconds before he began to fade and pop in and out in erratic flashes. When he seemed to be gone for good, I realized the urge to pee, which had brought me into the bathroom in the first place, had departed. Also, it would be best if I changed out of my soaked pants.

The rest began with little things. Out of the corner of my eye, I'd see movement—turn my head and nothing would be there. I'd reach for my coffee cup and it would be gone, only to turn up a minute later right where I had left it. My shoes were often an Easter egg hunt, though I learned that if I took a breath and waited a few minutes, they'd be back in the closet where they belonged. It spooked me, sure. But only in the sense that I might be losing my mind.

The physical manifestations to my own body came a few weeks later.

I was standing in my living room when the whole world seemed to lurch sideways. I snapped my arm out and clutched the back of my recliner for balance. The air whooshed out of my lungs, and my stomach tightened like I'd been punched. The hard edges in the room lost definition and smeared like a child's watercolor painting. The pressure in my ears felt as if all the windows in the house had been slammed shut simultaneously.

And then it stopped.

I stood like a fool, one hand clawing marks into the leather chair, the other braced against the unmoving wall. All was normal—colors, shapes, and edges were sharp and innocent of funny business. The light fixture above my head held steady—no swaying to give away tectonic activity. An earthquake would have been a relief.

Something was seriously wrong.

I considered going to see a doctor. What could he possibly say to me? Either I was losing my mind or was terribly ill. In either case, I couldn't imagine what he could do about it. My faith in science has always been a bit weak, especially in the medical field. We think we know so much, but time and again, current theories are proven wrong. For all the new technology we've acquired, we might as well still be using leeches and waiting to sail off the edge of the earth.

There was also the possibility that I wasn't the problem. Maybe something was happening, and we were all in a lot of trouble. But a doctor wasn't likely to tell me that.

I admit, I'm no genius. Quantum physics is a little beyond my scope. I know they've been theorizing about alternate universes for some time, but that's all it really is—theory. I have my own ideas. While they're busy measuring waves and particles, I look for a simpler explanation. Something my non-scientific mind can comprehend.

According to the Bible, God created the universe in seven days. What has He done since then to amuse Himself? I see no reason why He couldn't be cranking out another universe every seven days, layering each one on top of the other like a vast, cosmic lasagna. The way I picture it, between each layer of universe-pasta, there is a barricade of ethereal cheese to keep them from sticking together and sharing space. When the cheese gets thin and the noodles touch, we get a sort of *dimensional slippage*.

I'll be honest. I'm not particularly religious. I picture God doing all this because I have to believe someone is in charge of cooking all this up. Otherwise, I get a little claustrophobic, picturing the weight of a million universes crushing down, compressing us like sprigs of baby's breath in the family Bible. In reality, I don't think there's anyone in the kitchen.

And the oven timer is about to go off.

At work, a few days after the bathroom incident, I found a redheaded version of myself sitting at my desk. He looked tired—much like I imagined I must have looked. I wondered if he'd encountered the blond as well. No. The blond was *my* cosmic neighbor. I wondered what version of us lived on the cosmic noodle two layers from me, on the other side of this tired, ginger me. Perhaps he was Asian or bald? How many of us were there?

There were framed pictures on the desk of a family I've never had. A pretty wife smiled at the camera, two pretty children in her arms. I stared at a snapshot of my brother and the other me. The photo seemed recent and showed the men in fishing gear with a river winding behind them. *My* brother died in a boating accident when he was sixteen. I dragged my focus to the other me, and he was staring back at me with weary eyes.

He wasn't as substantial as I'd assumed. I could see the light from the computer monitor shining through him. He gave me a tired smile, and then he was gone. No flicker or fade, no theatrics. He was there, and then not.

Two days ago, I woke up with blond hair. The bed was much more comfortable than the one I'd gone to sleep in the night before. When I wandered into the unfamiliar kitchen, I stepped in the dog's water bowl, sloshing it onto the elaborate mosaic tiles on the floor. I don't have a dog. I have cheap linoleum floors. I tried to make coffee, but I couldn't figure out the fancy, expensive-looking coffeemaker.

Photos lined the walls. Blond-Me bungee jumping. Blond-Me water skiing. Blond-Me in a tux, dancing with a woman in a red evening gown. I examined the pictures for some time, standing bare chested in silk pajama bottoms, my beer gut replaced with abs of solid rock. I wondered how I had wasted my own life. I wondered how long I'd be able to keep this one. I wondered where the dog was and if he would recognize that I had stolen his master's body.

I blinked and found myself standing in the middle of the hallway, staring at peeling paint on my own blank wall. My shabby underwear road low beneath my sagging belly. I turned in disgust and pulled out my $20 coffee pot.

There was a puddle on the floor where no dog bowl had ever been.

I was never particularly dissatisfied with my life until these events began. I'm a moderately good-looking, outgoing guy. I have friends. I'm a good employee. Maybe I'm not top salesman, but I'm never at the bottom either. My house is comfortably furnished, and my clothes, while not expensive or high fashion, aren't exactly bell-bottom leisure suits and wide ties, either. I was fine before all this. I didn't regret not having a wife and kids. Sure, at thirty-five, maybe time was ticking a little faster than before, but I wasn't over-the-hill. I had time.

Then the cheese started to dry up in the cosmic lasagna. It showed me everything I could have been. Everything I could have done. Everything my life wasn't.

This morning I woke up next to my pretty wife. Her eyes are sapphire blue with tiny crinkles at the corners when she laughs. The kids squabbled over the cereal-box toy while we ate breakfast. Against my wife's protests, I opened another box from the pantry and pulled out a second toy to make it fair.

The girl has my red hair, and the boy looks a lot like my brother did at his age. We're all supposed to go fishing this weekend with him on his boat.

I hope I can stay.

Oh, I hope I can stay.

"Undercover Gorgon"
A Mount Olympus Employment Agency Short Story

Patrice is sort of the anchor character for the entire Mount Olympus universe. Expect to see her show up in everybody else's stories, though probably not often as more than a background player. This, however, is Patrice's story. It's probably not her last.

At 12:01 AM on my twentieth birthday, I lost my humanity.

Okay, maybe that was a little dramatic, especially since I was never human to begin with. I'd thought I was human. Clearly, I was not.

I didn't notice at first. I sat on the foot of my bed, drying my hair with a towel and watching Kathryn Hepburn toss a withering look at Humphrey Bogart as they drifted down the Amazon. I glanced at the clock. One more minute of being a teenager. I tried to think of something immature to do in my final seconds of pre-adulthood.

I couldn't think of a damn thing.

I'd never been a very good teenager anyway. I didn't drink or smoke, slam doors, sneak out at night, or moon over boys. Twenty wasn't likely to be much different from any other age. I'd still go to class on Monday, I'd still be working a shitty job at a drug store, and I'd still be living in my old bedroom in my parents' house.

At least, that was my thought at midnight. At 12:01, everything changed.

I gave my hair a last rub, then dropped the towel on the foot of the bed. My wet hair hung to my shoulders in heavy strands. Once it dried, it would lighten to a dishwater, nothing color, which went well with my eye-colored eyes and my pallid skin. Not a looker, as Bogie might have said. I wasn't ugly, exactly, but I wasn't noticeable—which was fine with me. I didn't care if anybody noticed me. Most people pretty much irritated me anyway.

Shadows moved on the wall in the flickering light of the television. My hair brushed my bare shoulder, and I scratched where it tickled.

My hair licked my finger.

I froze and peered at my hand where it hovered over my skin. A thin, emerald snake slid over my knuckles and flicked its tongue. I frowned and glanced at the terrarium across the room.

"Daphne, how did you get out?" I let the little grass snake weave between my fingers and headed toward the habitat I kept for her. "The lid is still closed. Did you slip out when I fed you?" I lifted the hinged door and tried to place her inside.

Several things occurred at once. First, I spotted Daphne already tucked in a corner behind an artificial rock. Second, the snake in my hand wouldn't come loose from my head. And third, several more snakes slithered across my hand.

Had I been a typical human, I might have lost my shit. But I'd loved snakes since I was a little girl, and I was studying to get a degree in herpetology. I was all about the snakes, reptiles, and amphibians. So, yes, I had a buttload of snakes crawling on me, but my initial reaction was that Daphne had somehow managed to lay a clutch of eggs when I wasn't looking.

"Okay, kiddies. You've had your fun. Time to get in bed with Mom. My parents will freak if you're running around the house." I took careful hold of several at once and gave a gentle tug to disengage them from my person.

They wouldn't come lose. In fact, I felt the tug all the way to my scalp.

With my left hand, I held out a snake, and followed it with my right hand to its origin. My fingers prodded the base. It appeared to be attached to my head. This was, of course, stupid. Snakes couldn't grow out of my head, even in the weirdest of Internet urban legends. Still, my entire head squirmed with them and, as many heads as I found, I could find no tails.

My heart raced and my mouth went dry. This was the worst nightmare I'd ever had—way worse than the dream about the rabid squirrel with the eye patch and the tiny hooked paw.

"Okay. Breathe. Wake up, Patrice. Just a bad dream. Wake up." I hit the light switch in an effort to get a better look in the mirror by my bedroom door. Pain raced through my head like someone had shot me through both eyes with a Daisy Red Ryder BB gun. I covered them with one hand and slapped at the light switch with the other until I got lucky and flipped the lights off.

Dream or not, the pain had been real. The snakes attached to my head squirmed and writhed in agitation, as if they, too, had felt the stabbing pain. I threw my bedroom door open and ran out in my cotton nightgown, yelling for my parents.

I was halfway down the hall when they heard me. Their light flashed on and I spun around, shielding my eyes. "Turn off the light! Turn it off!"

The light went out and my parents stepped into the hall, the low light of my television giving us enough to see each other. I rose and stared at them, waiting to see if they saw what I thought I'd felt—hundreds of snakes growing from my head.

I expected either bewilderment at my odd behavior or horror at what they saw. They gave me neither. I certainly hadn't expect an apology.

Dad took a step toward me. "Sweetheart, I can explain."

Mom gave me a watery-eyed smile. "I am so sorry, honey."

I frowned. "Sorry? I have snakes on my head. How is that something you did?"

Mom glanced at Dad and back at me. "It's not exactly something I did, but it did come from me."

The snakes settled over me, curling around each other and laying still.

I gave a nervous laugh. "What? You planted snake seeds in my scalp?"

I was still going with the idea that this was a terrible nightmare. Even worse than the one about the blood-filled water balloon fight with Christopher Walken.

She shook her head and walked toward me. "It's a recessive gene. Somewhere in my family, way back, we're related to gorgons."

I snorted. "What are you saying? Medusa is my great-grandmother?"

"Something like that." She took my hand. "Come sit down."

In a daze, I followed my parents into their room. Dad turned on the bathroom light and closed the door enough to shield my eyes from the light, yet give us enough to see each other.

A terrible thought occurred to me, and I squeezed my eyes shut. "Don't look at me! I might turn you to stone if you look me in the eyes."

Dad patted me on the arm. "You wouldn't do that to us. We trust you. Just don't look straight at us."

This was insane. I noted, as if from a far off, detached sort of way, that in the more natural bathroom light, my skin was a sort of translucent, sea-foam green. It was kind of pretty.

"I don't understand." I twisted my arm in the light to see the color better. "Why am I only seeing this now?"

Mom and Dad glanced at each other again, then Dad looked down at his hands. "We were contacted when your mother was pregnant. The situation was explained that you wouldn't appear human. They gave us a choice between giving you up to be raised as a gorgon in a foster home for mythological creatures, or raise you ourselves with you having no knowledge of what you really were."

I pointed at my head. "But I didn't look like this."

Mom brightened. "The man who originally contacted us sold us Deity Springs Stealth Insurance for you. It disguised you so well, no one would ever know. Including you."

I scowled. "You bought me a disguise that was mousy and unattractive? Thanks a lot." I shook my head and the snakes hissed in objection to the movement. "So, why am I seeing this now? What changed?"

Dad took a deep breath. "Your insurance lapsed. We can't legally cover you anymore."

~*~

The next few days were pretty rough. The light sensitivity was an easy fix. Sunglasses did the trick, and it kept me from turning anyone to stone by mistake. But no hat was big enough to cover all those snakes, and I wasn't about to do a full-body spray tan every time I left the house.

So much for my degree in herpetology.

Dad called the stealth insurance company and got the runaround. Since my parents had let the insurance lapse instead of actually telling me what the hell was going on so I could transfer it to my name, getting the insurance started again was enormously expensive. I didn't have enough in my account, and neither did Mom and Dad.

I'd have to save up for months to have the money. The catch to that was I couldn't go to work anymore, not without the insurance. People prefer to buy hand lotion, mints, and toilet paper from people who don't have green skin and a head full of snakes. I had no choice. The life I'd been living was over. I'd have to go to wherever non-human folks lived and start over.

Oddly enough, I wasn't too upset by that. Sure, I'd miss my parents. I couldn't think of too many other things I *would* miss, though. And this might sound crazy, but once I got a good look at myself in the mirror, I was thrilled. Seriously. For the first time in my life, I was *hot*. Maybe not the kind of hot that would get a guy's attention or make other women jealous, but that never mattered to me. I liked what I saw. The skin color. The snakes. The curve of my cheek and the fullness of my lips.

I was finally comfortable in my own skin—proud, even. Ironic that I couldn't go out in public like that.

So, when Garmond Schumacher, the six-foot tall minotaur, showed up at my front door in a snazzy business suit, I was ready to leave with him before he'd finished his spiel.

The bull-headed man sat on my sofa and cleared his throat. "Temporary housing will be provided for you, and you'll meet with a career consultant to find you a good match." He braced his hands against his knees and gave me an earnest look with his large cow eyes. "I know this is all new and difficult. We'll do everything we can to ease you—"

"I'll go pack my suitcase." I leaped from my chair. "How much stuff can I bring?"

He flicked an ear and blinked. "Pack a bag, and we'll send for the rest once you're settled."

My parents gave him sheepish smiles.

"She's been cooped up for a few days," Mom said.

I ran up the stairs and tossed clothes into a suitcase as fast as I could pull them off hangers and scoop them out of the dresser. I threw my toothbrush, toothpaste, and shower gel into a toiletry bag and stopped. What else could I possibly need? Hair products were out. I'd never need those again. I never wore much makeup before, and now that I wanted to, nothing was appropriate for my new coloring.

I shrugged and zipped the bag. Fairyland—or wherever the hell I was going—had to have drugstores, right? Oh, gods. I truly hoped I didn't get stuck working at a supernatural drugstore for the rest of my life.

Once my suitcase was packed, I paused and looked around my room. With the exception of the snake habitat in the corner, the room looked more like a guestroom or a motel room. It was as if no one had ever lived there.

In a way, I never really had.

I pushed my sunglasses up the bridge of my nose. "I'll send for you, Daphne. I promise."

~*~

The bull guy had promised me housing. He hadn't promised I'd have it to myself. Two giggling nymphs and a siren shared my dorm room with me. The nymphs were afraid of me and stayed clear whenever possible. The siren used up all the hot water while she sang entire operas in the shower.

Other than that, though, she was pretty cool. Her name was Lizzy, and she helped ease me into my new life from the first day of my arrival.

"One thing's for sure, we need to get you some better clothes," she said, wrinkling her nose. She flipped through the hangers in my closet, scowling at the sensible skirts and blouses. "Clothes are meant to decorate your body, honey, not hide it." She took a sip from her wine goblet, one finger sticking out toward me. "And we need to get you some makeup. Seriously. Look at that gorgeous complexion. I've got some lavender lipstick that will totally pop against that lovely green."

I perched on the edge of my bed and watched her scurry around, humming softly to herself. She snagged a huge cosmetics case and dropped it on the bed next to me. Her face screwed up in concentration as she dragged a chair close to me.

"Okay. First, I need you to take off those ridiculous sunglasses." She reached toward me to take them away.

I pulled away from her reach. Several head-snakes hissed and drew back. "What are you doing? I could turn you to stone."

Her eyes widened in surprise, and she stared at me. "What?"

I pointed at me head. "Hello? I'm a gorgon!"

Her lower lip quivered. "Honey." She put her hand on my knee and pressed her lips together while she inhaled through her nose. "Oh, honey."

"What? Don't you know anything about mythology?" I sat straighter, offended. She wasn't laughing at me, exactly, but she was close. "I can't take these off when people are around." I paused as she pulled herself together. "Besides. The light hurts my eyes."

She nodded. "Okay, that one's legit." She waved her hand. "The stone thing? Totally bogus. That was specifically Medusa's curse. Haven't you ever met another gorgon before?"

I folded my arms across my chest. "I only met *me* a week ago."

"Ah." She patted my leg. "I see." She tapped her finger on her thigh, thinking. "Okay. You need a makeover and a full tour. Have you met with your career counselor yet?"

"I just got here. I have an appointment tomorrow afternoon."

She snapped open her makeup case. "Good. We've got a lot of work to do before I can take you out in public. Let's get started."

~*~

I began my new job looking fabulous. The lavender lipstick was a great contrast to the green eye shadow Lizzie taught me to use as blush. We found some small, round shades that shut out enough light to protect my eyes without covering half my face. The slit in my pencil skirt showed off a whole lot of hot green leg. I learned to coax the snakes into a side part with a few of the smaller ones hanging seductively over one eye. Never in my life had I felt so confident.

And it was all wasted on the shitty receptionist job they assigned me in the career center.

I glared through my glasses at the skinny girl in front of me. "Yes?" I pressed my lips together as if she'd done something terribly wrong. The only thing she'd done wrong was have the bad luck to be there when I was there.

One of my snakes hissed, and the girl twitched and slid paperwork toward me. "I think I filled it out right." Her voice quivered and her hand shook.

I felt sorry for her and glanced over the page. "It'll do."

I regretted my grumpy tone and offered a small smile. "Follow the gold line on the floor to Athens. Orientation begins in ten minutes." I stamped her paperwork with a flourish and dropped it in the outbox. "Next."

There wasn't much to the job. I sat behind a desk and handed out maps of the building, registered newbies for orientation, took complaints, and answered general questions. Better than retail, I supposed. At least I got to sit down.

But it wasn't what I wanted to be doing with my life. I wanted to study reptiles and amphibians. I wanted to learn things. I wanted to go back to school. The moment I turned green and sprouted snakes from my head, my options became limited.

It turned out, the job did not actually require me to be nice to people. That was at my own discretion.

Within a month, I ruled the reception desk and all who stepped inside the brightly lit, domed atrium of the Mount Olympus Employment Agency. If someone wanted something done, they had to go through me to get the proper paperwork. If a new hire showed up, they couldn't get to orientation until I stamped their application. How long it took to accomplish anything depended solely on my good will.

If I couldn't have the career I wanted, I'd take what I was stuck with and make it mine.

"Next." I always kept my voice low and cool, sometimes adding a little hiss where I could. It made people nervous.

A human guy, kind of cute but nothing remarkable, stepped forward and placed a pile of paperwork on the chest-high counter. I gave him a long look until he squirmed, then picked up the papers, slowly tamping them on the counter.

"I filled in what I could," he said. His voice shook a little. "I didn't know the answer to a lot of the questions."

Of course he didn't. No one knew the answers to all of the questions on the intro-forms. Questions like "Which parent is the dominant deity?" and "What powers have you manifested?" weren't meant to be answered by the majority of newcomers. Most of them had no idea what was going on. They'd hit rock bottom in their lives, which propelled them into Mount Olympus. They had no idea they had the blood of a god or hero in their ancestry. Like regular humans, they didn't know any of this existed. The paperwork was meant to give them their first clues in order to ease them into their new reality.

I grunted and pretended to examine his paperwork. Frankly, as long as his name, address, and social security number were on the form, that's all that was required. Anything else was bonus.

"I didn't understand half of what's on it," he said. "What do my parents have to do with any of this?"

I looked down at him through my glasses, and he shifted from foot to foot. "You'll have to ask someone in personnel, sir." I leaned forward. "Did you want me to give you the form to fill out for an appointment?" There was no form for that. But I made it sound so ominous, he'd never ask for it.

He took a step back—they usually did that when they were afraid I'd take off my shades and turn them into stone with my stare. I loved that part.

"No, no. That's fine." He stuffed his hands in his pockets and pointed his gaze somewhere over my left shoulder. "I was just wondering, that's all."

I grunted at him again, then slammed a stamp on the top page of his paperwork and dropped it in the outbox. "Follow the copper line to Thebes for orientation and further instruction. Next."

My favorite part was always the way the finality of my words fed the confusion and panic on their faces.

After a moment of hesitation, he spotted the colored lines on the floor, chose the thick, copper one, and followed it out of the atrium down a hallway. Three more new hire humans stood in line behind him. I sighed and gave the next one an impatient signal to step forward.

The morning dragged in what felt like an endless stream of newbies to be sent to orientation. By ten, though, even the stragglers were checked in and on their way. Mondays always went that way—an influx of brand new humans bound for training for the first few hours, then everything went back to business as usual.

I dropped a *Be Right Back* sign on my desk and took my ten-minute break without saying a word to the four people standing in line. I heard a centaur clomp one foot in agitation, but I ignored him. I couldn't intimidate a Mythic with the threat of turning them to stone, since they knew I didn't have that ability. But I still had all the power. I was the receptionist. If they wanted me to straighten out whatever their problem was, they'd have to suck it up.

I might have liked the job more than I let on.

After a quick trip to the ladies room, I refilled my coffee cup and took a few minutes to watch the other folks meandering in the Mythics cafeteria. Two satyrs sat hunched over a game of checkers, laughing at some joke or other. A minotaur in a jogging suit blew on a cup of ramen noodles, then tipped it back and drank it all in one gulp. The snuffling noises he made were…unlovely. I wrinkled my nose, a little grossed out. A stray noodle had squirmed from the side of his mouth and lay flat against his hairy cheek. I took a sip of coffee and looked away.

A naiad and a dryad sat in a corner together, the naiad drinking water through her graceful blue fingertips, and the dryad with both green hands buried in buckets of soil. The naiad's cerulean hair shimmered as if wet, and the dryad's hair sprouted flowers as she ate.

I tried to take another sip of my coffee, but it was gone. While I'd been otherwise occupied, my snakes had dipped their tiny faces into my cup and drained it.

Fantastic. Now my hair's all caffeinated and won't stay in place.

TRANSMONSTRIFIED

I poured a second cup of coffee and returned to my desk. It turned out, spazzy snake hair was far more disconcerting to the clients than when I gave them the stony stare. I'd have to consider saving up for an espresso machine.

First in line when I came back was a cyclops with corrective lenses—lens. Really, it was a monocle. It was held in place around her head by a string of pink and yellow beads. She had her hair pulled into three pigtails, one on each side and one on top.

I made no attempt to hide my smirk. "Next."

She slapped an employee ID card on the counter. "I need this changed."

The card had a picture of a similar cyclops, but with a little goatee and a black plastic frame around the monocle.

I pushed the card toward her with two fingers. "You can't make changes to another employee's card. This person…" I bent closer to look at the name and my hairsnakes gave a warning hiss at everyone near enough to scare. "Charles Leech. Charles will have to come in himself if he wants a new ID card."

The cyclops's single eye grew wide, and the single eyebrow rose. She slammed her fist on the counter, her voice rising with each word. "I *was* Charles Leech. You're not listening. I'm Charlize Leech now, and I need the name changed and a new photo taken. I've been getting the runaround for weeks." With each word, the pigtail on the top waggled and bobbed.

The entire atrium had fallen silent. If I didn't take back control of the conversation, every person who witnessed the situation would take advantage of me from then on. I blinked. "Ma'am, in order to process your request, I'll need to see some photo identification."

Charlize groaned in frustration. "The only photo ID I have has the wrong information on it. That's why I'm here."

"I see." I reached under the counter and thumbed through a file. "Fill out these forms and follow the red line to Crete. Please make sure you answer all questions completely or they won't be able to help you." I slid the forms into a clipboard with a pen dangling from a string. On top, I added a yellow sticky note on which I wrote "Ask for Peg." Peg would make the transition go smoothly, and the cyclops wouldn't get the runaround.

What? I did nice things for people all the time. I just didn't make a habit of letting everyone know about it. I had a reputation to uphold.

"Did you say the red line?" Charlize asked.

"Yes, I said red." I handed her the clipboard and dismissed her. "Next."

She hesitated—they all did when I wanted them to leave—and I ignored her. She glanced at the clipboard, then found the red line and stomped off.

She'd be fine. But seriously, how often do you get such a perfect opportunity to roll out the red tape? She was lucky I didn't draw out the situation.

I should have drawn it out. The rest of the day droned on forever with nothing quite so interesting as a transgender cyclops in a beaded monocle. Plumbing complaints, transfer requests, lost time cards—it all had to go through me before I funneled it through to the correct department.

I glanced at the giant clock embedded in one of the enormous pillars across from my desk. Ten more minutes and I could bug out of there. All the clients had been taken care of, and with a little luck, no one else would come in. Five minutes later I bent over to grab my purse from a built-in shelf. Maybe I could cut out early. Who would care?

My headsnakes hissed, alerting me to the presence of another person at the desk. I sighed, bracing myself, and sat up. "Yes?"

A small woman with nervous eyes clutched her bag against her chest. "I need an exterminator."

I frowned. "Pardon me?"

"An exterminator. You're new." She glanced past me, standing on her toes. "Is there someone else here? Where's the man who was here last month?"

"Samuel?" I gave her a polite smile. "He was reassigned. What sort of exterminator do you need?"

She gulped. "I have a basilisk living under my porch. The exterminator came out to take care of it, but there must've been more than one. All the grass around the house is dead, and I'm afraid to let my cat out."

"Uh huh." I reached for a form in a cubbyhole under the desk, only half listening. I stopped and blinked. "Wait, basilisk?"

"Yes. Apparently, there were two."

My heart pounded in excitement. "What happened to the other one?"

"The exterminator took care of it."

I frowned. "Took care of it?"

She nodded. "Chopped its head off right in my yard. I doubt anything will grow there now. Might as well pour cement and make a patio in that spot."

My pulse pounded in my ears. Basilisks were small, peaceful creatures. I'd read about them—roosters with poisonous spurs on their heels and the long tails of snakes. *Snakes.* I couldn't let another one be harmed. I had to do something.

I pushed the paperwork into a clipboard with an attached pen. "Fill this out for me, please. I'll see to it the basilisk is removed and does no further harm to your property."

"Thank you." She sighed with relief and went to sit in a chair while she wrote down her information.

Five o'clock came and went, and I watched people from other departments brush through the atrium and out one of the two doors, off to wherever they lived in either the human world or in Mount Olympus.

As the last of the stragglers exited the building, my client returned to the desk with her completed paperwork. "You're sure they'll take care of it this time?" The skin under her left eye twitched. "I'm so afraid it's going to come out and bite me or turn me to stone."

I glanced at the paper she'd given me. She lived in New Mexico. It figured. Basilisks liked warm, dry places. "I'll see to it myself," I said. "Everything's going to be fine."

~*~

A lot of logistical problems stood between me and saving my first real, live basilisk. The first being location.

Mount Olympus was in a separate dimension from the human world. The front door led to wherever a person came from. I'd originally arrived from downtown Philadelphia. The building I'd entered looked, on the outside, like an abandoned department store. Once I walked through the door, I was in the atrium where I worked. All major cities had an access building that looked abandoned but led to Mount Olympus. If I walked out that door, I'd be in Philly, not New Mexico.

Now, of course, I didn't leave through that door. I didn't live in the human world. I left through the other door on the other side of the atrium. It led to other parts of Mount Olympus, like the residential and shopping districts.

The only ways to go to a different human location were to apply for a transfer, go with someone as a guest, or work in the courier department.

Since transfers took weeks and I couldn't let anyone see me, that only left one option. I'd have to become an unofficial member of the messenger branch.

After hours, the building was dark and echoed with every footstep I took. The ding of the elevator and the sound of its doors opening bounced around the atrium and made me cringe. My hand shook as I pressed the button inside, and I held my breath when the doors opened for me on the seventh floor. Nobody stood waiting to catch me.

I stuck my head out and peered both ways, then stepped into the tiled hallway. A directory on the wall across from the elevator advised me to turn left, and I followed the arrow until I reached the correct door. Gold letters on frosted glass read *Courier and Travel*. Beneath that was a picture of a pair of gold, winged sandals.

The problem with breaking into a god's office is you can't whisper a prayer before trying the doorknob to see if it's unlocked.

To my surprise, the knob turned and the door swung open. I ducked inside and closed the door behind me. A bead of nervous sweat trickled from my temple, and my headsnakes shifted and coiled tightly against my head.

The room's overhead lights had been turned off, but all along the far wall pockets of ambient light kept the room from total darkness. I crept over to inspect the light's source and found a row of glowing sneakers hung on pegs by their laces.

Perfect.

Every department had specific tools its employees used to do their jobs. Cupids had their wings and arrows to encourage love, muses had their bottles of thought-bubbles to offer inspiration, and messengers had their sneakers for travel.

I found a pair in my size, tucked them into my purse, and got the hades out of there.

On the way back downstairs, I nearly ran into a harpy pushing a mop bucket and humming to herself off key. I ducked behind a potted plant as she passed by, then made a run for the elevator. By the time I made it back to my desk, I was out of breath and panicky.

I'd only been a part of this world for less than two months, and I'd already stolen something from a god. I'd never done anything wrong in my life. I'd never so much as stolen a stick of gum. This was insane.

I berated myself for my terrible behavior the entire time I was changing into my ill-gotten sneakers. I lectured myself thoroughly all the way across the atrium, out the door, and out into New Mexico.

I glanced at the address on the paperwork the woman had given me and rebuked myself for risking so much without a thought to consequences as I flew over Albuquerque and landed at Mrs. Swanburg's house.

And then I forgave myself. No use ruining a perfectly good adventure.

The minute my magic-covered feet touched the dry earth, my headsnakes became alert. Something under the porch had their undivided attention.

One of the advantages of using one of the departmental tools—like the traveling shoes—was they disguised the user. What I'd lost when my stealth insurance had lapsed was returned when I put on the shoes. I looked human. The only difference was, I wasn't human. My headsnakes were still present and, to my eyes, my skin was green. But to anyone else, I was the mousy, unremarkable girl I'd always thought I'd been. At least, that's what I'd read would happen. Fingers crossed the material I'd read in training hadn't been outdated or incorrect, because I was in a New Mexico suburb pretending to be someone—something—I wasn't. Eileen Swanburg was obviously a part of the Mythos world, but I was betting none of her neighbors were. If a gorgon showed up and crawled under her porch, that would be bad for everyone.

I glanced around. A blue, four-door sedan pulled in across the street, and a man got out. He gave me a smile and a wave, then turned and went inside.

Obviously, he hadn't seen a green-skinned woman with a head full of hyperactive snakes. I was in the clear, so I turned my attention to the Swanburg house.

Four painted steps led up to the wraparound porch. A pair of whitewashed wooden chairs with pink cushions sat beneath a picture window, and hanging plants and wind chimes swayed from the overhang. Pretty in a kitschy, overdone sort of way.

The space beneath the porch was skirted in flimsy latticework, and one corner on the right hung loose. I assumed it was where the exterminator had gone in the last time. I tested it and found the decorative barrier came off without any resistance, so I set it aside and took off my glasses to peer into the darkness under the house.

Something moved in the shadows. I tapped a flashlight app on my phone and used the light to get a better look.

Two tiny eyes like liquid tar stared back. Silky black feathers glistened, and the creature snapped its beak open and closed several times. It shook its crimson rooster wattle at me and scraped its clawed, poison-spurred feet in the dirt, then ruffled two dark wings.

"Don't be silly." I kneeled in the dead grass and ducked my head inside. "I'm here to help you." I crawled inside on all fours, hoping the dirt wouldn't ruin my skirt.

The rooster bobbed its head up and down, then it stretched its neck toward me, beak clacking in warning. But the front half of the basilisk was a distraction. Aside from the venomous spurs, the rooster portion was no more harmful than its barnyard cousins. The problem was the back half. It slithered next to me in silence, fangs dripping with the same poison that had killed the grass outside.

My hand touched something wet and stiff, and I shone the light at it. A dead rat lay curled in on itself, as if it had died in agony. I wiped my hand on my skirt. I'd probably have to toss it after this anyway.

I turned and addressed the snake as it crept closer. "Look. I really don't want to hurt you. Give me a second." I sat up and removed the stolen sneakers so the basilisk could see my true form. "See?" My snakes coiled and uncoiled, the movements making my scalp itch.

The snake end of the basilisk pulled back, its eyes wide in surprise. The rooster stepped toward me, head turned to the side to examine me with one piercing eye, and the snake's tongue flicked to taste my arm.

I smiled and held still while the creature judged me. I must have passed the test. A moment later, my lap was filled with scales and feathers. The rooster end buried its head under my arm, and the snake end climbed my body to commune with my headsnakes.

"There you go." I cuddled the rooster with one hand and rested my other hand against the snake's skin. "Everything's going to be okay, sweet boy. I know. This was scary. I don't know how you got out here, but I'll get you someplace safe."

We sat like that for a while, until the basilisk was ready to go.

If I'd had a choice, I'd have taken him back to my dorm room. But I doubted my roommates would appreciate him the way I did. As it was, they already didn't like having my Daphne there in her tank. Besides—basilisks weren't pets, and certainly not indoor pets. I'd already thought it through, though. I knew exactly where to take him.

"Now, I have to change how I look before I we can go. Don't be alarmed, okay? It's still me."

The basilisk's rooster head bobbed a few times, and the two ends climbed from my lap and waited while I put the sneakers back on. Once I'd tied the shoes, the snake portion drew closer and flicked my cheek with its tongue to verify it was still me.

The rooster portion of the basilisk followed me out from under the house with the snake riding patiently on its back. The gods were a strange bunch, making such awkward creatures.

The sky had turned dark, so no one saw us emerge. I scooped the basilisk into my arms, replaced the lattice work over the hole, and flew into the sky.

The only way back to Mount Olympus from the human world I knew of was through the front door to the main building, right past my desk in the atrium. Despite my earlier expedition to steal shoes from the courier department, I felt pretty ballsy walking into the empty building with a basilisk tucked under my arm. Still, I strode through the door and across the atrium like I owned the place, then exited through the opposite door out into the rest of Mount Olympus.

Five minutes of flight later, I was in a clearing in the wilds of the land of the gods.

"This is it." I gave the basilisk an affectionate squeeze and set him on the ground. "You'll do a whole lot better here. I promise."

The basilisk nudged me with both its heads and gave me a sorrowful look from four eyes.

I hunkered down so I could get closer. "Now, don't be like that. I'll come visit when I can. I promise."

The bushes across the clearing shook, and clicks and hisses came from within it.

Another basilisk stepped into the clearing, this one with a purple rooster wattle and green tips on its wings. It hesitated, then stepped forward. My creature met it in the center of the clearing, and they eyed each other, circling and ruffling their feathers.

The two snakes slithered toward each other, tongues flicking.

After a moment, the two roosters crowed, the snakes twisted together, and the two creatures settled in a patch of grass to doze.

My heart gave a little tug, but I left, satisfied that I'd done a good thing.

That satisfaction carried me all the way back to the atrium and up to the seventh floor.

"No exterminators today," I whispered, as I hung the magic shoes back on their peg in the courier office.

~*~

The next day, I sat at my desk feeling particularly smug as I stamped unnecessary paperwork and directed people the long way to their appointments.

I'd totally gotten away with it. I'd broken several huge rules, stolen the shoes of a god, and robbed some exterminator out of a job. Not too shabby for a shy girl who'd never even driven over the speed limit in her previous life.

A lot more had changed than my skin color and a head full of snakes. I had a lot of catching up to do. I barely knew who I was yet. But I had plenty of time to find out.

"Next!" I bent my head and glared at the nervous man standing at my counter. "Can I help you?"

"I need a supernatural pool cleaner." He glanced past me, then at my desk, at his hands, the ceiling—anywhere but my eyes. "Or something."

I crooked an eyebrow, and the snake hanging over my left eye hissed at him. "What seems to be the problem?"

He bit his lip and looked at my hairsnakes. "I have a hydra in my pool, and it won't come out."

My heart sped up in excitement. "Did you ask it nicely?"

"Yes, but then it tried to bite me. My son threatened it with a knife, you know, to scare it off. He accidentally cut off one of the serpent heads and two more grew back. I don't know what else to do. Please. My mother-in-law is coming to visit next week. She doesn't know anything about this stuff."

I smiled and pushed a form toward him. "Don't you worry, sir. I think I can help you."

Relief spread across his face. "You can?"

"Sure. I think I might be able to get someone out there tonight." I checked my watch. Two more hours till everybody went home.

Maybe my job wasn't so bad after all.

"Voices on the Wind"

When I wrote this flash piece for the Confabulator Cafe, the challenge was to draw a random picture from an open source as a writing prompt. The photo I grabbed was of a lonely train trestle in the middle of a forest. This is where I went with it.

When the first trees fell, the entire forest stilled with the tragedy. Men dragged away the empty husks to clear space for the new railroad, their voices raised in celebration.

Under the full moon that night, dryads gathered around the ragged stumps and mourned the loss of their sisters.

In the distance, Elder Stagfather watched in silence. His hooves and antlers shimmered gold in the moonlight. He clenched his meaty fists, and his great, black eyes turned stony with resolve.

The men returned the next day, their hearts full of mirth and murder, and Elder Stagfather stepped out from the brush to greet them.

"Leave this place," he said. He flicked his enormous ears and waved a polished stick at them. "Or pay the price."

The men were startled by Elder Stagfather's appearance, but quickly recovered. They found reassurance in their numbers. Strange as the stag-man may seem, he was but one. They laughed and turned their backs on him, returning to their work.

Many dryads perished that day, their stumps left to sap themselves dry. The men dragged off the carcasses, which they stacked in cords for future use as slats and pilings for the trestle of the coming tracks.

When the men reached the village, their homes were in disarray. Fresh milk had soured, meat was rancid, and bloated rats and flies filled every well. The women fed the men stale bread and moldy cheese for their suppers and begged them not to anger the forest spirits further.

The men laughed. "You women are superstitious," they said. "The stag-man is trying to frighten us. He will tire of it." They slapped each other on the backs and drank ale, since there was no water.

The next day, they returned to the forest, their heads aching from too much drink. Elder Stagfather waited for them.

"What will you pay for the lives you have taken?" he asked, stomping a golden hoof. "What will you give for the lives of those you love?"

One man stepped forward and waved his ax in a threatening manner. "Be gone, spirit. Have you nothing better to do than bother men with honest work?"

A tear slid down Elder Stagfather's muzzle, and he shook his head. "There is nothing honest in this work. Do you not hear the trees screaming while you cut?"

The men waved him away and went on with their chore, though one or two paused in the act of chopping, heads cocked, listening.

When the men returned to their homes in the village, they found their woman and children huddled in closets and under beds, terrified. Thousands of mice had come through the village, spilling over each other in a wave of greedy eagerness. They ate every scrap and crumb, leaving the villagers nothing for themselves. Every woman and child was peppered with tiny bites from the passing vermin.

"Now will you listen?" they asked the men. "The forest is angry."

Because the next day was Sunday, the men stayed in the village. The cows gave fresh milk, freshly hunted meat remained unspoiled, and the villagers hauled clean water from a nearby stream. The people attended services in the little chapel and ate well enough that night.

Believing their misfortunes were poor luck and nothing more, the men went out again into the forest the next morning. Elder Stagfather waited for them in the widening clearing.

"What do you offer to pay for what you have taken?"

The men shifted their feet and glanced at each other. One stepped forward, shaking his fist. "Listen here, Stag Man. We are not afraid of you. Step aside so we may do our jobs." The other men mumbled their agreement.

Elder Stagfather snorted from his wet, black nostrils. "Then the price is set." He flicked his tail and walked away on his two strong legs.

The men returned to the village that night, dragging trunks and leaves and branches behind them. The village was deserted. Not a woman or child remained. They searched in the cupboards, the root cellars, and out in the fields. They never found a living soul.

Elder Stagfather wept in silence from a distance. The dryads hummed over their work, their bloody hands toiling carefully to place a sister-seed within each human heart. Some of the work was difficult, the hearts so small and the blood so slippery. With all the seeds buried deep, they dug holes in the earth and placed the already-rooting saplings inside.

Satyrs came for the husks. They played their pipes and danced a slow march, and the bodies turned wooden. The goat-men dragged them off and stacked them in cords for future use as slats and pilings for the trestle of the coming tracks.

The men never returned to the forest, but the satyrs saw to it that the trestle was built using the materials they had collected. It stands to this day, transporting goods and travellers from one side of the country to the other.

Late at night, when the train whistle blows, the voices of women and children rise on the wind.

And the voices of the trees cry back to them.

"Just Right"

This was originally written for the Confabulator Cafe. The challenge was to take a common fairy tale and do something different with it. I'm afraid I got a little silly, but I had a good time writing it.

I knew the dame was trouble the minute she blew into my office. Any Suzie Next Door comes with a measure of problems, but a gal this gorgeous is ten times more likely to land you in a heaping mess.

Unfortunately, her looks made it hard to turn her away.

She shook the rain out of her blonde curls and gave me the doe-eye with her big baby blues. "Are you Mr. Frank Grimsby?" she asked. Her voice came out all breathless-like, as if she'd hoofed it up the stairs instead of taking the elevator.

I nodded and dropped the stub of my smoke into a day-old cup of joe. "That's me."

She leaned over my desk, giving me an eyeful of her goods. "You gotta help me, Mr. Grimsby. I'm desperate."

Of course she was. By the time anybody made it into my office, they were desperate. That's just how it worked. Besides, a skirt like her was always desperate about something.

I lit another cigarette. She shook her head when I offered her one.

"Why don't you sit down and tell me about it? See what we can do?"

She sat on the edge of the chair, clutching her pocketbook. "Someone's trying to kill me," she said.

"Why don't you go to the police, then? I'm not a bodyguard."

"Don't you think I tried? The cops don't care." Her eyes filled with tears. "Nobody believes me. You just gotta help me, Mr. Grimsby."

She pulled a lace hanky out of her purse and sobbed into it. I waited for the waterworks to finish. One thing I've learned, there's no point in trying to stop a broad from crying if she's stuck on it. You'll just end up with a wet shirt.

When she was done, I poured her a drink from a bottle I keep hidden in my bottom drawer. She threw it back like a pro, then hiccupped.

"What's your name, doll?"

"Marigold Locke. My friends call me Goldie."

Of course they did. "Who's after you, Goldie? And why?"

She dabbed at her eyes and put the handkerchief in her purse. She was stalling. I could see it in the way her eyes darted away from me.

She sighed and settled into the chair. "You see, it all started when I took a job at the Bruin Club."

I groaned. This dizzy dame was involved with the mob. Whatever her trouble was, it would be big. "Showgirl?"

Goldie smiled and dimples popped out. "No, I wait tables. The Baehrs are quite kind to me. Well, the men are, anyway. I don't think Milly Baehr much likes me. Pauly and Junior are aces."

That didn't surprise me. "So you waited tables. Then what?"

The dame knew how to work a story. She went quiet for a minute, wringing her hands and biting her lip before spilling the next bit. "It wasn't enough. My brother's sick, and I'm all he's got. What I made waitressing didn't go far enough. I asked Pauly if there was anything else I could do, and he gave me extra shifts washing dishes in the back."

I leaned back in my seat. "Seems like a downgrade to me. Waitress to dishwasher."

"Oh, no. Not a downgrade, Mr. Grimsby. An addition, you understand."

"Sounds exhausting."

She nodded. "That's where the trouble really began. Junior started making eyes at me and asking me to dinner. But I was too tired to even consider it, so I gave him the brush off."

"I hear he doesn't take that sort of thing very well."

"Junior Baehr does not like to be told no. In the end, I was worried for my job and finally agreed to a drink after my shift ended."

"When was this?"

"Last night." Her voice went even more quiet-like, and her eyes flicked to the window. "It all happened last night."

"So, I take it things didn't go so well."

Goldie looked at me square. "That's just the problem, Mr. Grimsby. I have no idea how it went. I remember getting off work. I remember sitting in Junior's booth with a drink. And the next thing I remember is waking up in Junior's bed this morning, fully clothed, with the entire Baehr family standing around me, yelling at each other."

It sounded to me like somebody—probably Junior—had slipped her a Mickey Finn. "What were they shouting about when you woke up?"

She shrugged. "I didn't understand most of it. Vandalism and theft, I think. They seemed to think I stole something."

I squinted at her through a haze of smoke. "Well, did you?"

Goldie frowned. "Of course not. I know I can't remember what I did last night, but if I'd stolen something, surely I'd have had it when I woke up, whatever it was. Anyway, I didn't stick around to find out what the fuss was all about. Milly pulled out a gun, and I high-tailed it through the window."

"I see." I grabbed my hat and coat. "Let's go."

She looked up at me in confusion. "Where are we going?"

"Back to the scene of the crime."

~*~

The Bruin Club was all glitz and glam at night, but in the light of day, it was just an empty gin joint that smelled like stale cigarettes and greed. Goldie didn't seem too keen on going in there, but I flashed her the bean shooter under my coat, and she relaxed.

The front door was unlocked, but nobody was around. Off in the distance, I heard voices arguing, and we followed the sounds down a back hall and into a private apartment. All three Baehrs were together, their faces pink with anger.

The door was wide open, and the family didn't see us come in. Milly held a butcher knife in her hand and kept waving the business end of it at her husband. Pauly's mitt was wrapped around a gun, which he pointed square at Junior's chest.

Junior held nothing in his hands but two white-knuckled fists to match the ugly snarl on his face that was directed at his mother.

Not exactly the picture of a happy family.

The place was a disaster. Broken furniture lay scattered around the room. Tables were overturned, dishes of food puddled on the floor. Something had happened here, that was for sure. But I had a hunch it was not what any of these people thought.

I cleared my throat, and all three swung around toward us. Their faces told their stories pretty clear. Junior's melted with relief. Pauly's lip twitched in a smirk while his eyes got a little friendly with Miss Locke's curves. And Milly just plain looked annoyed.

Nobody here seemed intent on killing my client—my non-paying client. Goldie had read it wrong.

They might kill each other though, if I didn't straighten this out.

"Darling!" Junior said, rushing to Goldie's side. He took both her hands in his. "I was afraid I'd never see you again."

Miss Locke blushed. "I was so frightened. I didn't know what else to do."

"Anyway, you're here now, Angel. I'll never let anything hurt you."

They gazed into each other's eyes in a sick puppy sort of way—a way that confirmed my suspicion that they'd been seeing each other a lot longer than last night's single drink.

"What's that floozy doing here?" Milly said, waving the knife in our direction.

"Maybe the little thief brought back what she stole," Pauly said. "To think, I gave her extra hours to help her out, and this is the thanks I get."

Milly turned the knife back to her husband. "Shut up, Pauly. You know you took it."

The gun in his hand hung lose and forgotten. "I didn't take it. How do I know you didn't take it so's you could blame me for it?" The gun came up again, pointed at her face.

"Nobody stole anything," I said loud enough to interrupt. "If everybody would just calm down and take a seat, I think I can clear this up."

They eyed each other for a moment, then lowered their weapons. Milly picked her way around a broken end table and sat on the end of the sofa. Pauly sat on the other end, as far away from his wife as possible. There was only one chair left in the room, since all the other furniture had been destroyed. Junior pulled Miss Locke into it, then stood behind her. All eyes were on me as I lit up a smoke.

"How long have you been seeing each other behind Mommy and Daddy's backs, Junior?"

Goldie gave him an alarmed look, but he squeezed her shoulder. "It's all right, sweetheart. We might as well come clean." He stuck his chin out and looked at his parents. "We're in love. We're getting married, and there's nothing you can do to stop us."

Milly rolled her eyes. "You're better than that, Junior. The girl doesn't have two dimes to rub together, and without me, you don't have much more than she does. Once she's been gone a few days, you'll get over her."

Junior's fists clenched at his sides. "I've been saving money for a long time, Mother. I have more than enough."

Milly's smile was smug. "I seriously doubt that, Junior."

I took another drag and blew out a smoke ring. "Last night, Miss Locke's drink was drugged. I see no reason, under the circumstances, why Junior would have done it." I flicked ashes into a broken dish. "Milly, you wanted her gone, though, didn't you? Your precious boy was getting too interested, and you'd do just about anything to get her out of the picture."

Milly frowned. "You think I drugged her?"

"No, actually," I said. "I don't. I think Pauly drugged her."

He made a choking sound at the back of his throat. "Why would I drug Goldie?"

"You wouldn't. You meant to drug your wife so she wouldn't catch you trying to steal the money she already stole from your son."

He looked like a cornered rat. "I didn't...that's the most preposterous...why, I only wanted..." He sputtered half sentences for a minute more before his wife finally cut him off.

"You tried to drug me so you could steal from me?"

He held his hands out to her. "Honey, I didn't mean anything by it. Honest."

She folded her arms across her chest and glared at him.

"Wait a minute," Junior said. "You stole my money, Mother?"

"I most certainly did not!" She had the gumption to look offended.

Pauly scratched his head. "Your story has a flaw in it, Detective."

"Oh?"

He nodded. "By the time I got up here, Goldie was already on the bed, out cold, and Milly was tearing up the place. She can't be the one who took the money."

Goldie swallowed hard and looked up at Junior. "I'm sorry," she said. "I was trying to protect you."

I took a step toward her. "You never drank last night, did you?"

She shook her head. "It smelled funny. I knew Milly didn't like me, and I knew she and Pauly were both up to something. So, I faked it."

"You were faking?" Junior had betrayal written all over his face. "I was so afraid for you."

"You were very sweet," she said. "I pretended to be knocked out while you put me on your bed to sleep it off. After you left, I searched the apartment. I checked everywhere, but in the end, I found it hidden in the last place you'd look—under your own bed. So I moved it. Just in time, too, because your mother came in a minute after I lay back down. Went straight to the bed and checked underneath me. When she didn't find the money, she started tearing things apart. Then your father came in and they shouted at each other for what seemed like hours."

"Oh, my poor angel." He pulled her out of the chair and put his arms around her.

"When you finally came in, I felt safe enough to pretend to wake up and escape through the window."

"So, where's the money?" Pauly said.

"I bet she had it on her when she left," Milly said. "You'll never see it again, Junior. That's what you get when you don't listen to your mother."

"I believe I know exactly where it is," I said. "May I?" Goldie nodded.

"Milly wrecked all the dishes, thinking it might be in one of the cereal bowls. I'm guessing that was the original spot Junior hid it in."

"Yes," he said. "Not very original, was it?"

"No, I'm afraid not. Then Milly hid it under your own bed, so moving it to another bed would be foolish. But each time, it was hidden in something of yours, Junior. Pauly's too paranoid. It's too hard to get into his stuff. And Milly's things are all too soft. You'd be able to spot the lumps the dough made. But this…"

I grabbed the chair Goldie had vacated and slammed it against the wall. The chair burst open. Bills large and small exploded into the air and floated to the floor.

They'd been so busy trying to play each other, the dumb saps had missed the obvious. And they'd underestimated the blonde. Never underestimate a dame, especially a blonde. She'd even suckered me into this mess so she'd have a witness when it all came out. Clever girl.

"This chair was just right, wasn't it Miss Locke?"

She smiled. "Yes it was, Mr. Grimsby. Just right."

"Ill-Conceived Magic"
A Monster Haven Short Story

This was the first—and so far longest—short story from the Monster Haven world. It picked up shortly after the first book, Monster in My Closet. *It was originally published as a single in 2013. My editor insisted we include it partly because it's where I got the title for this collection.*

As soon as I stepped out of my car, the fairies were on me—and those little buggers move pretty damn fast. They swarmed my driveway, buzzing around my head and grabbing tiny handfuls of my hair. I swatted at them, but my objections were as ineffectual as trying to dart between raindrops in a downpour.

"Guys, let me at least get my stuff out of the backseat. What the hell is your problem?"

Their voices were too high-pitched for me to understand anything they were saying, but I was an empath. Words weren't always necessary for me to get to the creamy center of a situation. I opened up my barriers and let in the emotions coming from the fairy flock.

Worry. Urgency. Alarm.

The emotions banged against me like miniature fists. Whatever had the little people's leafy panties in a bunch needed my immediate attention. I left my purse and bag of groceries behind and slammed the car door.

"All right," I said, rubbing my head. "Quit yanking. You're making my scalp hurt. I'll follow you."

They let go, and several darted ahead faster than my eyes could follow. The rest stayed behind to lead me around to the side of the house, keeping up the sonic chattering.

I picked my way through the grass, cursing at the wet soil sucking at my high heels. When I rounded the corner, I found the fairies clustered around a small basket of laundry.

No. Not laundry.

"Hell, no," I said.

I bent over. Two bright eyes the odd blue-green of algae stared up at me. One chubby fist had escaped the swaddling and grabbed at the air.

The baby's skin was a soft sage, its hair a dark olive.

I let loose a heavy sigh and took hold of the basket's handle. Its inhabitant gurgled at me.

"Sure. You say that now. Wait till you get inside and find out I have no idea what to do with you."

I scanned the yard and the edge of the nearby woods, hoping to spot the owner of the package I carried. No one lurked in the area, not even my skunk-ape bodyguard, Iris. Usually, he stepped out from behind a tree and gave me a wave when I got home each day.

"Coward." I was pretty sure he could hear me. Iris might be out of sight, but he was always nearby.

The fairies, having done their part in the Great Green Baby Unveiling, scattered. It was nice they had so much faith in me. Too bad I had none of my own.

I circled around to the front yard, grabbed my purse and bag of groceries from the car and trudged up the porch steps, balancing everything with the basket of unidentified child. Muffled music trickled out from the house, so I knew somebody was home. I kicked the door with my foot, hoping my housemate would hear and let me in. After a minute or so, no help was forthcoming. I dropped the groceries on the porch and left them there to free up a hand and let myself inside.

What greeted me shocked me far worse than finding a green orphan on my lawn.

Maurice, a tall, gangly closet monster dressed in black and white checkered pants and a green and yellow paisley shirt, occupied the middle of the living room. Phil, his enormous gargoyle brother-in-law, stood next to him in blue sweats and a tie-dyed T-shirt. Both were going through a divorce, and while Maurice was staying indefinitely, Phil was only with us for a few days.

Though I was a bit peeved that neither of them heard me banging on the door, I was used to seeing Hidden creatures and accustomed to the unique fashion choices they often made, so their appearance was no cause for concern. People can adjust to almost anything.

Almost.

The two stood side-by-side, arms across each other's shoulders, swaying to the music.

And singing "My Heart Will Go On" into a microphone.

I rested the basket on the back of the couch with one hand keeping it steady. I cleared my throat, but the songbirds didn't notice me standing four feet away.

Maurice's voice, being higher, carried the loudest. "Near, far, wherever you are..." His left arm waved around in the air for emphasis, the mic traveling with it.

Phil's voice was lower and sounded like chewed-up gravel. Worse, gargoyles—or at least Phil, I wasn't sure if he was representative of his whole species—didn't speak in any kind of sentences I could understand. Sure, it was English, but the words and sentences he used to convey his thoughts had nothing to do with any kind of meaning the rest of us had agreed on.

He moved back and forth with Maurice, pumping his fist into the air. "Yawn, stew, forget my old shoe..."

I glanced down at the baby and shrugged. "At least it rhymed."

The infant blew a rainbow-colored spit bubble at me and burped.

The music faded away, and the boys patted each other on the back in congratulations—of what, I'm not sure.

I cleared my throat again. "Guys? Where the hell did the karaoke machine come from?"

Finally, they noticed me standing there.

"Zoey's home!" Maurice said. "Phil, find us a song Zoey can sing with us."

Phil grabbed a book that was dwarfed in his big hands. He had difficulty flipping the pages with his thick, granite fingers.

"Don't bother," I said. "There's not enough alcohol in the house for me to even consider it."

Maurice's grin faded. "Not even a ballad?"

"Not even a Disney song will get me to sing karaoke."

Phil held up the book, pointing to a song title. "Naked Sand Castles?"

I frowned and looked at Maurice for a translation, but no translation came. Maurice's enormous yellow eyes were wide and fixated on the basket in front of me.

"Zo?" His hand came up in slow motion, pointing. "What's that?"

"I was hoping you could tell me." I picked up the basket and shoved it at him. "It's green."

Behind him, Phil laughed. It was a grinding sound, like a handful of rocks rubbing together. A few seconds later, he started the music again. The words to "Defying Gravity" from Wicked skittered across the television screen.

Maurice snorted and leaned over to give Phil a high five. "Good one, dude."

I rolled my eyes. "Can you focus, please? Somebody abandoned a baby in our yard, and I don't even know what flavor it is."

The monster from my childhood closet plopped the basket onto my coffee table. "Let's see what we've got." He pushed away the blankets and lifted the baby. It cooed at him, and he pulled it close, rubbing noses and cooing back.

Phil came over to examine it, too. He poked the infant in the belly with a fat finger, and the baby laughed. "Garden apples are jogging away."

Maurice nodded. "I know. She's adorable, isn't she?"

"She?" I craned my neck to see what he was doing. He'd unwrapped her down to the makeshift diaper made from a dishtowel and clothespins and was rearranging the material after peeking inside for a gender check.

Freed of all constraints, her little legs kicked and stretched. They were covered with a fine down of silky green. Maurice brushed her dark hair back from her forehead and found two tiny bumps.

"Uh oh," he said.

"Uh oh? I don't want to hear uh oh. What's wrong?"

He frowned. "I think I know why she's here instead of with her mama and daddy."

Aside from the odd coloring, hairy legs, and nubs on her head, she looked perfectly normal and healthy to me. Not that I knew much about babies, monster or otherwise. "Problem?"

He re-wrapped her blanket and cradled her against his shoulder. "She's, um…" He covered her ear with one hand, as if she could understand him, then spoke in a whisper. "She's a crossbreed."

I shrugged. "Why is that a problem? The Hidden don't strike me as particularly prejudiced. You married a gargoyle."

He winced. "That didn't go over so well with Pansy's family, but it really wasn't a big deal. This, though. This is a big deal. From what I can tell, she's half dryad and half satyr. Dryads and satyrs hate each other. I can't even imagine how this little one is possible."

Nothing was ever simple. "So what do we do?"

"Check the basket. Is there a note or anything?"

I sifted through the extra blankets. "Nothing." The bottom of the basket didn't reveal any secrets either. "So, what exactly does that make her? A tree goat? A fawn vine? Drytyr? Sataid? Why wouldn't her parents want to keep her?" I touched the soft hair on the back of her head. "She's beautiful, in a weird, freaky sort of way."

Maurice sat down on the couch and laid the baby across his legs. "It's complicated. Her daddy must be a satyr. Satyrs are nasty little pervs, always male, and totally obsessed with their dicks. The closest troupe is up on Mount Tam. There's a clan of maenads on the other side of the mountain. When the wild women want a baby, they get one from the satyrs. Satyrs don't generally care, as long as they get laid."

"Okay. So a goat-man had a good time. What about the mother?"

"Dryads mate with other dryads in arranged parings. The children stay with the mothers, and the fathers go off somewhere to sleep for a few decades. The females stay active through most of the year, but they don't ever mate outside their pairing."

"Until now. Somebody had a fling and now nobody wants this little one." I sat in the overstuffed chair across from Maurice and tried to think what to do next.

Phil shut off the karaoke machine and sat next to Maurice, holding his hands out. "Artichoke is the best way to heat up a casserole," he said.

"Sure, Phil." He passed the baby over.

I scrubbed at my face and groaned. "My mom was good at dealing with stuff like this. She found you a new home when you were a kid, right? So, how do we do that?"

"Beats me. I'll talk to my foster parents and find out how it works."

"Good. Yeah." I frowned, thinking. "How do I find her parents?"

Both men stared at me and spoke at the same time.

"How is a mushroom like a fiesta?" Phil asked.

"Why would you do that?" Maurice asked.

I stood up. "Because if the Hidden want me to act like a supernatural social worker, I'm going to do the job right. I'm not handing over a baby to strangers until I'm sure the birth parents really don't want her."

They glanced at each other and shifted in their seats. Maurice ran his hand through the sparse hair on his head. "Did I not mention what total pervs the satyrs are? Start with the mom, at least."

"Fair enough. I'd rather not deal with horny goat-men if I can help it."

Phil lifted the baby from his lap and held her at arm's length. "There's never enough lip balm when you need it."

Even I could understand what he was saying based on the wet spot on his shirt and the dripping dishtowel drooping from the baby's butt.

"Looks like I better go back to the store," I said. "We're going to need some supplies. Somebody grab the stuff on the porch while I'm gone?"

~*~

By the time I got back, Maurice was cowering in the kitchen, and Phil was rocking the screaming baby, his eyes wide and distressed.

"I have a hankering for an alligator and a trampoline," he said. Of all the bizarre things that had come out of his mouth so far, this made the most sense, in a crazy, desperate way.

Maurice darted out of the kitchen and grabbed the bags from my arms. A second later, Phil shoved the wailing baby at me.

I held her with stiff arms, not sure what to do. I was an only child, and since we lived in a more or less isolated area, I hadn't babysat as a teenager. I liked kids. Molly's were great. But babies were a mystery.

"What's wrong with her?" I shifted her to a better position and the question answered itself all down my arm. I made a face. "Okay. Got it. Dishtowels aren't nearly as absorbent as diapers." They'd replaced the towel she'd arrived in with a fresh one from my linen closet. So much for that towel.

Maurice rummaged through my purchases and set up a spot on the floor. I pinched off the clothespins and slid the soggy towel away, dangling it in midair. Maurice, always at the ready for any situation, scooped it into a plastic bag and ran from the house with it held aloft, as if it were a hand grenade with the pin removed.

The baby continued to cry. The sound tore through my head and made it difficult to focus on the task at hand.

I surveyed the array of products spread on the floor around me. I'd bought everything that looked useful, with only a vague idea of what to do with them—wipes, rash cream, powder, oil, lotion. Logically, I knew if I put them all together, they would make mud. That couldn't be right.

I pulled a diaper from the pack and fanned her butt with it in an effort to create a dry surface to work with. Sweat trickled down my neck.

Next to me, Phil gave a low rumble of laughter. I looked up at him, annoyed. "You think you could do better?"

He grinned and nudged me over, squatting his bulk on the floor. "Never swallow a burrito whole," he said. "The mongoose wins by a landslide."

The words made no sense in any possible context, but judging by their inflection and the twinkle in his eye, he was making fun of me. Apparently, Phil had kids of his own. I hadn't thought to ask.

"Fine. Show me how it's done, then."

He took me through all the steps, and I assisted, since his big, stony fingers couldn't manage things like opening the container of wipes or pulling the tabs on the diaper. But he managed to get her dry and securely covered up before Maurice returned from his trip to the garbage can. I thought I could probably manage on my own the next time.

The baby was still fussy and made tiny whimpering noises of distress, but she wasn't screaming anymore. Phil had saved the day.

Maurice paused a second on his way through, then flew into the kitchen to scrub his hands. He reappeared a few minutes later with a bottle of formula.

"Hope this works," he said.

I snatched up the bottle and offered it to her. "Why wouldn't it work? Did I get the wrong stuff?"

He shrugged. "Beats me. But it's for humans. She's half dryad, half satyr. Who knows what they eat?"

I stared at the content, tiny green face. Her chubby hands clutched at the bottle, holding it with me. "She seems okay with it."

Ten minutes later, the diaper was soaked and she was wailing again.

I changed her all by myself this time, taking pride in my accomplishment. The crying didn't stop.

"What's wrong with her? What else can she want?" I paced back and forth, patting her back and praying she'd fall asleep.

Phil took her from me and walked through the house, rocking and humming. After an hour, Maurice took over and sang to her. No change. I wasn't sure if my hearing or my mind would snap first. It was hard to think. Mind-numbing, heartbreaking shrieks interrupted every thought I tried to complete. One full thought did make it through eventually: After this, I'm never having kids.

Maurice's face was pinched in desperation. "Zoey, I can't take much more of this. Maybe Aggie knows what to do. Or we could call Andrew. Somebody we know must be able to figure this out. The three of us are failing miserably."

"How can anybody know what an infant is thinking? She can't talk, and it's not like any of us are psychic." I stopped, stunned at my own stupidity. No, I couldn't read her mind. But I was an empath. I could do the next best thing.

"Here. Let me try something." I took her from Maurice and held her close against my body, whispering nonsense words of comfort in her ear. Focusing inward, I envisioned my protective walls and opened up a window to let the little one in.

Hunger.

That was it? She was still hungry?

"Maurice, she's just hungry. Let's try another bottle." I paced and rocked while he got it ready. The minute the nipple went into her mouth, my ears rang from the silence. She guzzled the formula down in no time, let out a window-shaking belch and smiled.

Ten minutes later, she was soaked through and wailing again. Hunger came off her in waves and tightened my own stomach.

"This isn't working," I said, taping the new diaper shut. "It's going right through her. She needs something else."

"I'm on it." Maurice ran out the back door in the kitchen, returning a few minutes later with a bucket. He was supernaturally fast. Either that, or he had the ability to translocate. I still wasn't sure. "Goat's milk. Maybe the half-satyr part of her needs that."

"Where did you get…?" I stopped. "Never mind." We'd discussed not stealing from my neighbors before, but this wasn't a good time to argue. If baby needed goat milk, she would have goat milk, no matter where Maurice got it. Maybe later I'd have time to wonder which of my neighbors raised goats.

We tried again. She seemed to like the goat milk, but ten minutes later she needed another change and was back to being hungry.

"What the hell are we missing?" I was desperate for an answer, and the baby, while still crying, was getting quieter. Her dark green hair lay plastered to her head and looked wilted. Her skin felt waxy. We'd spent most of the night feeding her, but the emotions coming through my shield were clear. She was starving in the most literal sense. We had to think of something soon.

We toyed with the idea of adding plant food to the milk, but that seemed like a dangerous experiment. I finally caved and called my friend Andrew, since he's an herbalist. He didn't have any ideas we hadn't already tried. If we didn't find a solution by morning, I would take the little one over to Aggie the Hag's house and see if she could drop a little knowledge on us. The woman was almost one hundred years old, and—I think—a witch. She had to know something useful.

The baby slept for a little while, having worn herself out, but in the wee hours of the morning, she awoke, whimpering and miserable. We tried again, and the milk went through her without giving any sustenance.

When the sun came up, we were all worn out, snappish, and still without ideas. I peered out the window and watched the first rays of light sparkle off the dew on my lawn. My arms were leaden with the listless, weakening bundle I carried. What does grass eat? How do you feed a tree?

If I'd had a free arm, I'd have smacked myself in the head.

"Maurice," I said, my voice quiet. "Can you get me another bottle, please?"

He nodded. "Milk? Formula? What do you want to try?"

I bit my lip. "I think goat milk is probably good for her satyr side, but cut it with half water."

He shrugged and went to the kitchen.

Phil's brow furrowed in thought, and he looked from me to the window and back again. His eyes cleared in understanding and he nodded. "Softball practice."

I smiled. "Exactly."

Maurice came out with a warm bottle. "You look like you have an idea."

I winked at him, sure I'd found the solution, and stepped outside. In the middle of my yard, where the morning light was most direct, I plopped in the grass and offered the bottle to the tired baby.

Seeing the change in her face was like watching a nature documentary. Her sallow cheeks plumped up first, and a bright, healthy green replaced the waxy dullness. She closed her eyes while she sucked, and a contented gurgle came from her throat. Halfway through the bottle, her lank hair puffed like green milkweed, and tiny buds formed in knots. By the time the milk ran out, the buds in her hair had opened into miniature pink flowers that wreathed her head in a halo of sweet perfume. She fell asleep, milk dribbling from the corner of her mouth.

Maurice and Phil knelt beside me, watching the transformation.

"What did you do?" Maurice asked.

"Photosynthesis," I said, grinning. "Biology 101."

~*~

Having unlocked the mysterious secrets to the care and feeding of a baby tree-satyr, I turned my attention to figuring out a long-term solution. Maurice said to start with the mother, so that's what I did.

There was one person in my little family who probably knew a lot more than he wanted to share about the goings-on in the woods near my house. But he was sure as hell going to, whether he liked it or not.

I walked through the trees, clomping around and shuffling leaves. Finding a skunk-ape is close to impossible, but I didn't have to seek him out—he would find me. I didn't really need to make so much noise. Iris always knew when I was nearby, but I was cranky from lack of sleep, and I wanted him to know I meant business.

I made my way deeper into the woods and leaned against the trunk of a eucalyptus, waiting. A minute or so later, he stepped out of the shadows, his hairy face tense.

"Hey, Iris," I said. "Anything you need to tell me?"

He scuffed a foot in the dirt and looked away. He grunted.

"You've been awfully scarce. Seen anybody new around? Maybe somebody with a delivery?"

He made a guttural wheezing sound from the back of his throat and picked at a twig stuck in his arm fur. He glanced up at me.

I gave him the stink-eye.

Iris chuffed out a lungful of air, and his shoulders sagged. His hand dropped and gave me a small, nearly imperceptible motion to follow. He turned away, slogging through the forest like I'd ordered him to the gallows.

I shook my head and stifled a smile. So dramatic.

We wove through the trees in a roundabout, circular pattern. At one point, I could see Aggie's cottage, but I didn't see my friend outside, and we didn't stop. The hike seemed to take forever, which was ridiculous, since the strip of woods bordering my house wasn't that big. Iris finally came to a stop in a small clearing on the other side of Aggie's house.

He folded his arms over his chest and grunted. I scanned the clearing and didn't see anyone. I gave Iris a questioning look, and he plopped down among the dried leaves in a furry hump.

No help there.

I stood still and listened to the wind in the trees. A faint humming carried across the clearing, and I shifted my gaze to find the source. I'd missed the woman at first because she blended with the foliage around her.

She was tall and thin, with long, brittle hair that resembled dreadlocks with bits of twigs and leaves woven through, as if they'd grown there. She had a pointed nose and rough, brown-gray skin. Her fingers plucked at a bush, pruning out the dead material. I thought she hadn't noticed me, but she looked up, scowled, and went back to what she was doing.

So that's how she was going to play it. I hated being ignored.

I stepped toward her. "Excuse me, ma'am." My policy had always been to lead with a polite greeting wherever possible. Sarcasm and accusations could come later. "I'm sorry to bother you, but have you lost a baby?"

The gnarled old woman stood up straight and glared at Iris. "Traitor," she said. Her voice echoed with a shushing sound like wind caught in branches.

Iris snorted and hung his head between his knees.

I gave him a reassuring pat on the shoulder, then took another step toward the woman. "So, the baby is yours."

She pushed her arm in my direction as if shoving me away, then turned her back. Stooping over, she ran her palms over the next bush, seeking out dead leaves and branches. "No, she's not mine. She's your problem now."

"If she's not yours, I really need to know where she came from before I can figure out what to do with her." Feeling daring, I took another few steps across the clearing.

She eyed me over her shoulder and spat on the ground. A clump of grass grew up from the damp spot. "Ask the satyrs. Maybe they can explain how my sweet girl was seduced by such filth. I didn't raise her to throw her life away on one of their kind." She grunted and returned to her pruning.

Refusing to budge, I watched her for a few minutes before she straightened up again and faced me, shaking her skinny fist in a menacing gesture. "Get out of my woods, you nosy busybody."

I ignored her theatrics. "So, the baby is your granddaughter?"

The woman drew in her breath with a hiss. "That child is nothing to me. It's a monstrosity."

I clenched my hands and tried to keep my voice steady. "She's a baby. And the circumstances of her conception aren't her fault. You could've at least left a damn note in the basket. She nearly starved while we figured out how to feed her."

The woman sniffed and flicked her nose with a pointy finger. "Not my problem." She walked away into the trees without another look. Her odd, whispery voice whistled from the darkness. "Don't even think about bringing her back here. I'll let the swamp bogeys have at her."

I debated following the miserable bitch, but I was afraid I might punch her in the throat. My hands shook, and my stomach clenched in a knot. It was probably too late, but I opened up the window in my emotional barricade and reached out in the direction she'd disappeared.

She'd left a faint trail of emotions—anger, disgust, irritation—but they didn't tell me anything useful. Nothing I could use to change her mind or force her to help me.

I turned to make my way back across the clearing while I sealed my feelings-bubble again.

Longing, sorrow, love.

I swung around to face the direction the old dryad had gone. No, those feelings hadn't originated with her. Before I'd finished blocking myself off, someone else had come through.

Spinning around, I scanned the woods. Feet shuffled to my left. I turned my head in time to catch the brush swallow up a head of long, silky, green hair. I tried to follow, but there was no path, and the brush wouldn't yield for me.

"Dammit."

Iris appeared next to me and poked at the bushes. He shrugged.

"Your baby is safe," I called into the dense foliage. I didn't know if she could hear me, but I hoped I could comfort her a little. "We'll work this out. I promise."

A gust of wind blew through the trees and lifted my hair in a gentle caress. I was pretty sure she'd heard me.

~*~

Back at the house, Maurice was irate.

"No. Absolutely not, Zoey. The old bitch may be dead wrong about our little princess, but she's right about the satyrs. You can't go up there."

He paced the carpet in the living room, jiggling the baby in a way that bordered on shaking. Phil and I exchanged a concerned look, and the gargoyle eased the little one out of the closet monster's arms.

"Maurice, I've got to find out what happened."

"It was probably a gang rape. You don't understand. Satyrs are horny assholes."

"I got the impression from Granny Treeface that Mama wasn't an unwilling participant. Besides, I can handle horny assholes." I smiled in an attempt to reassure him. "I've dated."

He stopped and frowned at me. "This is not a joke, Zo. Seriously. Iris can't exactly hop in that tiny car of yours and ride up there with you. You're not going."

I toyed with the "you're not the boss of me" argument, but decided he wasn't in the mood for more humor. "Fine. You come with me, then."

He sputtered and blustered before finding real words. "You can't be serious."

I shrugged. "I'm going to visit those satyrs. If you want to escort me, you're more than welcome to ride along."

~*~

I decided to wait until the next day to make the trek up the mountain. None of us had slept, and I wanted to be on my toes when I faced down a herd of perverted goat-men.

I figured once the sun went down, we'd need to be better prepared for night feedings, so I scrounged in the garage and found a UV lamp I'd used in a college botany project involving a bladderwort and a flytrap.

It wasn't necessary. We fed her in the dying light of the sunset, and as the sun disappeared, the tiny flowers in her hair closed up tight, she shut her eyes and slept until morning.

Best baby ever.

I debated whether to take her with me to visit the satyrs. They might demand proof of my claims, and she was adorable. How could the father resist her? In the end, the lack of a car seat or baby carrier decided the matter. I couldn't exactly have Maurice crouched in the back holding her and trying to avoid being seen at the same time. It was a safety issue for him as well as for her.

Maurice had it tough enough already, with his tall, skinny frame, having to curl up in the barely accessible backseat of my VW Bug. Once we got through Bolinas, which didn't have much traffic anyway, he didn't have to scrunch so much. His knees still stuck up around his ears, and he made miserable, put-upon faces at me in the rearview mirror.

"When are you going to get a real car?" He sighed and readjusted himself across the seats in an attempt at spreading out. His head tilted to the side to avoid hitting the roof.

"I like my little car."

"It's not practical."

"It was plenty practical when I lived alone. I have a long commute, and gas isn't cheap."

He grumbled to himself the rest of the way. Maybe I needed to rethink the Bug. This probably wouldn't be the last time someone enormous would have to accompany me somewhere. I had a family to think about now. One filled with skunk-apes and closet monsters, fairies and brownies. And visiting gargoyles. Tinted windows and more space would make this much easier.

I shivered at the thought of trading in my beloved Bug for a minivan.

Halfway up Mount Tamalpais, Maurice directed me to a side road I would have missed without him. It wound around to the northern face and up into the thick forest. At the dead end, we abandoned ship and hiked the rest of the way.

My purple Doc Martens crunched on pine needles, and I breathed in the scent of clean air and earth. Lagging behind, Maurice continued to argue.

"You know, there's one other option." He gave me a hopeful look. "We could keep her. I could clean out the junk room and make it into a nursery. This could all be settled. I'll make a quiche for dinner to celebrate. A nice salad. A bottle of wine. Come on, Zoey. I'll race you back to the car."

I ignored him, so he dragged his feet in the gravely dirt.

I tugged on his shirt sleeve to get him to walk faster. "How would you feel if she were your baby and nobody told you about her?"

"Satyrs don't care, Zo. You don't understand. They're like animals."

"Most animals don't abandon their young. That's more of a human trait."

He shrugged. "Okay. Then let me rephrase. Satyrs don't care. They're like humans."

I was working on a rebuttal, but we'd reached the clearing. Any words I had in my mouth slid down my throat and landed in my stomach with a thunk.

Maurice had warned me—more than once. But nothing he'd told me had given me a true idea of what lay before me now. Horned goat-men populated the clearing, reclining, dancing, standing still, leaning against trees.

Every last one of them sported an enormous erection. And every last one of them was doing something with it.

It wasn't exactly pornographic. They weren't engaged in any monkey spanking or meat beating. What they were doing can only be described as party tricks. Juggling, balancing objects, playing penile Hacky-sack with pinecones. It was the most bizarre and uncomfortable thing I'd ever seen.

I wanted to avert my eyes, but there was nowhere to look without seeing something I couldn't un-see. I took a step back, hoping to avoid notice.

My voice came out as a dry whisper. "Maybe you were right, Maurice. We weren't doing anything with that back bedroom anyway."

At least ten pairs of eyes locked on me as I tried to retreat. Pine cones, leaves and pebbles fell to the ground from their precarious, engorged perches.

The satyrs drifted toward us, their expressions dreamy. We had about fifteen seconds to make a choice. We could either make a run for it, or I could stand my ground and do what I'd come to do.

I've never been a runner.

I took a step into the clearing. "In for a penny…" I nudged Maurice with my elbow. "Cover me. I'm going in."

Maurice groaned and followed.

One satyr, hairier and taller than the rest, broke from the looming pack and clomped toward me. His horns were impressive black spirals growing back from his forehead and curing around his ears. "Well, hello there, pretty lady." He looked me up and down, waggling his eyebrows.

I crossed my arms over my chest, grateful that Maurice had made me wear the baggy grey Mickey Mouse sweatshirt. I stood my ground. "Hi. I'm looking for someone in charge."

The satyr grinned, showing flat, even teeth. He bowed low, but still kept his eyes on my chest. "Then you're in luck. I'm the king of the Tamalpais satyrs." He grabbed my hand from where it was tucked. He sniffed it. I was afraid he was going to lick me or do something even more disgusting, but he planted a kiss and let go. "Mad Dog Armadillo, pretty lady. How can I service you?"

I ignored the odd wording, and refolded my arms. "I believe I have a baby fathered by someone in your troupe. I'm trying to find who it belongs to."

His face sobered. "You're not sure if he's one of ours? Don't you remember? I assure you, if you'd been with us, you'd remember."

Maurice tensed beside me. "Zoey's not the mother, you idiot. We found the baby on our doorstep. We're trying to figure out who she belongs to."

"She?" The king relaxed, and he shook his head. "We have no interest in girl babies until they're grown. Drop her off with the maenads on the other side of the mountain. They keep the girls."

Behind him, several satyrs battled for my attention. Two tossed a ball back and forth between them, no hands. With each pass, they checked to see if I was watching, grinning at me and waving. One enterprising fellow climbed a tree and did the satyr version of planking. I shuddered. He stretched out straight along a branch, balancing all his weight on his erect member. When he started to do pushups with it, I looked away.

I cleared my throat. "Mr. Armadillo, this is not a maenad baby. She came from a dryad and a satyr."

King Mad Dog Armadillo paled. "Satyrs don't mix with dryads. I'm sure you're mistaken." He waved at the nearest goat-man, a younger satyr with ruddy skin and a dark gold pelt. "Leatherneck, get our guests some refreshments."

"That's not necessary," I said. "Please. Someone here must know who spent time with a dryad. We only want to be sure this baby isn't wanted before we find her another home."

He squinted at me. It was the first time his eyes weren't zeroed in on my chest. "She isn't wanted. Is that clear enough?"

Leatherneck appeared, carrying three golden cups filled with what appeared to be a dark red wine. Only two of the cups were in his hands.

I refused to look at how he balanced the third cup in the center.

"It's clear," Maurice said. "All the fun. None of the responsibility." He put a hand on my elbow and tried to guide me away. "I warned you about these guys, Zoey. This is pointless. Let's go home."

"Wait," I said. I concentrated on my emotional barrier and opened a window. Something wasn't right here. Okay, to be fair, there was a lot here that wasn't right. But there was more to the situation than King Mad Dog of Clan Raging Hard-On was letting on.

The first thing that hit me, of course, was arousal. The horniness in the clearing was so thick my throat constricted. I cringed and pushed through it, feeling soiled and a little violated at the mental contact. The king's excitement was superficial. Beneath it was caution tinged with haughty arrogance. And under that, I tasted a lie.

Without thinking my actions through, I shook off Maurice's hand and moved into the center of the clearing. Satyrs gathered around me, pressing closer. I ignored them.

Their emotions were thick and wet like a humid afternoon in a rainforest. I tuned out the sexual feelings bombarding me from all sides and focused past them. Somewhere in the forest something—someone—different hid among the brambles and leaves. A different kind of need cried out, an agony of heartbreak and desperation. I spun around, trying to locate the source. Dozens of eyes met mine, hungry for my attention. None contained anything but a skeezy cloud of lust. I turned to the king and he waggled his eyebrows again.

"Who else is here?" I asked.

"Who else do you need? There's more than enough of us to satisfy you, pretty lady."

He reached for my hand. His fingernails were caked with grime, and his knuckles were covered with coarse, reddish hair.

I backed away and stepped into the waiting arms of another satyr who proudly displayed a wreath of daisies around his erection. His arms circled my waist, and another satyr took the opportunity to reach out and cop a feel.

"Hey, knock it off," I said. I pushed them both away and shoved through the crowd, attempting to locate the source of the emotional distress call. The herd followed, and hands grabbed at my arms, my shoulders, my ass. I kept moving. A part of me knew I was getting deeper into trouble with each step, but the danger felt detached. Maurice's voice floated through the crowd, calling me back, warning the satyrs to leave me alone.

Muffled moans came from the bushes on my right. I turned toward the sound. It was entirely possible someone, or several someones, were having sex back there, but that's not what it felt like. I heard words, disconnected from sentences, words like baby and quiet and no. The brush stirred, as if someone were struggling, then what sounded like a fist connecting with flesh and breath expelled in a forced rush.

I tried to move to the bushes. Someone needed rescuing. But I'd misjudged my own situation. The someone in need of rescue was now me. With my attention elsewhere, the satyrs had closed in on me, pressing tight. Hands yanked at my sweatshirt, and the fabric tore at the neck. Multiple fingers tugged at the waist of my jeans, and I lost my footing. I was going down. And that was a terrible figure of speech, considering all the raging hard-ons now pointing directly at my face. I struggled to regain my feet, but the satyrs grasped and groped and pushed with hands and fingers and lips and tongues.

My own fear rose to cover any other emotions coming from outside of me. I scrabbled in the dirt and grass, breaking contact with one sex-starved beast-man, only to have him replaced by two more. I felt the screams coming from my throat, but my ears didn't register the sounds. My sweatshirt shredded. My jeans, now unfastened, inched down my hips. I grabbed at them, and someone pulled up my tank top, exposing my belly. I let go of my jeans with one hand and tried to recover the remnants of my shirt before I was left with nothing but a flimsy bra protecting my breasts from tongues and teeth and whatever else they had in mind.

A thunderous growl split the crowd, distracting them from their orgy.

I thought I'd been frightened a minute before, but what stood before me was the most terrifying thing I'd ever seen. The satyrs seemed to agree. Several scattered. The rest froze, jaws hanging loose.

Whatever this creature was, it stood at least eight feet tall, with broad shoulders and bulky muscles. It took a step toward me, teeth bared and fists clenched. Wicked-sharp canines dripped with drool. Drops spattered on the ground and the grass smoked and burned where the spit landed.

The thing roared again. Monstrous yellow eyes, rimmed with blood, cast around and glared at the satyrs that were left behind.

I was going to die. There was no question. First I was nearly gang-raped by savage goat-men, now I would be torn apart and eaten by a monster from hell.

I scooted out of reach of the frozen satyrs and pulled my legs in close, trying to make myself small. As big as this thing was, it looked fast. Running away would only draw its attention. I wrapped my arms around my knees and held tight to fight the tremors in my body. A sob caught in my throat and stayed lodged there.

The creature howled and tore after the remaining satyrs. Its hands were like over-sized slabs of grey meat, and they swiped at anything in their path. The satyrs churned the dirt and grass as they fled from the monster's blows.

King Mad Dog Armadillo stood several feet from me, clutching tattered grey cotton embellished with Mickey's left ear and part of a nose. The monster turned its attention on him, snarling, and acidic drool whipped across the clearing and sizzled through leaves and twigs.

All color drained from the king's face, and his cloven hooves stumbled as he back-pedaled.

In two pounding steps, the monster stood before Mad Dog. It lowered its head and brought their faces close. A roar like the grating metal of a derailing train tore from its jaws, and tiny drops of acid rained onto the satyr.

Mad Dog Armadillo, king of the Mount Tamalpais satyrs, turned and ran, still clutching a chunk of my favorite Mickey Mouse sweatshirt.

The monster watched him go, then swung around to view the empty clearing. There was no one else for it to target. Its blood-rimmed eyes met mine.

They teach us about the fight or flight instinct in school. I'm not a runner. Running gets you killed. But I'm not a fighter, either. This thing was so much bigger than me that I had no chance of defending myself, even if I did know how to fight. And I'd left my purse in the car. I couldn't even whack the monster with my handbag. Maurice had been swallowed up by the crowd of satyrs when I walked off. I didn't see him anywhere, and I hoped with all my heart he was okay. I had nothing and no one, because I'd waltzed into a crazy situation unprepared, thinking I could handle it. All I could hope for now was to stay beyond notice.

But it was even too late for that.

Tears streamed down my face, and my arms locked harder around my legs to keep my body parts from shaking loose. I'd been frightened by the closet monster when I found him in my kitchen that first morning. I'd been startled by a family of brownies in my linen closet. I'd been terrified when I thought an incubus was going to kill me. All of those scares were minor in the end. I adjusted. I dealt with them. I learned that I could handle anything.

Almost anything.

This beast standing over me was too much. I was going to die. In that moment, I learned that, no matter how cool I might seem in accepting the weird and scary into my life, at my core, I was a coward.

In my defense, who wouldn't be? Faced with something so big and ferocious and terrifying, who wouldn't squeeze their eyes shut and wait for the final blow? I lowered my head against my knees and shivered.

No matter how tight I squeezed my eyelids, I couldn't do the same for my ears. I could hear its ragged breaths, and I heard twigs snap under its feet as it drew near.

Moments ticked by. Its breathing was still clear, though the breaths were softer now, more even. My arms and legs were cramping. If the monster didn't do something soon, I was going to have to move anyway.

I loosened the stranglehold I had on my legs and wiggled my fingers to get the blood circulating. The monster didn't immediately pounce on me. That was a hopeful sign. Without looking up, I moved my neck a little, side to side. Still no attack.

Maybe if I lifted my head but didn't make eye contact, it would be okay. Treat the thing like a silverback gorilla and keep your eyes lowered out of respect. That might keep you safe.

My eyelids cracked open, and I took a minute to adjust to the light. I could do this.

On three. Take it slow. One...

The monster grabbed my shoulder.

I screamed and propelled myself backward, slamming into a tree. Hard. My breath blew out of my chest with an audible chuff.

So much for that flight instinct. It had finally kicked in, and I totally muffed it.

"Zoey, it's me!"

It took me a few seconds to get my breath back and my racing heart under control. I was nauseated from the buckets of adrenaline still coursing through my system.

The clearing was empty, except for Maurice. The monster was gone.

We were okay. Both of us. Maurice was alive. I was alive.

He helped me to my feet, and I craned my neck around, terrified the monster would return any second.

"We have to get out of here before it comes back," I said. I tugged at his hand to get him moving.

Maurice didn't budge. "Zoey." His face was sober, and his bony shoulders sagged.

"Come on. What's wrong with you?" I tried to pull my hand loose. He wouldn't let go. He stood there looking at me, waiting for something. Bushes rustled in the distance and I panicked again, yanking at his arm. "It's coming, Maurice. We have to hurry."

Still, he refused to budge.

I looked at his face again. Really looked. Even without my empath skills, his sadness was clear. What was there to be sad about? We were alive. Yay us.

I looked into his eyes. Big and yellow and filled with love and concern.

And still rimmed with blood.

This time, he let go when I tugged my hand away. Too much adrenaline. Too much fear. Too much information about a dear friend I'd invited to live in my house. I bent in half and horked up my breakfast. It wasn't pretty, but something had to give.

Maurice touched my arm, and I jumped. He pulled his hand back as if I'd burned him.

"I'm so sorry, Zoey." His voice was soft and unhappy. "I never wanted you to see that."

I was the worst friend in the world. I could feel his misery pooling at my feet. My own guilt beat against the inside of my chest. I turned away again and dry-heaved.

"I'll go, Zo." Over my shoulder I heard his feet scuffling in the leaves.

"Dammit, Maurice, could you just give me a minute to process this?"

He stopped and waited, silent. I took a few deep, cleansing breaths and pulled myself together. I straightened my tank top, buttoned my jeans, and swept my hair back from my face. As best as I could, I closed up the opening in my shields. I needed to be alone with my own feelings for a while.

"Okay," I said. "Let's get the hell out of here." I wanted to reassure him that we were all right, but I wasn't ready to reach out and grab his hand. He was still my Maurice. But the monster I'd seen was lurking and salivating in the back of my mind. I wasn't ready.

He hesitated. "Are you sure?"

I attempted a smile. It felt small and awkward. "You scared the shit out of me. Folding you up into the back of the Bug will make me feel better. Besides—I have no clue where we are. You have to get us out."

The smile he gave me was a little stronger than mine. He took the lead through the forest and out to the parked car.

My hands still had a slight tremor, but I got the door unlocked without dropping the keys. Points for me.

I had a lot of questions, but I wasn't certain I could handle the answers just yet. Still, he was getting into a tiny car with me. I didn't want to have doubts about Maurice. He was my friend. I had to know.

I swallowed and turned to face him. He stood a few feet away, giving me space. My heart broke at the hang-dog look he wore, as if any moment I would yell at him and chase him away. But there was something I'd missed before. I frowned in suspicion.

"So," I said, pointing at his un-torn clothes. "Why don't you look like Bruce Banner after he's de-Hulked?"

He shook his head. "It wasn't real, Zoey."

I frowned. "I saw you. You were huge. Your drool burned the ground and the satyrs went flying through the air."

"No. The ground smoking was fake, and the satyrs ran off on their own. I barely touched them." He scratched his ear. "Everything was an illusion."

I stared at him in silent disbelief. Then I punched him in the arm. "You might have warned me. I nearly peed myself."

He looked down at his feet. I could see his jaw working while he tried to put the right words together. "I'm sorry I scared you, Zoey. I don't like to transmonstrify, but you were in trouble. It's the only way I had of defending you." He refused to meet my eyes, as if he'd done something shameful.

I felt terrible for being angry with him. It was my fault I'd gotten us into a mess bad enough to need a rescue that big. "Get in the car."

"Really?"

I ran my hand through my hair and sighed. "I'm not going to lie to you, Maurice. I'm kind of freaked out. But even if you really had turned into a big snarling, scary beast, you're still you. And it's not the first time you've pulled my ass out of a fire, especially when it was my fault my ass was on fire in the first place. Let's go home."

He moved toward the car door and raised his hand on the way past me, as if to touch my arm. I held very still, trying not to flinch.

He dropped his arm and ducked into the car, folding up into an origami version of himself. Neither of us spoke as I got in, then guided the car around to the road.

We would be okay. I needed a little time was all.

The tires crunched on the gravel road, and we pulled out.

Before I'd managed to get up to more than five miles per hour, something big slammed into the back of the car.

I screamed and slammed my foot on the brake pedal.

A face peered at me through the driver's side window, and I screamed again.

The satyr's eyes were frantic, and one was bloodshot, the area around it puffy and already beginning to bruise. He slapped at my window and tossed a worried look over his shoulder.

"Please," he said. "They're coming back. Let me come with you!"

I looked at Maurice through the rear-view mirror. He shrugged and glanced back at the forest. I didn't see anything.

I rolled the window down a crack. "Who's coming?"

"The king. And everybody else." Voices spilled from the trees, and he jerked his head in their direction. "Ma'am, I know you don't have a reason to trust me, but you have my baby. I need to see her."

That did it. Maybe the trip wasn't such a waste after all. I reached across and unlocked the passenger door. "Hurry."

He came around and slid in as the horde of satyrs poured onto the road behind us, dicks and arms waving. I didn't wait for my passenger to buckle up. I'd seen enough. We pulled out and flew down the mountain as if all the minions of hell were on our asses. Because they sort of were.

We drove in silence for a while, each swallowed in our own thoughts. It was the satyr who finally spoke up first.

"I'm Nick," he said.

My eyebrows rose in surprise. "Nick what? Nick the Blade? One-eyed Nick? Slick Nick Barracuda?"

He stared at his hands in his lap. "No. Just Nick."

It was then that I realized Just Nick was wearing a pair of blue Bermuda shorts. I stole looks at him while I drove, noting the clean fingernails, the shaven jawline, and the tidy haircut.

A freak among satyrs. I approved.

"I'm Zoey." I pointed a thumb over my shoulder. "That's Maurice."

Maurice grumbled from the backseat. "Can somebody please explain why I have to crumple myself up in the backseat to avoid being seen, but the guy with the big ram horns is okay to ride in the front?"

Well, shit. I hadn't thought of that, and we were coming up on a main road. "You're right. I think I've got a hoodie on the floor back there."

Maurice dug around and found my pink hooded fleece wedged under the passenger seat and passed it forward. Nick gave me a doubtful look, then put it on, easing the hood up over his horns. Between his larger build and the protrusions from his forehead, my shirt would never be the same, all stretched out and weird.

I really needed to think about getting that bigger car with tinted windows.

"So, Just Nick," I said. "What's your plan?"

He grinned. "I'm going to meet my daughter. And then I'm going to go get my girl."

I nodded. "Finally we're getting somewhere. I like your plan very much, Just Nick."

Looked like maybe I hadn't screwed up so bad after all.

When we pulled into the driveway, Nick was out of the car so fast, we hadn't even come to a complete stop yet. Maurice untangled himself from the backseat, and we followed Nick up the front steps. I opened the door for him, and he hesitated, peering into the living room.

"Go on," I said. "We're right behind you."

His cloven hooves clopped softly on the hardwood floor, and I shut the door.

Phil stood in the dim light, cradling the baby in his arms. One of her tiny hands had escaped the blanket and patted at the rocky surface of his face making soft slaps.

Nick didn't move, his eyes a little misty.

I touched his pink sleeve. "Would you like to hold her?"

He nodded and shrugged off my hoodie. His jaw worked, as if trying to form words, but none came out. He stepped forward with his hands out, and Phil placed the baby in her father's arms.

The faun's grin lit up the entire room. "Hi, Fern," he said. His voice was barely above a whisper, and he leaned in to nuzzle her face. "She has horns." He looked at me, eyes wide. "She has my horns."

At home, I didn't keep my emotional walls as strong or focused as I did in the outside world. It was a habit to lower them a bit as I came up the driveway. As a result, Nick's outpouring of love and happiness at first contact with his child washed over me in a warm rush. The swelling of emotions cradled me with affection and pride, and my eyes welled up. My own father's love had felt like this in the years before he died.

I reached forward and pulled the blanket aside to show him her furry legs. They kicked out, and she gurgled, delighted at the freedom.

Maurice laughed. "Fern. Perfect. Now we can stop calling her *the baby*."

After a few minutes of pure magic between daddy and baby, Fern's fussing started up again.

"Minor incident in Flapjack Waffletown," Phil said, his face apologetic.

I raised an eyebrow and looked at Maurice for a translation.

"He couldn't change her diaper or feed her while we were gone," he said. "She's probably wet and hungry by now."

"Ah." I reached to take her. I was now an expert at such things, despite my extreme ineptitude the day before. Practice makes perfect.

"No, let me," Nick said. "It's my job."

He changed her with none of the awkwardness I'd shown on my first try, and when Maurice handed him a fresh bottle, he went straight outside to feed her.

"Great," I said. "We couldn't figure it out for a whole day, and he knew all along."

Phil eyed us both and crossed his arms. "Can you play kickball in the microwave?"

Maurice cast his gaze at his feet, his face stoic. "I'd rather not talk about it, Phil. The mountain isn't safe. Let's just leave it at that."

No, the mountain wasn't safe. But the most terrifying part had come home with me. Phil gave me a questioning glance, and I looked away. I didn't want to talk about it any more than Maurice did. I wasn't sure how we would get past this thing he'd revealed. He was my friend. My good friend. He'd saved my life, cleaned up after me, cooked for me, and held me when I was afraid. I didn't want him to be the thing I was afraid of. I didn't want him to know I wanted to sleep with the lights on for a while.

I would get over it. Time would work it out. In the meantime, I couldn't let Maurice know how uncomfortable I was. Soft wisps of shame rose from him and spread through the room. Would he leave because I'd seen a side of him he never wanted to show? Had anything truly changed? He was still my Maurice. It was up to me to show him we were okay. I didn't want to lose him.

I put an arm around his shoulders and gave him a gentle squeeze. "I could really use a drink. How about you?"

His head came up. "A drink would be nice." He smiled at me. It was weak, but it was a start.

Phil shook his head. "I want Charles in charge of me."

~*~

This time, Iris didn't try to fight me. When the three of us—me, Maurice and Nick, plus Fern—showed up in the woods, he took us straight to the crazy tree lady. She pretended not to notice us, at first, and continued to dig in the dirt, dropping seeds into the holes.

We waited. I had all the time in the world as far as this bitch was concerned. Five minutes, ten—she was methodical in her seed sowing. As she worked her way around the clearing, it became more of a challenge for her to keep us at her back.

Fern gurgled and crazy tree lady's head snapped up. She scowled at me. "I told you not to bring that thing back here."

I shrugged. "I don't listen very well."

Her eyes slid over Nick, and her mouth curled in a crooked line as if she'd tasted something especially rancid. She spat on the ground in the direction of his feet. Where the spittle had landed, a seedling pushed its head from the earth, and in motion-capture glory, rose to full height, formed a bud, and unfurled the petals of a small daisy.

Really hard to keep a straight face when somebody makes a rude gesture and flowers pop up. I would have said so, but I didn't have the chance.

Nick stepped forward, his arms in a protective shield around his daughter. He brought his face within inches of the old crone's. "She's not a thing. She's your granddaughter. You don't have to like me, but you won't ever hurt her." He took a step back, but he kept up his threatening glare. "Where's Mari?"

The woman sniffed and tried to turn away. "Marigold is not your concern. Leave."

Nick grabbed the woman's arm and held her in place. "I'm not playing with you. I don't care what you think of me or my people, I'm not leaving until my family is together."

She shrugged him off, her face cold. "So be it. You want to stay? Then stay."

She waved her arms around her head, and the trees lining the clearing us shuddered. Green fire oozed from the tips of her fingers and into the ground under Nick. Small roots took hold of his hooves.

Nick's eyes went wide with panic. He tried to pull free, but for every root he snapped, two more took its place. "Zoey, take Fern. Please! Don't let her get swallowed up with me!"

I grabbed the baby, and Maurice and I each took one of Nick's arms, trying to tug him free. The growths had already twined their way halfway up his calves.

From somewhere outside the clearing, a shrill scream split the air. "No!"

A cloud of silken green hair flew from the trees and rushed the old woman. The two dryads toppled to the ground, knocking the wind out of each other. They were a blur of browns and greens and elbows and knees, rolling in the grass and leaves.

Roots continued to climb the satyr's body, and I could hear his labored breathing as the tendrils wrapped around his chest.

The women scrabbled in the dirt, shouting incoherent words, biting and scratching.

"We don't have time for this," I said. I let go of poor, strangling Nick and shoved the baby at Iris. Maurice and I yanked the women apart.

The crone stood panting and swatting at the hand I'd fixed on her upper arm. Marigold shook loose from Maurice's grasp and glowered at the other woman. "Let him go, Mother."

Nick's breath sounded raspy and weak.

"You'd better hurry," I said. "He's only got a minute or two." Maurice and I returned to the satyr and worked at loosening the roots. They weren't going anywhere.

Mari's eyes brimmed with tears. "You're killing him, Mother!"

The old lady shrugged. "It's your own fault. Next time you'll do as you're told."

Nick gasped and his head lolled backward. Mari narrowed her eyes at her mother. "No," she said. "No, I don't think I will."

Her arms shot up, and the trees and bushes rustled with life. Eyes blinked from the darkness. I stepped closer to Maurice.

A wild boar trotted out of the trees, its sharp tusks and pink eyes both aimed at the old woman. From behind us, two coyotes and a wolf entered the clearing, trotted past us, and joined the boar. A mountain lion boxed the woman in on the other side.

Her face lost its nut-brown color, becoming ashen.

Marigold the dryad stood firm. "Let him go, Mother. I won't ask again."

Mari's mother opened her mouth to object, and the animals snorted, grunted, and howled as they drew closer. Her mouth snapped shut. Defeated, the older dryad waved her arm in Nick's general direction. The roots let go, and Maurice and I grabbed him before he fell. We eased him to the ground, giving him room to regain his breath.

Mari was by his side in an instant, smoothing his hair and repeating his name again and again, as if it were a mantra.

He smiled up at her. "I'm okay." He ran his hands up and down her arms. "We're okay."

I tore my eyes from the reunion and glanced over at Mari's mother. She squatted in the dirt, watching the couple. The animals must have determined for themselves she was no longer a threat, and one by one they disappeared into the foliage.

Mari helped Nick stand, and they both turned to face Iris. The skunk-ape, clearly uncomfortable with the infant I'd fobbed off on him, handed Fern over to her mother.

The love I'd felt earlier from Nick had been a taster of the total package. With the entire family united, love exploded through the clearing like a clap of thunder.

Birds sang, flowers bloomed, leaves sprouted from bare branches. My knees went weak with it, and I was forced to sit while we all bathed in the very real glow of a family reunited.

Mari's mother rose from her stooped position. She looked a little puzzled, but a smile touched her lips. Her eyes met mine, she nodded once, then disappeared into the woods.

Maurice helped me up, and we gave a last look at the new family. Mari and Nick cooed over their beautiful girl, and Fern giggled at them, her green hair in full, glorious bloom.

We didn't say goodbye. They needed time together, and they knew where to find us. Iris led us out of the woods and chuffed in satisfaction.

I swatted at his furry arm. "Don't act like you fixed this. I had to force you to help."

He snorted and left us at the edge of my property.

Maurice and I trudged together toward the house.

"You did a good thing, Zoey," he said.

"We did a good thing."

He shrugged. "I nearly wrecked everything."

"No. You saved me. As usual." I so didn't want to have this talk. I wanted the awkwardness and fear to go away on their own.

"I never wanted for you see me like that."

"I know."

"I didn't want you to think of me as a monster."

"I didn't want you to see me eat half a bowl of chocolate chip cookie dough after my horrible date with Riley, but you saw it."

"It's not the same thing." He ducked his head and stuffed his hands inside his pockets.

I stopped him and made him look me square in the eyes. "It is the same thing. Friends see each other at their worst, and love each other anyway. This transmonstrification thing is part of you. Friends accept each other as they are." I was desperate for that to be true. I was reassuring Maurice, but who would reassure me?

We continued walking toward the house. It was getting dark, and we could see Phil had every light blazing to guide us home.

I stopped again. "Shit."

"What?"

"Do you hear…is that Bon Jovi?"

Maurice beamed at me. "Yes! Karaoke tonight!"

"No."

His grin expanded three sizes. "Oh, yes. You. Me. 'Islands in the Stream.'" He winked at me. "It'll be epic."

I stuffed my hands in my pockets and dragged my feet toward home, muttering under my breath. "Lots and lots of alcohol."

"Prune Juice Sestina"

My editor really, really wanted me to include this bit of weirdness. I gave in.

In case you're not familiar, a sestina is a fixed verse form, six stanzas of six lines each, followed by a three-line stanza. The same six words are used at the end of the lines in each stanza, but the position of those words has to be different in each stanza—sort of like poetic Sudoku. The final, three-line stanza also uses those same six words, two per line.

When I learned that such a horrendous thing existed, it pissed me off. I know. Totally irrational reaction to a form of poetry. Once I got over my anger that someone would actually make something like this up, I decided to write one as penance for my behavior. I used a spreadsheet to get the word positions right. Seriously.

It's highly unlikely I will ever write a sestina again, but at least this one gave me the opportunity to rant about a conspiracy theory I've been suspicious of for over twenty years.

Like an old woman, wrinkled and sweet,
filled with wisdom and concern for your health,
a prune, newly dried in the sun,
hides within its shriveled skin, a secret.
Packed with nutrients and all that is good,
it cleans your pipes and wards against evil.

To misuse this simple gift would be a thing of evil.
We never wonder what is in our glass of sweet
prune juice. You might think it vile or think it good,
but no one doubts its benefit to their health.

Question it they should, for the juice is a secret
spirited away by the rays of the sun.

When the juice of a grape is stolen by the sun,
an offering of a glass of raisin juice would be evil,
for the liquid is hidden in the heavens, evermore kept secret.
Someone, somewhere, thought it might be sweet
to create a mystery concoction for our health,
and trick us into believing it is for our own good.

Thick and viscous, how anyone can think it's good
is a mystery passed down from father to son.
We wander the grocery, thinking of our health,
never suspecting on aisle twelve lurks a tremendous evil.
Only dreaming of how it would be sweet
to rid ourselves of the buildup we must keep secret.

That the elderly drink the most prune juice is no secret.
Old people die every day, leaving this world for good.
A coincidence? No! A foul smelling plot that's made to smell sweet.
All the warnings they give, (eat less fat, exercise, stay out of the sun,)
are merely diversions meant to trick us into falling for this evil,
designed to undermine our health.

We reach for anything that boasts improved health,
but the origins of prune juice are mysterious and secret.
Ignorance and complacency are a tremendous evil.
They give us false hope and conceal what is good.
Storm the supermarket, expose the conspiracy to the sun!
Demand to be heard, let the truth ring sweet!

For the good of your grandmother, preserve her failing health.
Find her secret stash and destroy the looming evil.
She has always been sweet and deserves more days in the sun.

###

About R.L. Naquin

Rachel writes stories that drop average people into magical situations filled with heart and quirky humor.

She believes in pixie dust, the power of love, good cheese, lucky socks, and putting things off until the last minute. Her home is Disneyland, despite her current location in Kansas. Rachel has one husband, two grown kids, and a crazy-catlady starter kit.

Hang out with her online:
Web: www.rlnaquin.com
Facebook: www.facebook.com/rlnaquin
Twitter: www.twitter.com/rlnaquin

Visit her website to subscribe to her newsletter.

Other Works by R.L. Naquin

The Monster Haven Series
published by Carina Press

Monster in My Closet, Book 1
Pooka in My Pantry, Book 2
Fairies in My Fireplace, Book 3
Golem in My Glovebox, Book 4
Demons in My Driveway, Book 5
Phoenix in My Fortune, Book 6

Additional Copyrights

The poems "Baked Goods," "Cast Off," and "Prune Juice Sestina" were previously published in the 2008 literary annual *Inscape*.

"How Greg's Chupacabra Became a Small Town Legend and Ended Up Between the Wooden Eye and the Wig Collection at the Caney Valley Historical Society" and "Cosmic Lasagna" were respectively published in the September 2010 and Fall 2010 Returning Contributors issues of *Seahorse Rodeo Folk Review*.

"Fool's Gold" was previously published in the March 2011 issue of *Daikaijuzine*.

Made in the USA
Columbia, SC
16 May 2025